THE
FIRST
GIRL

Jennifer Chase

BOOKS BY JENNIFER CHASE

JENNIFER CHASE

THE FIRST GIRL

bookouture

Published by Bookouture in 2023

An imprint of Storyfire Ltd.
Carmelite House
50 Victoria Embankment
London EC4Y 0DZ

www.bookouture.com

ISBN: 978-1-83525-020-4
eBook ISBN: 978-1-83525-019-8

For Glen and Buna

PROLOGUE

The soft breeze blew through the open bedroom window, ruffling the sheer curtain. The evening was still warm from the sizzling day and was now gently cooling into the July night. The crickets played a harmony of music that filtered around the farm and across the acreage.

Lara Fontaine suddenly awoke, a loud sound interrupting her sleep. She sat up in bed and looked around the small bedroom but wasn't sure what she had heard. In the other twin bed, her best friend Desi was still asleep and breathing evenly. What had disturbed Lara? Her first thought was to wake her friend because it was Desi's house and she might have some idea what the sound had been, but she decided against it. She swung her legs over the side of the bed, where they dangled, not quite reaching the floor. Still contemplating if she should go investigate, she stared at the closed bedroom door. Even though she was twelve, almost thirteen, she had developed a curious mind and wanted to know the answers to so many things. Everything she saw in her world made her more inquisitive.

Lara stood up, feeling the wood floor against the soles of her feet—it too was warm, like the evening air. Wearing only a white cotton nightgown, she decided to explore. Glancing back at Desi, who was still sound asleep, she went to the door and slowly turned the knob. To her relief, the door hinges were well-oiled and didn't emit any sound.

A breeze hit her as she stepped into the hallway, which seemed strange. It was as if someone had left a door or a window open. She didn't slow her pace as she moved forward. For the first time since she woke, she heard a noise, as if a chair was sliding across the floor. It was high-pitched and had an eerie quality about it.

As if being pulled by an unknown force, Lara crept toward the sound. She headed down the hallway, passing closed doors, to the kitchen. The farmhouse plank floors creaked beneath her slight weight. She stopped and listened. Leaning her body toward the sound, stretching on her tiptoes, she assumed she would hear more, but it remained quiet. As Lara let out a breath, her previous curiosity had now diminished, she decided she would return to the bedroom and try to go back to sleep.

But suddenly a strong arm grabbed her around the waist and clamped a hand over her mouth. She instantly struggled, but the man's strength easily overpowered her as he carried Lara to the back door. She could smell stale cigarette smoke on him and some kind of whiskey. The more she struggled against him, the more she weakened. Her whimpers were the only thing she could express.

The outside air hit her. She kept struggling, hearing her attacker's rattled breathing next to her ear. Realizing they were heading toward the large barn, she tried to put her legs out in front of her to stop their progress, but it was no use.

"Stop fighting," hissed the man directly into Lara's ear. "It'll be over soon."

Those words resonated in her mind.

What did he mean?

The crickets abruptly stopped.

Silence.

Holding Lara with one arm, the man pulled open the barn door. The hinges made a terrible squeak, interrupting the quiet.

"Stop!" Lara managed to say. "Please, don't..." Her arm felt as if it would break.

They moved deeper into the barn.

Lara could smell the hay and the alfalfa. But there was a low murmuring sound that she didn't recognize. She was forcibly put into an old metal chair and immediately her hands and ankles were secured, and a piece of duct tape covered her mouth.

It was difficult for Lara to focus through her tears, but she forced herself to look around. There were wooden crates filled with metal items, tools, and miscellaneous parts from various pieces of farm equipment. Then she saw her.

In a corner, there was a dark-haired young woman. She too was tied to a high-backed chair, unable to free herself. Her arms, legs, torso, and neck were secured. Her eyes were wide in terror, swollen from crying, and blood ran down her arms and neck from struggling against the restraints.

Lara locked eyes with the woman. So many emotions gripped her. Panic. Desperation. Fear.

The man moved around the area, he was dressed in jeans and a white, stained T-shirt. He appeared to be conflicted, confused, and even a bit panic-stricken as he ran his hands through his hair. Moving back and forth, he went from one box to a table, and then back to another box until he decided what he wanted. He carefully plucked out a long instrument that appeared to be some type of sharp, thin knife and stared at it with curiosity and wonder as if seeing it for the first time.

To Lara's horror, he turned and approached the woman. With his back to Lara, he attacked the woman with vicious intent. She heard muffled screams as the woman writhed in her seat.

Lara could barely breathe. She thought she would pass out, but her unrelenting terror kept her awake as she shook violently in her chair, watching the horrifying ordeal until it finally came to an end.

The man turned slowly, his shirt soaked in crimson. He looked at Lara as if he wondered why she was there. Still with the bloody tool in his hand, he slowly moved toward her. The weapon was still drenched with the woman's blood.

"No..." Lara tried to say.

He stood in front of her like a monster, reaching out.

Lara took a short breath. It was the last thing she remembered before passing out.

ONE

Tuesday 0945 hours

Detective Katie Scott drove with purpose as she steered the police sedan. She merged onto a country road off the main highway leading out of the Pine Valley area to meet with the family of a missing cold-case victim, Abigail Andrews. She glanced at her partner, Detective Sean McGaven, and smiled as he busily scoured his tablet looking for more information surrounding the case. She loved the way he was so thorough before they talked to anyone.

The landscape quickly changed to the dense forest that Pine Valley was known for. The morning was overcast with clouds obscuring the sun and a blustery wind blew. The view began to darken as they weaved along the country road where in addition to the dreary weather the tall pine trees acted as a giant canopy. The automatic headlights switched on, casting shadows among the dense trees.

"Anything?" Katie asked McGaven.

"Nothing new," said McGaven. "Hopefully, Mrs. Andrews

will be able to give us more insight into the time her daughter disappeared. Maybe she's remembered something."

Katie had read the missing person's report several times. It wasn't as detail-oriented as she would have liked, but there was the basic information and leads had been followed up. Apparently, Abigail had left her house with her dog and said she was going to see a friend. It was unclear where she went or who the friend was until her car had been found a week later parked in a rural area.

Katie couldn't get Abigail's face out of her mind. The photo in the file showed a beautiful young woman with long dark hair and dark eyes. Her smile was slight and there seemed to be a sadness about her.

"The file said that Abigail was falling in with some bad influences. Like substance use?" Katie asked.

"Yeah, but the two friends considered the bad influences were ruled out when the original investigation began."

"Still," she said, "there may be other friends her family didn't know about and she was going to meet up with them. And people are more likely to talk about things when enough time has passed."

"True. We'll see if we can track them down. If they kept doing bad things, they might not be around anymore either."

Katie frowned. "We need to check out where her car was found and triangulate the area to see what pops."

"Don't worry, we will. A little bit longer isn't going to make any difference." He smiled at his determined partner. "Wait," said McGaven. He turned up the scanner to hear the dispatcher. They usually had it turned down or off because they weren't on patrol.

"Motorist reported a woman on the south side of the Pine Valley Bridge. Appears to be a jumper," said dispatch.

"We're close," said Katie.

"Dispatch, this is Detective McGaven and I'm less than

three minutes from that location. We're on our way. Request assistance."

"Ten-four. Backup on the way."

Katie pressed the accelerator harder, and they headed for the bridge. "Maybe a kid or a prank."

"Maybe, but we can't take any chances." McGaven's face was solemn as he watched the road in anticipation.

As they jetted around the sharp turns in between the thick tree line, the sky seemed to lighten up ahead. They were just seconds from the historical Pine Valley Bridge, which connected Sequoia and Pine Valley counties. The bridge was sturdy, constructed with concrete supports with large rocks anchoring it, not like a county passing. It was almost a hundred years old but had been renovated twice. The bridge traffic was generally light, so they were lucky the concerned motorist had been passing at the time.

"We're almost there," Katie said.

"There," said McGaven.

They could see a woman standing on the bridge on the left side—she was still, with her arms at her sides and her head looking straight ahead. She wore a pale yellow, full-length dress and had long dark hair loose and blowing behind her. The breeze rumpled the dress. She was barefoot, her shoes lying on the ground neatly placed next to each other. She looked more like a subject in an expressionist painting than a woman in distress.

Katie pulled to the side of the road just before the bridge entrance. "I don't want to spook her," she said as she cut the engine.

"How do you want to proceed?"

She eyed her partner and decided it was best for her to confront the woman—McGaven was tall—over six-foot, six-inches—and might seem intimidating.

Both detectives got out of the car.

"Keep your cell on after my call so I can hear the conversation," McGaven said as he called his partner's phone.

Katie nodded, answering the call and keeping it open. She carried it in her jacket pocket. "Can you hear me?" she said.

"Yep."

"How long before backup arrives?"

"They said about fifteen or eighteen minutes. Hurry," he stressed, feeling his partner's concerns and hoping for the best. "I'll see if I can get a unit to stop any traffic from the other side."

Katie gave McGaven a quick look before she turned and faced the bridge. The woman was still standing on the ledge and seemed to be unaware of their presence. Dread filled Katie. She had never been a crisis negotiator, but they couldn't wait for backup. They needed to get this woman off the bridge in order to obtain the help she obviously so desperately needed.

Katie felt her pulse quicken as she walked toward the woman. The closer she got, the more she realized that the woman was young, about her age. It struck a chord with her. She remembered what it was like for her when she received the news that her parents had died in a car accident. We are all faced with tragedies at some point in our lives, but sometimes people don't know how to reach out. Maybe this was the case for this young woman.

As Katie neared, she saw that the woman's legs were shaking, and her toes gripped the edge of the bridge. Katie kept her distance. Not quite knowing what to do or say, she said, "I'm Katie. What's your name?"

The woman didn't move or respond.

Katie could hear the water rushing from below.

"I'm a detective with the Pine Valley Sheriff's Department." Katie thought she sounded lame, but she wanted to try to build trust by telling the woman the truth and giving her support. "My partner and I were on our way to interview someone." Katie took a deep breath. "Can you tell me your name?"

For the first time, the woman turned her head toward Katie. Her light-colored eyes were puffy, obviously from crying.

"I'm here to listen. Why don't you come down and we can talk?"

"You're a cop," said the woman.

"Yes."

"You'll just arrest me." Her voice lowered to barely a whisper.

"No, I won't. I'm here to help you." She paused a moment, not quite knowing what to say. "Is there someone I can call for you?"

The woman shook her head.

"Do you live around here?"

She nodded.

"Is it far?" Katie didn't see any car or a way the woman had come to the bridge.

The woman turned her attention back to the deep ravine, ignoring Katie's question.

Katie took two steps closer.

"It's best you leave," said the woman. Her voice was calm and even now.

"I can't do that."

"Why not?"

"I've sworn to protect this community—protect all citizens and to obey the law."

"Just walk away." Her voice began to crack. "Please..."

"I can't do that," said Katie and she took another step forward. "What's your name?" She glanced behind her to see that McGaven had moved closer to the bridge. "Please tell me your name."

"Lara."

Katie was relieved. "Lara... I'm Katie. Why don't you come down and talk? I will do everything I can to help you..."

"No one can help."

"Lara, I'm here to listen."

The woman began to cry.

"It's okay. Whatever it is, we'll work it out—together." Katie took another couple of steps.

"No..."

"Lara, please come down so we can talk."

"I can't..."

Katie estimated her distance and how fast she could grab Lara to take her down safely. She had to do something to disarm the escalating situation.

Lara leaned slightly forward and almost lost her balance.

Katie, with quick thinking and fast reflexes, took the opportunity and lunged toward Lara, grabbing her around the waist and pulling both of them safely to the ground.

Instead of Lara fighting her, the woman broke down and cried. Katie sat with her, comforting her until she stopped.

McGaven had run down the bridge to meet them. "You okay?" he managed to say, breathless.

"Yes, we're fine." Katie helped Lara up, still holding her.

McGaven stopped and stared in disbelief. "Lara?" he said. "I can't believe... it's..."

Katie watched her partner's reaction, intrigued by his response.

Slowly the woman turned her gaze and looked at McGaven, glancing at his badge and gun. She seemed to search his face for a few moments. "Sean?" she said.

"It is you, Lara," he said.

Katie watched the recognition spark in their eyes. "You know each other?" What a surprise.

"Uh, yeah," said McGaven gathering his thoughts. "We grew up together. I haven't seen Lara in years. I thought you'd moved away a long time ago."

Lara suddenly moved toward McGaven and hugged him tightly. "Please, Sean... please help me."

TWO

Through the many small cracks in the walls the darkness lifted once more inside the deep bunker and the man could see the general outline of his prison. No windows. One door. Low ceiling. He tried to keep track of the days, but now it had turned into months, so he had no way of knowing just how long he had been held against his will. But he did know that no one had come to give him food or water in days. He had rationed his portions, but they too were almost depleted. There was only a little bit of water, which meant he would be dead in days. He didn't know how much longer he could hold on.

He had been drugged so many times it was difficult to really know for sure if he was lucid and fully awake in the real world. After a lot of hard work, his wrists and ankles were finally freed from the restraints, but he was now seriously weak and fatigued. The muscles in his arms and legs were taxed as he stood up and began to search his confinement—again. There had to be a way to get out, but he wasn't really sure where he was. He wouldn't last much longer and had given up hope of anyone finding him.

He staggered around the perimeter, which was about four-teen-foot square. Stopping at a place where he could feel the slight air coming in from outside, he paused, taking a deep breath, hoping that it would revitalize him and give him a boost of energy.

He listened intently. Almost having the feeling that he had lost his hearing, because he hadn't heard any type of sound for days, he took a breath then cleared his dry throat, allowing sound to reach his ears, giving him a brief reprieve in his soon-to-be-silent tomb.

He had accumulated in the corner a small pile of food and miscellaneous items. He had managed to make weapons from the plate, plastic fork, and to-go box he had been given.

Staggering to the reinforced metal door, he ran his hands along the sides, trying to discover anything that would be pene-trable. But there was nothing. He kept his emotions and failing positive attitude in check, but there was going to be a point when he would sit down, give up, and wait to die.

He leaned back against the cold wall. His threadbare clothes hung on his thin body. Racking his brain for a reason why he was drugged, abducted, and then left alive this long was almost the only thing on his mind. It made no sense. He wasn't sure if his thoughts were coherent as they once again rambled over everything that had happened. The blaring question that always echoed through his thoughts: Why?

The man touched his bearded face and ran his hands through his dirty hair. He was losing hope and his faith wavered. He knew that there would be only one moment that would give him what he needed to escape, and he had to be ready. For now, he waited.

He sat down on the cold floor and dozed off like so many times due to his weakness. His dreams were filled with what his life was like before. Sweet memories. Friends. Family. Happiness. Joy. Looking forward to the future and her beautiful face. These dreams kept him going.

He was abruptly awakened.

There was the sound of someone coming through an interior door. It was distinct, as it slammed with a slight echo. Footsteps approached and then a key was inserted into the lock.

He took several deep breaths for strength and grabbed one of his makeshift weapons, clutching it tightly in his hand.

He readied himself.

THREE

After a devastating loss of not knowing what happened to a loved one, where there is no closure, love is the one thing that stays constant in your soul. Even if you only experience that love for a short period, it stays with you for a lifetime. Reminders are everywhere if you know where to look— mementoes, places, memories, a sound, a fragrance, and dreams are just a few things that help keep that love alive.

Tuesday 1140 hours

Katie watched as paramedics checked out Lara. She sat motionless with a blanket wrapped around her body, seemingly in her own world, unaware of the activity around her, her eyes vacant as she stared past the emergency workers. It was unclear if she really had been about to jump.

Lara would be transported to the county psychiatric hospital for a seventy-two-hour observation where she would get the help and, possibly, the medication she needed. This was normal protocol when someone wanted to hurt or kill themselves.

McGaven hovered around her as he spoke with patrol officers. Katie wondered how close they had been, and if he knew anything about her wanting to hurt herself in the past. She decided to let him come to her when he was ready to talk about it.

Katie walked back to the area where Lara had been on the bridge. She looked from one side to the other. It appeared to be almost in the middle. Katie leaned over the railing and looked down. There was a creek running beneath the bridge, deeper than most. The annual rain had been higher than average and had brought much needed water, which had filled up local waterways.

The lush forest and low-lying shrubbery were close to the creek banks. A plastic bag with something in it caught Katie's eye. The trails didn't end at the edge of the water, but trash could have blown from just about anywhere or out of a passing car. The bag floated down the creek until Katie lost sight of it.

"Hey," said McGaven.

"Everything okay?" she said.

"Yeah, they're transporting her now." His expression appeared despondent, and his voice was downcast.

"Did you talk to her?"

"Not really and I won't be able to speak to her until her observation time is over."

"Oh," said Katie. She wanted to ask more, but instead she looked at her watch. "So... we can still speak with Mrs. Andrews if we hurry."

"Let's go."

Katie drove to Mrs. Andrews's house, which was about fifteen minutes from the Pine Valley Bridge. She glanced at her partner who remained quiet for the entire drive. McGaven stared out the window at the tall trees, but it was clear he wasn't looking at the scenery.

The detectives had worked cold cases—both missing persons and homicides—for the past year and a half. Katie headed up the cold case unit at the Pine Valley Sheriff's Department. She had been a patrol officer at Sacramento Police Department and had done two tours in Afghanistan as part of an Army K9 explosive team. Upon returning to her hometown in Pine Valley, she stayed to make a difference as a cold-case detective.

There was a definite law enforcement buzz about the two detectives due to their record of solve rates, with other departments around the state having taken notice. To date, they had closed a hundred percent of their cases.

Katie wasn't immune to tragedy. Almost six months ago, her fiancé Chad Ferguson had mysteriously disappeared from their cabin getaway and had not yet been found. As difficult as it had been, Katie remained hopeful that he might still be. She got through the heartbreak of Chad's disappearance by focusing on investigating cold cases and leaning on the support of her uncle and her friends.

Katie turned onto Lavender Lane and looked for 3328. The house came into view. It was an older, one-story, blue home with white trim, modest, with a simple landscaped yard with rock, steppingstones, and planted pots.

Katie parked and got out on the quiet street. She noted that there wasn't any sound, no birds chirping in the trees, no barking dogs, and no car noise. It seemed strange, but she realized that it was an out-of-the-way home and quiet seemed to be its main attraction.

"What do you think?" said McGaven as he stood next to her.

"Not sure. Just taking a look around." Katie took another moment before walking up to the front door. She could smell the yard as if it had been recently watered. It was fresh and had a healing quality to it.

Katie knocked. Within moments, the door slowly opened, and an attractive older woman greeted them.

"Yes?" She had shoulder-length brown hair and wore a pale blue sweater and blue jeans. Makeup had been applied, accentuating her vivid blue eyes. She looked too young to have a daughter who would have been in her thirties today.

"Mrs. Andrews?" said Katie.

"Yes, you must be Detectives Scott and McGaven." She smiled.

"Yes."

"Please come in." She opened the door wider. Katie could smell freshly brewed coffee.

"We apologize for being late."

"It's fine. I work at home and planned on being here all day."

The interior of the home differed from the ordinary exterior. Inside, it was decorated with modern furniture and artwork. There were two large beige leather sofas and glass bookshelves and low end tables. The paintings on the wall were stunning abstracts in bright blues, yellows, and reds.

"Would you like some coffee?" Mrs. Andrews asked.

"Yes, that would be great, thank you," said Katie still looking at the furnishings.

The detectives sat down on the couch waiting for Mrs. Andrews to return. Katie gazed at a cluster of framed photographs along a table. She could see pictures of a couple, assuming it was Mr. and Mrs. Andrews with two young girls—one of them was Abigail. They were smiling and it appeared that they were at a lake.

Mrs. Andrews returned with a tray and three coffees. "Do you need milk?" she asked, handing the mugs around.

"Black is fine," said Katie.

"This is great coffee," said McGaven after his first sip.

"I noticed you looking at the photos," Mrs. Andrews said.

"Yes," said Katie.

Mrs. Andrews took a sip before she continued. "My husband died six months ago, so I'm still getting used to being alone. You plan for every type of possible event, but nothing prepares you for the loss of your partner."

This comment shook Katie to the core for a moment. She regrouped. "I'm so sorry for your loss."

"Thank you. But I do have closure at least. That's why I was so glad when you called about Abigail's case. There's no closure there. Even though her body hasn't been found, I had given up on the hope that she's still alive. That's just the reality after all this time."

For some reason, this case was hitting Katie hard, but she wanted to get to the truth. "We've reviewed the case, but we always like to re-interview everyone."

"Of course. I'm just thankful that the case is still being considered." Mrs. Andrews looked away from the detectives. It was clear her pain was always at the surface.

"Can you tell us about the last time you saw or talked to Abigail?" Katie asked.

"As you know, Abi had been struggling with substance use, so she didn't have the best influences when it came to friends. She hadn't always been that way, but she seemed to be lost and was looking for something. What it was wasn't clear."

Katie and McGaven waited patiently as the older woman gathered her thoughts.

"It was a Thursday, during July, and she said she was going to meet friends. She had Sadie with her."

"Sadie?"

"Yes, her dog, a lab that went everywhere with her."

"Do you know where Abigail went?"

"No, she never gave any details. And if she did, it wasn't the truth." Mrs. Andrews took a sip of coffee.

"About what time did she leave?" said McGaven.

"It was three p.m."

"Are you sure?" said Katie.

"Yes. My husband and I were getting ready to go to our friends' house, which was a couple of hours away. We wanted to be there about five."

Katie looked at her notes. "Kyle and Annie Stewart?"

"Yes."

"I see they were questioned to verify your timeline."

Mrs. Andrews sighed. "Yes. The police spent a fair amount of time concentrating on both me and my husband."

"I'm sorry to say, unfortunately, that's common. Statistics show that when someone disappears, a family member or close friend is usually involved." Katie hated how this sounded when they were talking to someone about the disappearance of their loved one, but it was the reality.

Mrs. Andrews nodded. "I've gone over that day a million times trying to think of anything that I might have missed. I just don't know."

"After they found Abigail's car, they said there was nothing inside. Everything had been cleaned up. There wasn't even anything in the glovebox, like registration. Did you know"— Katie read the names—"Teri Butler and Anthony Drake?"

"No, I'm sorry. Abigail never brought any of her friends around—or mentioned them."

"I see." Katie made a couple of notes to try to find them.

"Detective, I know this is a case that you might not solve. But, please, for me and my remaining family—my daughter Kayla—please find Abigail so we can give her a proper funeral."

"We will do everything we possibly can," said Katie. "We're going to retrace what we know and move on from there."

"We will keep you informed every step of the way," said McGaven.

The detectives rose from the couch.

Katie asked, "Mrs. Andrews, I know it's been almost fifteen years, but do you have anything from Abigail? From her room, storage, or anything?"

"I kept her room for two years just the same, but when it was clear that she wasn't coming back I cleaned it out and put her things into boxes. They are in the garage. I just didn't have the heart to throw anything away. You are welcome to look through them and take anything you might need."

"Thank you."

"They are all marked Abigail."

Katie paused a moment. "Mrs. Andrews, thank you for seeing us today."

She nodded. "The side door to the garage is open. Please take all the time you need."

Katie and McGaven left through the front door, made their way to the side of the garage, and stepped inside. It was organized and neat with just one car, a workbench, and a good-size storage area.

"Over there." McGaven pointed.

Katie walked to the storage area and easily found several stacks of boxes with "Abigail" written in dark blue ink. She sighed. "Let's get started."

FOUR

As the key rattled the padlocks from the other side, there was a pause. The door didn't open but the lock wasn't fastened again. There was no sound. It was as if the person on the other side of the door sensed someone was waiting for him.

The man leaned his body weight on the left side of the door, hoping to surprise the captor. He only had moments to get the upper hand, to use his dwindling energy. He gripped the meager plastic utensil tightly... and waited.

What seemed like an hour was only about thirty seconds. The person on the other side began to move, shuffling heavy-sounding boots, and only then did the reinforced metal door slowly begin to open. At first, barely two inches, then it pushed wider.

That was all it took for the man to react. Propelled by adrenaline, pushing him to attack mode, he launched into the unsuspecting captor, shoved him, slamming his fists into his face, throat, and eyes, stunning him. The much-needed food and water the intruder had been carrying plummeted to the ground. But the man didn't stop as he hurled his body to slam the captor once more, and both went down.

The man, breathless and dizzy, stared into the eyes of the person who had kept him captive. He held his elbow at the captor's throat and leaned his knee against his chest, hearing him wheeze. It was the first time he'd seen his abductor's face up close. The man usually had his eyes covered, and when he didn't, the jailer's face was covered with a red bandana. Now the bandana had slipped, and the man saw the terrified face of the person who had treated him so callously. His jailer was now in the vulnerable position of not knowing if he would live or die.

Dark eyes stared back at the man. So terrified, the captor didn't speak, but merely trembled and sweated.

"Who are you?" demanded the man, barely recognizing his raspy voice. "Tell me!" He leaned harder on his jailer.

"No..."

The man pushed the plastic implement against the captor's throat. "Who are you? Why did you kidnap me?"

"I didn't..."

The man realized that who he was staring at wasn't the person pulling the strings. "Give me a name! Who's behind this?"

It was no use.

The man struck the captor several times, rendering him unconscious. He then dragged the body inside the room and looked through the jailer's pockets. There was no phone, money, or identification.

The man stood up and steadied himself. The exertion of the scuffle had almost completely depleted his energy and he had to continue searching for his way out. There was no way of knowing if there was another person waiting—or possibly an entire team of people. He grabbed some of the spilled crumbs of food and quickly ate it for energy.

Looking down at his bare feet, he realized he needed to take the captor's shoes and jacket if he was going to move fast. The man took a few moments pulling the boots and the jacket off the dazed jailer on the floor and tying him up with the bandana, and only a few more moments to catch his breath, not knowing what waited outside for him, but moving quickly out the door.

FIVE

Katie had shed her jacket and rolled up her sleeves to go through the boxes of Abigail Andrews's possessions. They had spent more than forty minutes going through ten boxes. Hoping for something that would give them the information they needed, she was met only with disappointment. She thumbed through trinkets; a jewelry box with butterfly necklaces, pins, and earrings; small teddy bears; and bank records.

"Anything?" said McGaven. He moved a couple of boxes and restacked them.

"Not yet. She didn't seem to have much money. Just deposits from disability. Looks like it was for an accident she had... and it was only for another six months. But nothing that seemed to indicate activities of a criminal nature. There were withdrawals every week for a hundred dollars."

Katie came across a framed photograph of Abigail and a man with her yellow Labrador. They looked happy together. It was unclear where the photo was taken, but it seemed that the background was a rural park area with no identifying buildings or structures. There was a partial view of the Toyota. Katie opened the back and pulled out the photo.

"Here's something," she said.

McGaven looked over her shoulder.

"It says, 'Me and T. Drake' with a heart drawn next to it. The files referred to an Anthony Drake, maybe his nickname was Tony?" She looked at her partner as he was already writing down information. "I'll take this with us," she said.

"There's nothing else?"

"No." Katie frowned. "It's almost as if certain things had already been discarded. Maybe important stuff, but we'll never know. This is just stuff that you end up keeping and gets stored in boxes until it's finally tossed."

"What are you thinking?" McGaven said.

"Let's just keep an open mind. But... what do we really know about Mrs. Andrews?" She glanced at the door.

"Fair enough. I'll run some background and see what shakes out."

"Thanks. I think we're done here," she said.

"Agreed."

Katie studied her partner as they readied to leave. He seemed a little bit distracted. "You okay?"

"Yeah, fine. Why?"

"I don't know. Maybe seeing an old friend wanting to jump off a bridge could be upsetting?" she said gently.

McGaven turned to his partner. "I know you mean well, but I'm fine. It was shocking but things happen. And I haven't seen Lara in years. I hope she gets the help she needs."

"Me too."

McGaven smiled. "I know I can count on you if I need to talk about stuff. That's what partners do. We have each other's backs. But I really am fine."

Katie met McGaven's gaze and smiled. "You got that right."

.   .   .

The detectives walked out to their car after returning the boxes and securing the door to the garage. Katie glanced around. She had a sense they were being watched, but she couldn't see anyone. Still, she felt goosebumps prickle her arms. She shook it off and continued.

Once inside the car, McGaven said, "Okay, we're not too far from where Abigail's car was found." He pulled up the area map from his phone and put a pin at the location.

"Let's go," Katie said as she started up the car.

"Then we can grab some lunch before heading back to the office," said McGaven. "My stomach is already grumbling."

Katie laughed. "Mine too."

As they drove away from the Andrews residence, Katie couldn't help but think that this cold case would test their skills and endurance. The strange circumstances and the age of the case made it more difficult.

SIX

The man didn't know exactly how long he had been running but couldn't stop his momentum, otherwise he wouldn't be able to go any farther. His lungs felt as if they would explode soon and his legs were unsteady, but he kept going.

After leaving his fourteen-foot-square jail, he didn't know what exactly to expect. There was no one on the other side of the metal door, and he seemed to be in a long tunnel that he guessed to be some type of old drainage culvert. He suspected he'd been held in what had once been some type of control room for a facility that was outdated and most likely sealed up.

As he ran through the culvert, the light around him became brighter the closer he was to freedom. It was so bright that he could barely stand it, closing his eyes except for a slight opening; he thought his vision would deteriorate because of the intensity.

Finally, he reached the end of the long concrete tunnel and stood on real ground. The dirt and surrounding trees were a relief and a wonderful sight. The fresh air hit him with intensity. The stale smell of his cell was finally gone. His first thought was to drop to his knees in overwhelming gratitude, but he was afraid that he wouldn't be able to get up and continue.

But he stopped for a moment and stood still, savoring his freedom. He slowed his breathing and took a quick inventory of the surrounding area, which consisted of dense trees and several trails. There was an overgrowth of foliage, as if the area had been long forgotten. He could hear every small sound. The slight wind. The rustling of the pine needles. Birds nesting in faraway trees. The noises and sights were unnerving and a bit frightening, but he coped as best he could.

The man staggered up to an immense tree trunk and leaned against it. He didn't know where he was, which direction to go, and if he would make it somewhere to get help before he collapsed. His strength and any endurance he had would soon run out. He pushed the inevitable thoughts of dying out of his mind. Instead, he thought of everything he had to look forward to.

Looking up, he slowly turned his head and studied each direction. He decided to move forward in what he figured to be south. He didn't know it was early afternoon for sure, but by the light of the sun, he was acting on his instincts.

The man shuffled along the trail, moving as quickly as he dared. He wanted to find help, someone, a hiker, a park ranger, a campsite, anyone. He let the feeling of freedom drive him as he followed the trail.

SEVEN

Life is a continuous struggle of ups and downs. It's what you do when things are tough, and you don't know if you will ever get back on track, that makes the difference. Things may not be what they seem. Your perspective may have jumped the tracks. But the best times are what ground you and will help you get back on track. Stay the course and keep your focus. When something doesn't seem what it appears to be—keep searching until you see everything clearly.

Tuesday 1530 hours

Katie eased the police sedan to a parking area on the shoulder near where Abigail's car had been found. The roadway was a little-used utility road that connected various properties to the main roads and highways. There were several farms and ranches in the vicinity, but nothing within at least a mile.

Katie and McGaven stepped out of the car and walked around the area, observing. It was midafternoon and the sun was shining and there were few visible clouds. It was quiet and peaceful. Katie walked to the side of the road where there was a slight downhill slope and she wondered why Abigail's car hadn't been driven or pushed down there where it wouldn't have been found for some time—if ever. It would have been covered by forest growth and slowly disintegrated into the wild landscape.

"Why would Abigail park here?" said McGaven, as if reading Katie's thoughts. "The car was in running condition. No flat. No engine trouble noted. Though her mom did mention some type of mechanical trouble."

"And the keys were still in the ignition. The crime-scene technicians noted that it started up," said Katie. She walked to the spot and stood for a moment.

McGaven walked across the roadway from where Katie stood, then he slowly walked back to his partner. "It was clearly staged."

Katie nodded. "The reports indicated that there weren't any identifiable fingerprints, most being smudged, and the only ones they could identify were Abigail's." She stared down the incline. "But still..."

"What are you thinking?"

"I know the detective at the time, Detective Jamison, had patrol canvass the nearby ranches and farms, and no one had seen her. But I think Abigail did go somewhere near here. I think *she* actually parked here alone."

"Based on?"

"If whoever Abigail met, or was meeting, wanted to get rid of evidence, why didn't they push the car down the slope? It would have been easy and made the most sense to try to hide their involvement. Why leave it on the side of a road where someone would find it easily?"

"I see your point," he said.

Katie remained quiet, contemplating what their next move should be. She slowly made a 360-degree turn, wondering what

Abigail had seen that day. Was she meeting someone? Did one of the neighbors happen to be here?

"So, I take it you want to check out the farms? And... basically have a look around?" McGaven smiled. It was his partner's usual method to revisit areas where abductions and murders took place.

She nodded. "I know it's been about fifteen years, and it may prove fruitless, but I think we need to follow all avenues, reinvestigate, wherever it takes us." Katie turned around to look across the street. "We need to try to trace Abigail's last steps."

"Have you considered the possibility that Abigail simply wanted to disappear?"

Katie thought a moment as her brows scrunched. "Of course, it's possible," she said slowly. "But she didn't have much money in her account, and it hasn't been touched since she was reported missing."

"Could she have come into some money? Stolen it? Met someone?"

Katie stared down the hillside. "Let's follow up with everything and then re-evaluate." She paused. "Until we find a body, there's no real way I can begin a profile."

"On it. I'll try to locate Tony Drake and set up a time to talk with Detective Jamison." He turned. "And I'll get a detailed aerial map of this area..."

As McGaven readied to leave, Katie remained. She looked down the hillside again. It had dark areas that never saw sunlight, making it difficult to see anything clearly. She studied the map app on her phone. North traveled to a large farm. She stood at the hillside and saw a glimpse of the trees and several structures. South headed back to the long road they'd driven to get here. East or west would be difficult to travel unless you knew exactly where to go.

"If Abigail's car stalled here," she said. "The file indicated that the car had an intermittent alternator issue causing it to not start. I could see how she might've walked to a nearby farm for help. Maybe someone from the county was out here near the utility roads and saw her that day."

"Nothing was noted in the initial search of the area."

Katie checked out the areas all around. "There could have been someone she was meeting." She looked down the ravine. "But..."

"What's up?" he said.

"I want to have a quick look around."

"Where?"

"Down there," she said, indicating the incline below the roadway.

"Don't you think that after all this time there's nothing to find?"

"Maybe, but I want to look. Just a few minutes or so. We've found things before."

McGaven shrugged. "Okay."

"Grab a flashlight."

Katie felt the breeze against her face and could hear birds calling. The sky had cleared from earlier in the day. Any residences would have plenty of privacy, and it would make it difficult to hear someone in distress.

Her thoughts were on Abigail again. She could see in her mind's eye the woman's beautiful smile and long dark hair from the cold-case file. She was young, barely twenty-one years old, and had so much of her life to live. Sometimes the reality of the cold cases they worked made it difficult to process, but they had to retrace and rework them if they had any chance of solving them.

Katie descended the hill. It looked easier than it was, the terrain filled with roots, dead bushes, partially buried pine cones, and decomposing trash from years of litter. She carefully placed her feet, taking a wider stance than normal.

Once she reached the bottom, she took a firm footing,

steadying her balance as she systematically looked around. It smelled of moist and decaying earth and looked untouched. It had probably been a mistake to come down here. They should head back to the office to coordinate their next moves and not waste time.

Just then, there was a flash of light near one of the bushes. The sunlight filtering through the tree canopies and branches had lit up the darkened, damp areas for a moment.

McGaven made his way down, his footsteps crashing through the undergrowth due to his tall stature. He grimaced as he neared Katie. "Here," he said, handing her the flashlight.

"Thanks." Immediately she switched on the light and swiped the beam to the darkened areas. Panning the beam, a section of the forest sparkled for an instant.

"What is that?" asked McGaven.

"I don't know." She stepped forward, trying to keep her balance. The dead debris from the underbelly of the forest crackled beneath her feet.

McGaven stayed in place as he watched his partner.

About three feet back, behind several dead branches, Katie could see something swinging slightly in the breeze. As she moved into the shade, she could feel the temperature drop around her and the sun seemed to have disappeared. Bending slowly forward, she reached her hand into the dry, weathered mangled mess.

"What is it?"

"Not sure," she said. Her hand grasped something metal, and she pulled it toward her. Wiping off the dirt, leaves, and debris, she shined the flashlight directly on the object. It was a butterfly pendant hanging from a chain. It was similar to the jewelry she had seen in Abigail's stored boxes.

"Is that like...?"

"It looks like the necklaces in Abigail's jewelry box." She

turned to her partner. "And I think it looks like the one she always seemed to be wearing in photos."

"It's definitely consistent, but there's probably a million of these kinds of necklaces floating around. Still, what are the odds that some random butterfly necklace showed up here where her car was abandoned?"

Katie nodded. "Exactly. What are the odds? And it means that forensics needs to search and sift through this area for anything belonging to Abigail Andrews. If we're lucky, we're beginning to see a trail and getting closer to finding out what happened to her."

EIGHT

The man had walked for almost an hour—stumbling along the trail and taking periodic breaks to catch his breath. His vision blurred. The beautiful forest around him seemed ominous. There was no sign of people. No sign of life. It was as if he was the only person left in the world. He kept moving in the same southerly direction and actually prayed he would find someone soon.

The sky was clear, and the warmth of the sun felt good, but he was still chilled on the inside. His mouth was parched. He needed water soon or he would blackout and the odds of someone finding him would be even less than they already were.

The man pushed forward, and his heart rate increased.

He stopped.

There was the sound of a car. He strained to listen. There it was again—the idling of an engine.

The man moved faster, falling once, but getting to his feet again. He followed the sound, but it suddenly stopped, making him pause. His head spun; he didn't know exactly where the sound had come from. The landscape faltered in and out. His legs were heavy, and the ill-fitting boots seemed to make him stumble more.

As he staggered around the closely knit trees, he saw it. There was a dirt parking area for people hiking some of the nearby trails.

"Help..." he said, but it was barely a whisper. "Please, someone..." His voice was raspy and weak. No one answered his call for help.

The man made his way to the SUV and used the high-profile vehicle as support. He tried the doors, but they were locked. Then he tried to shake the car to make the alarm go off, but nothing happened.

He turned and saw some fist-size rocks near the car. He bent down but lost his balance and fell. Grappling for the rock, he managed to get back on his feet. He swung his arm several times until the driver's window shattered. Clearing a space around the window, he managed to unlock the door.

Trying to desperately catch his breath, the man climbed into the seat and began looking for anything, keys, a cell phone, or the vehicle help assistance. Underneath the passenger floor mat was a cell phone.

The man activated it and called 911.

"911, what's your emergency?" said dispatch.

"Help me..."

"Sir? I can't hear you."

"Please..."

"What's your emergency?"

"I need help... I can't..."

"Where is your location?"

"I don't know... near Pine Valley forest... maybe..."

"Sir, I need your location."

"Please send police and ambulance..."

"Are you hurt? Do you have any injuries?"

"I've been held captive... I can't..." His voice was fading, and he had a difficult time breathing. He fought the urge to pass out.

"I'm tracing the call now. Stay on the line as I alert fire and rescue. What is your name?"

"My name..."

"Sir, what is your name?"

"Chad Ferguson," he managed to say before passing out.

NINE

Katie and McGaven had coordinated their interviews for the next day and were now looking at a full-size map of the area where Abigail's car was found. They stood in their cold-case command center, which, due to the space constriction, was located in the forensic division at the Pine Valley Sheriff's Department. It worked out well as it was a quiet space and close to the evidence of cases they worked.

McGaven's phone chimed, alerting to a text.

"Anything?" said Katie.

"It looks like John and Eva are processing the area and finding miscellaneous artifacts that might belong to Abigail—clothes, a dog leash, one shoe." He read further. "Nothing to indicate her body was dumped."

"Did they do a complete search at the time when they found the car? Maybe Abigail's things were tossed later after the car was towed." she said. "That could indicate that the area was a dumping ground and reasonably close to where the perp either worked or lived."

McGaven's phone chimed again. He read it with concern on his face.

"Everything okay?"

"Yeah. It was social services letting me know Lara has been checked in and will be under supervision until Friday. And if I wanted to see her, it wouldn't be until then."

"Are you going to see her?" The information seemed to upset McGaven more than she thought it would.

"I don't know."

"That's three days away. Anything can happen and hopefully she'll get the help and services she needs." Katie tried to sound optimistic, but the truth was if Lara had been living with a mental illness for a while, it could take some time for her to accept help and begin to recover.

They were interrupted by a knock at the door.

"Detectives," said Sheriff Scott. He was tall, distinguished, and commanded attention. Not only was he the sheriff, but he was also Katie's uncle. He was her only family since her parents were killed in a car accident when she was a teen.

As soon as Katie saw him, she immediately recognized he was extremely concerned about something and knew that he had some important news. His jaw was clenched, his eyes focused and unblinking. Something had happened.

"What is it?" said Katie as her entire body tensed.

McGaven remained quiet but had noticed the seriousness from the sheriff as well.

"We have some news," said the sheriff.

"About?"

"Chad."

"What? Is he...?" Katie could barely speak. Since her fiancé had disappeared during a romantic evening at a secluded cabin several months back, she had spent every day trying to find new clues as to what had happened to him. Her life had ended up sideways, her PTSD resurfaced with a vengeance, but she kept working... and waiting to hear anything. But now... she wasn't so sure she wanted to hear what her uncle had to say.

The sheriff took a step toward her. "He's alive."

Katie felt her world turning upside-down again. Her hands shook and her heart raced. "Where has he been? What happened? Is he okay?" Some part of her wondered if it was really him, or if some kind of mean joke was being played on her. "Have you seen him?" she asked.

"Yes, and he's stable. He had been held captive all this time and was finally able to escape and managed to call dispatch for help."

"I want to see him," she said and began to pack up to leave. "Take me to him."

"Wait a minute. You need to know a few things. We've been putting together everything."

"I want to see him now." Katie's mind ran in several directions. She had been allowing herself to grieve, believing he had to be dead. "Please..."

Sheriff Scott looked at McGaven.

"Please take me to him now!" she said firmly.

"Okay. They're examining him and he's dehydrated and weak. He's going to need some time to recover." He lowered his voice. "I'll take you to him."

Katie turned to McGaven. "I'll call you when I know more."

"Of course," he said as he watched the sheriff and Katie leave.

Katie rode with her uncle to the First Memorial Hospital of Pine Valley, quiet, tense, and alert. If she relaxed or let her guard down, she would break and start crying, unable to stop. Sheriff Scott didn't push his niece, letting her process it all.

When they parked in the visitors' parking lot, Katie jumped out of her uncle's large SUV and practically ran to the entrance.

The sheriff gently took her arm. "Wait a minute."

"Why?"

"You need to understand something."

Katie searched her uncle's usual solemn face and realized that he wore a look of genuine concern. It was unusual. He could usually hold his emotions to do his job. "What haven't you told me?"

Her uncle guided her to a quieter area near the hospital entrance. Katie felt her breath stick in her throat.

"Chad is living with physical and mental stresses right now," her uncle said. "Not only is he severely dehydrated and malnourished, but he's also exhibiting signs of extreme anxiety and stress."

"You mean PTSD?" Even though Katie had her traumas during her two tours in Afghanistan, she knew all too well what it was like. She imagined Chad being imprisoned for the past months were similar to being a prisoner of war. Her heart ached not knowing what he had endured during that time—and that he had been alone not knowing what was going to happen.

"He's under observation right now, but I've managed to get permission for your visit."

"Permission?"

"Katie, you know he's a part of an ongoing investigation."

"Yes, and I want to—"

"Let me stop you," he said. "I know you mean well, but you can't investigate this."

Katie took a breath and stepped back.

"I know how you feel," said her uncle.

"Do you? I've been living with the fact he was taken right out from under my nose. I've been following every lead until there were no more. And after the arrest of Terrance Lane and the death of Sean Hyde it has been a whirlwind of nightmares."

Hyde was a serial killer in cold cases spanning twenty years and Lane his willing accomplice. Hyde had claimed to know about Chad's disappearance and had taunted Katie before his death.

"I know. Katie, you need to take it easy, not only for your sake but also for Chad's. We've only been allowed a short visit."

Tears welled up in Katie's eyes, and she desperately wiped them away. She knew that things would never be the same, but her love for Chad was real and forever. "Okay. Let's go."

Katie and the sheriff walked into the main entrance to the hospital, but they didn't go to the usual area in ICU. She followed her uncle into the elevator, and they ascended to the fifth floor. When the doors opened, she realized it was part of the psychiatric unit. Katie looked questioningly at her uncle.

"It's okay. We wanted to have him here where there is more security than an officer stationed at his door."

Katie nodded.

There were two security guards that more resembled seasoned SWAT officers than hospital security. Passing several doctors and nurses, they continued, walking down two more hallways until they came to Chad's room where two uniformed officers were stationed.

Katie stood at the closed door, frozen. Her nerves were frazzled, and she felt uncomfortable in her surroundings. Even though she'd thought about this moment for months, now that she was actually here it seemed almost paralyzing. So many questions fired through her mind.

"Go on. It's okay," said the sheriff, moving back to let her proceed.

She took a deep breath and pushed the door open.

The medium-size room resembled a small studio apartment or motel room more than a hospital unit—except for the typical hospital bed. The sides were drawn up and it was elevated, apparatuses monitoring blood pressure and heart rate.

Lying in the bed with a white sheet covering him was Chad. At first, Katie wasn't sure if it was him. Chad's appearance was drastically different—he was considerably thinner, his face gaunt. His sandy hair was long; he had a beard. He reminded her of some of the soldiers she'd seen who had been in combat for more than a couple of tours. But staring at his face, she knew it was him.

Katie's heart shattered. What had they done to him? Just because she had investigated serial killer cases, someone had wanted to up the excitement by kidnapping the lead investigator's fiancé to make it a game. The horror. The heartbreak. The deep sadness she felt in her soul came crashing down on top of her. She couldn't breathe.

She moved next to the bed. Her hand touched his cheek. "Chad?" she said softly. "It's me. I'm so glad you're home." She kept her voice steady, but her body trembled slightly.

At the sound of her voice, Chad's eyes opened. His blue eyes stared at her as if he was seeing a mirage. "Katie?" he said as he tried to sit up.

"No. Just rest. I'm here. I can only stay for a little bit. But I'm here now." Katie tried to stay stoic and not cry, but the tears flowed.

Chad lifted his hand and touched her cheek, wiping away her tears. "It's okay."

"We're going to get to the bottom of this... I promise. The sheriff is making it a priority."

"I love you," he whispered.

"I love you more," she replied. "I'll stay as long as they let me." Katie pulled a chair closer to the bedside, holding his hand as he closed his eyes again and fell back asleep.

Katie didn't know how long she remained at his side listening to the hypnotic beeping of the monitors, observing the saline drip, and watching Chad's restful breathing when her uncle appeared at the doorway.

"Katie," he whispered, "we have to go. You can come back tomorrow."

The last thing Katie wanted was to leave Chad. What if he simply vanished without a trace again?

Sheriff Scott patiently waited.

Katie stood, looking down at Chad. Her heart still ached, but her soul felt lighter. She leaned over and gently kissed his forehead before joining her uncle and leaving the room. The two uniformed officers still stood watch. They nodded their respect to the sheriff as Katie and he passed by.

Her uncle didn't say a word until they were back at his SUV in the parking lot. It was getting dark and the lights from the hospital seemed alien, like a weird beacon.

Before getting into the vehicle, the sheriff stopped Katie. "I know this is hard for you. And I also know you very well. You have to let the investigation run its course. You cannot be the investigator on this for the obvious reasons."

"Did he tell you where he was being held?" she asked.

The sheriff hesitated. "Not the exact location, but he explained the surrounding area, which is the Pine Valley Hawk Ridge region. And that he knocked his captor out. We will find the location and the man. We're looking through old maps that would have outdated culverts and drainage areas. That's what Chad thinks he was held captive in."

"You need me on this," Katie said. She was determined to help in any way she could—any way she was allowed. "Me and Cisco. That man who held him is probably long gone by now."

"I know you mean well."

"You don't think we could find it?"

"I know you and Cisco could find it."

"Then why not? It would be in the best interests of the investigation." Katie tried to keep her emotions in check. "Is anyone searching now?"

The sheriff looked around. "No, daylight is gone."

"I respectfully request to head the search with Cisco at daybreak." Cisco was her retired military working dog that she was able to take home with her after her honorable discharge from the Army. He had been more than helpful in other forensic searches in the past, not to mention the dog was Katie's protection as well.

Katie and her uncle stood silent, as if in a standoff. It was almost a full minute before Katie spoke again.

"You know I'm right and the clock is ticking," she said. "McGaven can continue to work the cold case for a day without me. He's more than capable."

The sheriff looked around the hospital parking lot as cars entered and left. "Okay."

"Okay?" Katie was relieved, looking forward to doing something constructive in Chad's investigation.

"But... you will be acting in the capacity as a K9 search team. Which means you must work under the authority of me *and* Detective Hamilton."

"Fine." Katie didn't like the idea that Detective Hamilton was heading the investigation, since she'd had confrontations with him in the past, but she had to learn to work with everyone at the department.

"I'm not kidding, Katie. You must work under the authority of Hamilton and me. No rogue work."

"Yes, I understand."

They both got into the SUV and the sheriff softened his tone. "You know I love you. And I love Chad like a son. I want to get to the bottom of what happened, but I have to go by the book. Understand?"

Katie nodded. Her mind was already beginning to process where and how they would conduct the search, and how difficult the Hawk Ridge region's terrain was going to be.

TEN

Tuesday 2200 hours

After Katie had called and updated McGaven about the morning search and had eaten dinner, she sat on the couch going over paperwork from Chad's investigation as well as the map of the area where he had been rescued. She wanted to make a plan of the search regions before morning.

Cisco, her large black German shepherd, was lying quietly at her side. His long, stretched-out body was completely relaxed. She had taken him on a short run so that he could get out all his energy. Tomorrow was going to be a big day and they both needed the rest.

Katie had a difficult time keeping her eyes open as she read and reread her account of their night at the cabin before Chad went missing, and she dozed off while she still held it in her hand.

Katie stood up next to the bed, her senses strangely heightened. "Chad?"

She expected to hear him return from the other room, but only silence greeted her. Fumbling beside her, she switched on the bedroom lamp. The room was still. The other side of the bed was made, and the pillow was arranged as if someone had recently composed it. Chad's clothes were gone, and his overnight bag was missing.

Katie moved slowly across the room and the wooden floor felt cold on the bottom of her feet. The planks creaked beneath her. "Chad?" she said again. Her voice sounded hollow and disconnected...

"Chad?" Her voice echoed strangely in the forest. Alone and distant. Pure adrenaline-fueled panic set in like a sword piercing her soul.

Looking down, Katie saw that she had stepped in something sticky. Immediately kneeling, she touched her fingertips to the floor. Turning her hand over, she stared at the crimson substance, rubbing it between her fingers. Blood. Sucking in a breath, she followed the trail of tiny drops, illuminated by the early morning light, outside and along the pathway, where they suddenly vanished in front of Chad's SUV. There were no footprints. Nothing.

Katie stood alone in the cool dawn air as mounting horror and confusion consumed her.

Katie startled awake, her breathing heavy, her skin perspiring. The memory nightmare had infused her consciousness. Sitting up, staring at the paperwork scattered all around her on the coffee table and the couch made her realize how important it was to have closure on Chad's case.

Cisco nestled his body closer to Katie, feeling her stress and heartache.

"It's okay, Cisco," she said, petting him as the dog softly panted. Katie knew her life would have been very lonely if she didn't have him. Her farmhouse had belonged to her parents, and she had inherited it from them after their deaths. Although she lived there alone, it gave her a feeling of being closer to them. Katie wasn't sure if she could ever sell the house and property. She and Chad hadn't worked out where they would live once they were married. She knew Chad thought it best to buy a new place together—but as Katie looked around at everything she had always known, and what had comforted her during some of her most difficult and complicated times—she wanted to stay right where she was.

ELEVEN

Wednesday 0630 hours

The sunrise colored a vivid morning sky with oranges and yellows, casting the first shadows of the day. The wind stalled as the difficult terrain spread out before the small group of law enforcement gathered for the joint effort to find Chad's holding area, seeming to say, "You can go ahead and find it."

Katie had already suited Cisco with his search vest, and she was wearing her heavier combat gear, ready for anything they'd encounter along the heavy terrain. She snapped on Cisco's long lead and was ready to begin.

They were at the parking area for Hawkeye Trail in the Pine Valley forest. It wasn't a well-used hiking trail, but many keen experienced hikers would venture up here for extreme privacy and the feel of the rural outdoors in a magnificent setting. It was indeed breathtaking, but today it was their starting point for trying to trace Chad's escape path back to where he'd been held.

As Katie looked out over the immense forest and the few open valleys in between, she was immediately struck by her memories of camping and hiking with not only her parents but also with Chad. She had wanted to visit him this morning, but the search was more important at the moment, and he needed his rest. The weather and time would soon diminish any trace of his trail—and the scent of that trek. The area they were going to search was where the trails were barely visible, if at all. That was why Cisco's nose was so important to guide them in the right direction. She stared at the tree line and smelled the intoxicating scent of the pine forest where they would begin their investigative search. There was nothing like it.

Her uncle walked up to her. He was dressed in his tactical uniform and had been briefing the few officers and forensic personnel. There were a half dozen different types of police vehicles plus Sheriff Scott and the detectives' SUVs. Detective Hamilton kept his distance but nodded to acknowledge Katie's presence. He wore clothes similar to the sheriff and had a baseball cap covering his sparse hairline.

"Okay, we're going to head north. It seems like the best direction according to Chad's statement. He felt like he was traveling south to get here," said the sheriff.

"We're ready," Katie said. She noted Cisco's body language, tense with his tail down and head high, indicating that he was focused and ready to go.

"You have your walkie in case we get separated?" he said.

"Yep." She patted her hip where it was attached to her belt, along with her gun, cell phone, and flashlight.

Cisco's energy began to heighten as if he sensed what was at stake and the surrounding energy of everyone involved.

"*Such*," said Katie in German, commanding the dog to search.

That's all it took for Cisco to begin his tracking. He first went up to an area where the overgrowth seemed to be packed down in places, keeping his head low, cataloging various scents, making a slight wave motion back and forth where the makeshift trail was located.

Katie watched the dog for any behavioral changes—a hesitation, a head snap, or a rigid body. Cisco's body was directed at the task at hand with some tautness, but his tail was low and his ears perked. His jet-black coat glistened in the morning light. A few minutes passed, and he kept a steady speed with a relaxed gait.

As she trekked, Katie could hear the footsteps behind her, but she didn't want to let the search crew distract her from concentrating on Cisco's movements. The team kept their distance and their formation wide so each member could examine the terrain for evidence of Chad as they followed. The land wasn't as difficult as she had first expected. The landscape was dense and dry making it steady under her feet.

As she watched Cisco easily pad up and down slight hills, he began to slow his pace, which indicated he'd caught a whiff of something important and it had become a stronger scent. Katie had given Cisco almost ten feet of leash ahead of her to begin, but now she gently reeled him closer to about six feet. Her senses were heightened as well, reminiscent of her time in the military on searches with Cisco when every footstep, every sound around them, could be potentially dangerous. Now in the densest forest of Pine Valley, Katie felt the same. Of course, she knew it wasn't as dangerous, but her intense reactions were the post-traumatic symptoms she brought back with her from Afghanistan. Every twig that snapped beneath her boots and every bird that fluttered from a tree branch made her twitch.

Katie watched Cisco slow even more where he seemed interested in something around an area.

"What's up, Cisco?" she said softly. She knelt down and examined a two-foot area that seemed to have dark drops spattered on dead leaves. Blood?

"What do you have?" asked the forensic supervisor, John

Blackburn. He had been a Navy SEAL and then studied forensics and chemistry to head up the forensic division. This, and his military stature, made him a force for the Pine Valley Sheriff's Department.

Katie looked up and saw John standing over her. "I think it's blood," she said.

"Let me see." John carefully knelt down and took a small swab from one of the droplets. He pulled a small vial out of his pocket and used a dropper to squeeze phenolphthalein and hydrogen peroxide on the swab. It turned pink, indicating blood. "Yep, it's blood."

"It makes sense," she said, remembering the blood droplets at the cabin when Chad had disappeared. "According to Chad's description of where he came from, and by his injuries from the fight with his captor, this seems like the right amount of blood."

"Can Cisco track the trail?" John asked.

"Yes."

The sheriff, the detective, and the other officers stood patiently waiting at a safe distance for Katie and Cisco to continue.

"I'll continue trailing behind you to keep an eye out for anything you need to be aware of, so you can completely concentrate on Cisco," John said.

Katie nodded. Her skin prickled as if the nerves were exposed. Her heart rate increased. She knew they were close. There was no doubt they would find where Chad had been kept all this time.

Even though the sun was shining, the area they were moving into was dim with shadows all around due to the thicker forest canopy. They had been walking for about an hour. This time the dog moved at a moderate pace and seemed to be following a strong scent. The canine didn't deviate back and forth, but rather kept to a track, similar to how a person would've walked.

Katie slowed her pace, but Cisco seemed to want to go faster, until he sat down, indicating there was something up ahead that was potentially dangerous.

She stopped.

"What's wrong?" said John in barely a whisper.

"I don't know," she said quietly.

Katie heard footsteps advancing from behind her as the sheriff approached. "What do you have?" Her uncle's voice was low as well.

She turned to the two men. "I don't know, but Cisco seems to have caught a scent that he doesn't trust. Danger."

The sheriff turned to John. "We need to surround the location and proceed with caution. Move as if there are traps."

"On it." John left to coordinate the others.

"You think there's really danger?" Katie asked her uncle.

"Don't know. It could be a wild animal."

"I don't think so. Cisco responded as if there were trip wires." Katie watched the group organize and move in. She scrutinized the area. It would be easy to imagine a hidden bunker within the forest or an old culvert that diverted excessive rain to keep the surrounding areas clear of flooding.

Katie looked to the left and the right of the trail and she thought she could see where someone might have walked. Was it Chad or his captor?

"Stay here," instructed Sheriff Scott. And before Katie could respond, he merged with the group.

Cisco whined and clearly wanted to join them; his wolf-like eyes wide as he waited for her to give him a command to continue.

"We have to wait," said Katie to the large dog.

Katie watched as her uncle and the rest of the group moved out of sight. There wasn't a sound, the forest eerily quiet. She waited. Her walkie-talkie was also silent. Her mind spun through all types of scenarios—booby traps, dead bodies, the captor lying in wait, and more people held against their will. Anything was possible in such a deserted wilderness area.

Katie was extremely aware of her surroundings and made slow 360-degree turns to make sure they weren't followed, tracked, or being ambushed.

She and Cisco waited another ten minutes before she saw the sheriff and John emerge from the thicket area. Their expressions were neutral, and their body language was relaxed.

When the sheriff was near, he said, "All clear. We found it. It's an old, decommissioned tunnel, probably from fifty years ago, leading to a drainage channel. There are a few around in these areas to help with watershed and to prevent heavy flooding."

Katie was relieved, but at the same time she was anxious. It was an unusual combination of feelings, but there was the obvious emotion of relief that they had found where Chad had been held, and then the deep sorrow of knowing what he must've gone through, not knowing where he was and not knowing if he would be rescued. He had been left to die. Alone.

Katie and Cisco began to walk toward the area.

"Wait," said the sheriff.

"I want to see it. I promise I won't get in the way of the investigation."

"I don't think that's a good idea."

"Why?" she said. "I'm not going in as a detective."

"That's what I'm afraid of."

"I think that with everything I've been through, and especially with what Chad has been through, I need to see where he was held. I can help." Katie took a breath. "If we're going to heal from this trauma, I think I should see the area."

Sheriff Scott looked out at the forest and glanced at the team behind him. He seemed to struggle with the decision for many reasons. "My gut instinct says yes, but professionally I don't—"

"Please," she said.

The sheriff looked up. Detective Hamilton was approaching. Katie knew that Hamilton's reaction might play a part in the process.

"Sir," said Hamilton, "we're ready to have forensics process the interior and exterior. I'm having everyone vacate the immediate area and canvass the surrounding sections."

"Thank you," said the sheriff. He still didn't answer Katie's question.

"If it's okay with you," said Hamilton to the sheriff, "I would like Detective Scott to run through the interior before forensics."

Katie could barely blink when she heard Hamilton wanting to include her.

"Of course." Her uncle turned to Katie. "Detective Scott?"

"Yes, of course," she said.

"I'll take Cisco," said the sheriff as he took the lead.

Katie nodded. Now that she had permission to go through the scene first, her heart sank. It was real. She would see where Chad had been held for months and that reality was difficult for her.

"I knew you were going to want to see the scene, but the fact is," said Hamilton, "you're the best at assessing crime scenes and this is no different."

"Except it's personal now. But I'm not going to let that get in the way."

"I know you won't." His voice was somber, but he still showed respect.

Katie realized Hamilton had more understanding than she'd originally thought. She didn't want to lose that respect from him because she knew there were going to be other cases they would have to work together on.

They walked up to the entrance. It was shrouded in vines and forest undergrowth. The doorway was barely visible except for the trampled areas from tactical boots. It appeared that the original door had been replaced at some point in the past few years with a reinforced metal one.

"Take your time," said Hamilton as he moved away. "I'll be just a bit behind if you need anything."

Katie saw John as he nodded to her as if to say he's there for her—and good luck. He had been there for many cases and for backup on some serious occasions and she appreciated his presence. She heard a quick bark from Cisco, probably because he wasn't getting to go in and search a scene.

Katie knew all eyes were on her as she reached the entrance, pulling on a pair of gloves, and pushing the door open. She stepped inside.

TWELVE

Wednesday 0900 hours

McGaven drove to St. Joseph's Church located in downtown Pine Valley. He was scheduled to meet with semiretired Detective Richard Jamison—who handled most of the church's local donations and headed up the support groups for police officers. He had been the detective assigned to the missing person's case for Abigail Andrews. It was customary in the opening of cold cases, if at all possible, to speak with the investigating officer at the time of the report.

McGaven's mind wasn't completely on the case as his thoughts fell back to how Katie was doing in the search and if there was progress being made. He had sent her a text earlier but hadn't heard back. She was in a rural area and the signal was most likely sketchy.

There was only a sprinkling of cars in the church's parking lot. McGaven stepped out of the sedan, glancing around him. The area was quiet and deserted. Walking to the back door entrance, there was a large white pickup truck with boxes neatly stacked in the back.

The door was slightly ajar, so McGaven pushed it open. "Hello? Detective Jamison?"

"Yeah, come on in," came a voice.

McGaven walked through the back area where boxes, bins, and large storage containers were organized by group and size. He still didn't see the detective.

"I'm over here," said the voice.

McGaven passed boxes identified as household, kitchen, clothes, and medical, until he came across a man in a corner organizing more boxes. He looked to be in his late fifties, heavyset around the middle, and wearing jeans and a T-shirt. His silver hair made him seem older, but his young-looking face said otherwise.

"Detective Jamison?" said McGaven. "I'm Detective Sean McGaven."

"Yes," he replied and came to McGaven to shake his hand. "Nice to meet you."

"You too. Need a hand?"

"No, thank you. I'm just getting some boxes ready for pick up."

McGaven looked around and was impressed by the dedication that the former detective had put into this work.

"I just made some coffee. Would you like a cup?" Jamieson asked.

"No, thank you, I'm fine," said McGaven. "I've had four cups already this morning."

"Where's your partner?"

"She's on a special assignment today."

"Too bad. I wanted to meet her. You know... you two are quite the topic among us old-timers." He smiled and moved a box to sit down on and gestured for McGaven to do the same.

"Really?"

"Of course. A one hundred percent cold-case solve rate is

impressive... and not to mention Detective Scott is quite the dedicated officer."

McGaven laughed. There had been so many situations they had been involved in—and some he hadn't been sure they would survive. "Yes, she sure is..."

"So, what's on your mind about the Abigail Andrews case?" the older detective asked.

McGaven coordinated his thoughts. "Well, we just reopened the case and have spoken to Mrs. Andrews and looked through some of Abigail's things. We've read through the reports."

"And you want to know my gut on the case. My impressions."

"That would about sum it up. If you can remember."

"Oh, I remember everything about my cases, especially when they were like the Andrews case."

"What do you mean?" asked McGaven, his curiosity piqued.

"Everything about the case seemed off. The initial report, the car location, and the area around it."

"We visited the area where the car was found, and it did seem strange. If there was foul play, why didn't the perp hide the car? It would have been easy and probably no one would have ever noticed it—especially at that location."

"You mean down the ravine?"

"Yes." McGaven reached for his phone and pulled up a photo of the butterfly necklace. He showed it to the retired detective.

Jamison put on his glasses and looked at the photo. "You found it where?"

"Down that slight hillside."

"I see." He nodded. "I remember those butterfly pieces of jewelry in her room at her mom's house." He examined the photo longer. "You think this was the girl's?"

"Don't know for sure. But one of the forensic techs is searching the area—just in case there is anything else that might have belonged to her. It could answer some questions, like if there was indeed foul play or not."

"What else could it be?" said Jamison as he looked at McGaven over the top of his glasses.

"We're just reviewing evidence and eliminating things—trying to generate new leads."

The older detective sighed. "Not to rain on your parade of a perfect cold-case solve rate, but this may be the case you can't crack."

McGaven chuckled. "I've thought that same thing about some of our other cases, but we manage to solve them. But we can only try." He wasn't going let anyone derail their cold case at the beginning.

Jamison scrutinized McGaven for a moment. "I like your attitude and your resourcefulness."

"What other things stuck out to you?"

"Well, the victim's friends for one. We couldn't really get solid alibis, but we searched both of their homes and work. Nothing we found seemed suspicious. But each one had the opportunity to make her disappear."

"You mean Anthony Drake and Teri Butler?"

"Yeah. Teri seemed genuinely upset that Abigail had gone missing and her car was found. But the boyfriend—Drake—acted a bit cagey about some of the questions we asked. I think it was more due to the fact he had been arrested on some minor substance use charges."

"What about the mom?"

"Nothing panned out from there. She seemed truthful and there was nothing that waved a red flag. And don't forget Mr. Andrews was still alive then. He was angry and frustrated. I get it. I've had my own problems with my kids in the past. Thankfully they've straightened up and are living great lives now." He smoothed some tape on a box and seemed to be rehashing things from the investigation over in his mind.

"Do you think that whatever happened to Abigail was because of her lifestyle? Or was it something else? Like wrong place, wrong time?"

"At the time I leaned toward her lifestyle. We couldn't get a beat on why she was at that location to begin with. We worked the case from the perspective that it had been someone close to her, like family and friends. I actually thought we'd find her body too."

"That's what makes this case difficult," said McGaven.

"The body is everything. It's what puts the pieces together of what happened and then leaves the who and why for us to figure out."

McGaven thought that was a good way of describing it. "If you were working the case today... what would you revisit first?" He waited patiently for the detective to answer. He already knew what he and Katie were going to do, but still, he respected the detective's opinion and experience.

"I think it starts at the car and finding a connection to it, whether it be some other location, someone who was linked to it, or one of the farms near where it was found. We did a canvass twice, but never turned up anything." He took his phone and made a note in his day reminder. "I have some of my personal notes from my cases that might have something that would help your case. I'll email them to you."

"Thank you." McGaven felt that Detective Jamison had been consistent with the reports, which meant he did remember his cases well. "Was there anything about the car you noticed at the time? Like if there'd been car trouble?"

"No, the keys were in it, which seemed odd."

"Did it start?" said McGaven.

"It did, but there was an intermittent starter problem. You

know, like when the alternator is failing. It was possibly what happened to her that day."

McGaven nodded and thought it was an interesting point.

"Anything I can do, let me know," said Jamison. "And if I remember anything else that might help, I'll be sure to contact you directly."

"Thank you, that would be great. It seems like this case doesn't have much to go on, but I'm optimistic we'll find something." McGaven smiled.

"After hearing and reading about your partner, I don't doubt it." He stood up. "I'm sorry that I wasn't more helpful. Oh, and please, let me know if you solve it."

"Of course."

"It would put an unsolved case to bed for me. One less thing to obsess about. You'll understand when you get older or when you retire. There are always those cases that haunt you."

"I appreciate your time. And it helps to get more perspective on the case. Thanks again."

As McGaven walked back to the car, Detective Jamison's words rolled through his mind. *The body is everything. It's what puts the pieces together of what happened and then leaves the who and why for us to figure out.*

THIRTEEN

Wednesday 0945 hours

Katie stepped inside the tunnel and was immediately hit with a heavy foul odor. It was a combination of rancid garbage, mildew, and stale air. The thought of Chad enduring this for months made her extremely sad, not to mention angry. She wanted to find the people who had done this and make them pay.

There was the distinct sound of water dripping somewhere, which echoed loudly in the long tunnel. She retrieved her flashlight and flipped it on. Even though she knew it was safe and no one was hiding, the entire area made her uncomfortable. If there was ever a time of fearing the unknown, this was it.

Katie could hear her elevated heart rate pounding in her ears. Instinctively, she took a deep low breath. It wouldn't do her any good if she hyperventilated. With the inhale, she took in more of the filthy aroma surrounding her, but her pulse returned to normal. Glancing back at the entrance, she saw that Hamilton patiently waited.

Turning around, she swept the beam of her flashlight across

the walls, ceiling, and straight ahead. It was just an outdated drainage channel that had been sitting for some time. It struck her as odd that someone would know about it, much less use it as a holding area for prisoners. Had Chad's abduction been planned for some time? Or had they kept someone else here against their will before Chad?

Katie walked ahead, looking from side to side. Nothing appeared to be unusual or gave any helpful clues. Maybe forensics would have better luck. She kept moving. The air became even more stagnant, causing her to feel a bit lightheaded. She saw a door up ahead that definitely appeared out of place for the old culvert. It was metal and seemed to have been retrofitted recently. It was an unusual shape and obviously specially designed, with expensive hinges and hardware. It had been planned for keeping something safe—or holding someone captive for an extended period of time.

Katie halted at the door. She flashed the beam on either side of it, looking for anything that might prove to be useful such as recent garbage, cigarette butts, contents from a pocket, or slips of paper—anything that might give some indication of why this holding place existed and who had created it.

As she stood at the door, Katie could feel Detective Hamilton's eyes watching her every move. He didn't say anything, but she knew he was lingering for anything she found in her search. It was going to be a difficult case if he only had Chad's recount of the incidents.

Katie put her gloved hand on the metal doorknob and felt it turn in her hand. She slowly pushed the door open. To her surprise, the room had light infiltrating through cracks, which gave it a weird atmosphere, almost a funhouse quality, with the walls looking taller than they were and the lighting resembling a sunrise.

She took a few steps into the room, approximately fourteen by fourteen foot. There was a corner where there were paper containers, which most likely had held food, a metal bucket in another corner, and a threadbare towel in another. Next to the towel were broken zip ties. Scattered across the floor were dark spots, appearing to be dried blood.

Katie studied the area, recalling what Chad had told the sheriff. Everything seemed to be consistent. However, there was no sign of the man who Chad had fought with or what he had used to defend himself.

She knelt down, taking a closer look at the dark droplets. Almost instantly, her mind went back to the cabin after Chad disappeared where the only clue was the droplets left behind. Trying to keep her emotions in check, Katie then saw there were scrape marks across one side of the floor, which seemed odd. She also noticed there were worn areas from feet passing over many times.

Katie closed her eyes and imagined Chad walking the room a million times, trying to find a way out. Not knowing where he was or if anyone would ever find him again. It smacked her in the gut with despair.

She glanced at the door, expecting to see Hamilton or the others at any moment since she was taking longer than they had probably estimated, but no one was there. Turning her attention back to the scrape marks along the floor, she followed them to where they appeared to end at one of the walls. Running her fingers along them, the indentations were superficial. Strange.

Katie stood up and studied the wall. As she ran her hand over it, she could feel an unevenness to the structure. What was peculiar was that the wall should have been concrete like the tunnel, but it wasn't. It was made of some type of fiberglass, she thought. It didn't seem to be new, but still something fabricated after the original construction. Although dense, there were cracks where the light shone into the room, indicating that the outdoors wasn't too far.

Katie kept searching until she reached the corner, where the two sections of the wall met. There was also a crack here, more defined, but this one appeared to have been made on purpose during construction. It seemed like a panel of some kind incorporated into the area. She tried to push in her fingertips and move it, but it was strong. There wasn't a way for her to pry it open by hand. Someone would need to force it with tools.

She stepped back and could see that it would be an opening about five feet across. It was difficult to see at first, but as she studied the wall under the flashlight it became more apparent.

Katie ran back through the tunnel and Hamilton met her.

"What's up?" he said.

"I think there's a hidden room and I need something to pry it open," she said.

Hamilton turned and yelled for John. After a few moments, the forensic supervisor entered the tunnel carrying a toolbox and a digital camera.

"Show me," he said to Katie. John followed her back to the small room. He hesitated, looking around. It seemed to make him upset.

"Here," said Katie. She ran her fingers along the crack. "I think there's something back here."

John scrutinized the section and he nodded. "I think you might be right." He quickly documented the wall with overall and close-up photographs.

It took John a few minutes to pry the area open. When he did, Katie helped him move the panel away from the wall. As they peered inside, Katie aimed the flashlight beam revealing an area about four to five feet. All they could see was some heavy plastic, partially rolled up.

Katie hadn't been expecting that. "It's just plastic," she said.

"We'll have to run tests to find out what else might have been stored in there."

Katie gulped. She wasn't sure she wanted to know.

FOURTEEN

Katie, Cisco, and the sheriff stood just outside the tunnel watching the team work. They had discovered an outside entrance into the secret area, which led to the room where Chad had been held. The room had access from the holding room to the outdoors. It would've been almost impossible for Chad, without a flashlight, to find the room unless he was looking for it, and then he would have needed proper tools; otherwise, he might've escaped sooner. It was difficult to see the seams of the hidden section even if you ran your hands over it. Katie had seen secret hidden compartments in the past and she systematically looked for these types of anomalies. In Chad's defense, he had been tied up most of the time and when he was free, his weakened state would search for the obvious means of escape, such as the door.

Many things ran through Katie's mind. *Had there been bodies stored here? Were there other captives? Why was Chad kept alive as long as he was? Who was the person Chad had fought in order to escape?*

Katie paced with Cisco, trying to make sense of everything they had learned so far, even though she knew that Detective Hamilton would be in charge of the investigation. No matter how much she wanted to pursue the case, she knew that the sheriff wouldn't approve it. Still, she ran scenarios in her mind.

Cisco whined and nudged her hand.

"Katie?" said the sheriff. He had been on his cell phone. "Chad is being moved to a rehabilitation facility across town."

Her heart almost stopped. "Everything okay?"

"Everything is fine. It's just a better place for him to heal and where we can have better security. You and McGaven need to continue *your* case," he said.

Katie frowned. She wanted to work the case and find the man who had kept Chad prisoner. But she said, "Of course."

Detective Hamilton approached. His expression was solemn, and he didn't look directly at Katie or the sheriff.

"Update?" said the sheriff.

"John is documenting, taking samples, and dusting for prints. Hopefully we'll find out the identity of the man who had been holding Mr. Ferguson."

"Are you going to talk to Terrance Lane again?" said Katie.

"Of course. I just spoke with your partner and he's forwarding all your files from the cases. Detective Scott, I appreciate your resourcefulness in finding the secret room."

Katie didn't respond.

"Thank you, Detective," said the sheriff.

Hamilton nodded before walking away.

"Katie, I think we're good here and we'll keep you in the loop. You can join McGaven and continue your case," said the sheriff.

Katie wanted to argue that she was the better person to investigate the case, but she knew it was pointless. She turned and started to walk back down the trail with Cisco.

"Katie?"

She turned.

"I'm so sorry for everything," her uncle said.

"I know. I'll be fine. Chad is who is important now."

As Katie and Cisco made their way back to the parking area, she rehashed what Chad had recollected about his walk. It didn't seem to take as long as she had originally estimated; twenty minutes at a moderate pace. She wondered if Chad had been mistaken, or if his condition had made a drastic difference.

She approached her SUV and loaded Cisco inside. Once she climbed into the driver's seat, she called McGaven.

"Hey," he said when he answered. "You okay?"

"I'm fine."

"I'm in the process of sending Hamilton the Lane/Hyde files."

"Good."

"You're good with that?"

"There's nothing I can do. I understand why the sheriff made the call."

"I sense a but coming."

She couldn't help but smile. McGaven knew her too well. "Let's just say I want to find the person who kept Chad hostage."

"You don't think Hamilton will?"

"Maybe. Maybe not. But I want to find him before he has a chance to disappear for good. Hamilton doesn't have what we have invested in this case."

"We have some interviews this afternoon for the Abigail Andrews case."

"I'll meet you back at the office in an hour."

"I'll be here."

Katie disconnected the call.

Cisco pushed his large head around her seat headrest.

"We're going to find him, Cisco, I promise."

FIFTEEN

Katie and her partner sat in the visiting area at Pine Valley Corrections waiting to speak with Anthony Drake. McGaven had tracked down the boyfriend of Abigail Andrews and found he was doing five years for substance possession and burglary. Abigail's other friend, Teri Butler, was nowhere to be found. Her last known addresses, phone numbers, and places of employment were dead ends. Her only family, a niece and a half-sister, hadn't seen or heard from her in almost five years. That would not stop McGaven from digging for any leads to her whereabouts.

There were only two other inmates visiting with family, so it was relatively quiet in the room. She noticed that there were two correctional officers conferring with each other and it seemed to be something important. They both kept glancing back at the detectives.

"What do you think that's all about?" said McGaven.

"Not sure," she said.

"Think it's about Drake?"

One of the officers gestured to the detectives. Katie and McGaven stood up and walked to the entrance where they had been let through.

"Detectives Scott and McGaven?" said one of the officers.

"Yes," said Katie. She noticed several emergency personnel and other officers rushing to another area. There wasn't an alarm blaring that would initiate a lockdown, but it was definitely an emergency. "What's going on?"

"There's been an incident."

"What kind of incident?" said McGaven.

"Anthony Drake was found dead in the library."

"What? How?" said Katie.

"Stabbed," the other officer said. "It's pretty bad."

"We were here to question him about a cold case. He was one of the last people to see the victim alive," she said.

"I don't know what to tell you, Detective. He's dead."

"Take us to the scene," said McGaven.

"I don't know if—"

"We need to see him," said Katie.

The officers looked at each other. Finally, one of them said, "This way."

Katie and McGaven were led down several hallways and into the library area. Katie glanced at her partner with a questioning look. She saw blood streaked along the floor leading to a man's body in a corner. Books were strewn across the tables, and chairs were overturned, along with bloody handprints on the wall. It was a violent scene and it appeared that Anthony Drake had fought back with everything he had—but ultimately succumbed.

"Murder weapon?" asked Katie.

"There wasn't one left," said a correctional officer.

The infirmary attendant came with a gurney.

"Wait," said Katie. She went to the body and knelt down next to it. Comparing his face to the photos, it was clear it was indeed Anthony Drake. His eyes were fixed, staring at the ceiling. Blood had spattered across his face and forehead. She saw the ragged tearing along his neck, which would have caused him to bleed out in minutes. There were also several stab wounds on his chest and defensive wounds on his forearms and hands. It seemed strange to her that someone would do both types of attack. Did they stab him in the chest first and when it didn't kill him, cut his throat? Or had they just wanted to make sure the job was done?

Katie looked up. "Why was he in here alone?"

"He would restock books that were brought in. And he did that mostly alone until the library reopened."

Katie looked at the body again before standing up and letting the infirmary staff take him away. She rejoined McGaven.

"I guess we can't question him about Abigail," said McGaven.

"Afraid not," she said, still seeing Drake's staring eyes.

Once back at the office, Katie and McGaven reread Anthony Drake's original statement.

"Do you think his murder has to do with Abigail?" he said.

"It does seem strange that he ends up dead when we start looking into it again. But then there are a lot of things that could trigger an attack in prison."

"Corrections will forward the report when it's done."

"There's nothing we can do about it now," she said. "It may end up being a loose end."

"I can do more digging on his last years before prison."

"Okay," said Katie. She stood up and studied the aerial map of where Abigail's car was found. She scrutinized the farms and structures nearby. The room where Chad was held floated in and out of her mind. It followed her everywhere she went, and it was difficult to concentrate on the cold case.

"What's bothering you?" said McGaven.

Katie snapped back to the present. "Where the car was found and the rural area. Something doesn't fit." She saw there was a ranch approximately two miles from where the car was found, but when she looked more closely it was different from how she expected. "What's that?" She put her index finger on the area in question.

McGaven looked over. "That's an abandoned property. It was foreclosed years ago. No one owns it; it's like a wasteland."

Something in Katie's gut told her they'd need to investigate it. "I think we need to check it out and search the area. Just to mark it off the list of uncertainties so we can move on to the next possibility."

"I guess it's the next step. With Cisco, I assume?" McGaven gave a slight smile. It wasn't a secret that he loved it when Cisco was part of the investigation.

"Yep." She couldn't stop yawning and tried to cover it from her partner.

"Katie, go, take off. Let's meet up early tomorrow morning."

"But, I—"

"No, you need to spend some time with Chad. And get some rest. Too much stress today."

She sighed. "Thank you. I do."

"Meet back here at 0700?"

"Sounds good. Thanks, Gav."

"We're partners. I've got your back."

She smiled as she left.

SIXTEEN

Wednesday 1835 hours

Katie hurried through the hallways of the rehabilitation facility. It was a newer building in the Pine Valley area with impeccable rooms. She tried not to think about her cases or the dungeon-like room where Chad had been held. Whenever she worked any case, it would always be a part of her days and nights until she closed it. After she stepped off the elevator on the fourth floor, Katie easily found Chad's room as there were two uniformed police officers stationed outside his door. She smiled, nodding at them, and they motioned for her to enter.

Katie slowly walked through the door, which closed behind her with barely a sound. The room had a full-size sofa and two easy chairs along with a small dining table with two chairs. Along one wall were counters, cabinets, and a sink with a glass and a plate in it. As Katie noticed the dishes, the memory of being at the cabin came rushing back. She quickly pushed those thoughts away and concentrated on the present—and Chad.

He was resting comfortably, tucked in a nice bed with a comforter. His eyes were closed. Now clean-shaven with his blond hair combed away from his face, he more resembled the handsome man she had known most of her life.

Katie stood next to the bed and watched him sleep—his breathing and his expression were peaceful. She contemplated whether to wake him but opted to let him sleep. If anyone needed to sleep and feel safe, it was Chad.

She pushed one of the oversize leather chairs next to the bed and removed her boots. Pulling her legs up, she pressed her body against the cozy pillows. She hadn't realized how exhausted she was until she'd stopped moving. The room remained dark except for a low watt nightlight near the bathroom and some light peeking around the doorframe from the hallway.

Katie closed her eyes and quickly fell asleep, dreaming of her cases.

"Hey," said Chad.

Katie opened her eyes and sat up. She saw Chad's beautiful smile as he stared at her.

"When did you get here?"

"Just a little while ago." She stretched and leaned forward. She must've dozed off for about a half hour.

He took her hand. "I've missed you so much."

"When I didn't know what happened to you... and if I would ever..."

"It's okay. I'm here now."

Katie smiled. "I didn't know what I would do without you."

"And you won't have to."

Katie leaned over and kissed him. It was a soft lingering kiss.

"Has anyone spoken to you?" he said.

"About?" she said, sitting up. Dread began to creep in.

"It's going to be a process for me to move on."

Katie kept quiet, barely breathing.

"There are some things I remember and can see as clear as sitting here with you, but there are other things I don't recall. It could be because I was drugged frequently—usually in my food and water."

"What are you trying to say?"

"I will be working with a therapist to try to put all the pieces together."

"That's great. I will be here for whatever you need," she said.

"And... they thought it might be best for me to get away."

"Okay. I have tons of vacation time accrued and under the circumstances I'm sure I can get the time off and—"

"Katie," he said softly.

She knew what he was going to say even before he said it. But she wanted it to not be true.

Chad squeezed her hand. "Katie, I'm taking a leave of absence from the firehouse to go spend some time with my mom and sister."

"In Florida?" Her heart sank.

"Yeah. I have some things to work through and it would be best until there's an arrest of the man who kidnapped me and held me captive." He averted his gaze. It was clear that the thought of being away from Katie caused him pain.

"Okay. That means you need a break from me as well. We've been apart for the past few months, and I don't want to lose you again..." She was barely managing to speak.

"Katie, I love you. But I agree with the therapist and the police that I need to take a break. I can't ask you to leave in the middle of an investigation—"

She interrupted. "You are more important—we're more important. There will always be another case."

"It's going to be for a couple of weeks, maybe a month."

Katie tried to listen to what Chad was saying, but his words hit her like knives to her soul—she had only just got him back and now he was leaving her again. "I want you to do what you need to do—and heal." She snuggled up with him as the images paraded through her mind: the victims, the prison room, and the cold case. "I love you."

Chad hugged Katie tightly. "I love you more. And I'll be back before you know it."

Katie closed her eyes, enjoying those precious moments of being together with Chad.

SEVENTEEN

Wednesday 2345 hours

Katie's sleep was restless and tormented as she dreamed of the Abigail Andrews cold case and her previous cases. Her house was dark with only the low light of her security system illuminating the living room, kitchen, and a portion of the hallway. As she tossed and turned, the security control pad on the wall at the front door blinked, indicating that there was movement outside in quadrant number four—the backyard section on the far side of the house.

She was suddenly awakened by a beeping, indicating that the alarm system had been tripped. Sitting up in bed, Katie took a moment to fully wake. The low-level beeping was still sounding. She glanced at the chair in the corner where Cisco usually curled up for the night, but it was empty.

Katie threw back the covers, her bare feet hitting the floor. A sense of urgency filled her. She grabbed her Glock from the nightstand and hurried from the bedroom and down the hallway to the kitchen. She saw the still outline of Cisco at the sliding door leading to the backyard. The dog's posture was tense, his hackles partially bristled.

Katie quickly opened the laptop computer on her counter and checked the area that seemed to have a motion disturbance. It was most likely an animal that had tripped the alarm, but she couldn't just ignore it and assume it wasn't more of a threat.

She turned off the alert, leaving the house to fall into silence, then rewound the video, but there was nothing out of the ordinary. The yard with a country fence leading to the rest of the acreage was undisturbed—no animals, tree limbs, wind, or anything else that might have caused the motion sensor to activate.

Cisco whined. He pushed Katie's leg and then returned to the sliding door.

"What is it?" she whispered. Something was making her uneasy. She wasn't sure if it was due to previous experiences or if there really was something to worry about.

But Cisco was on edge too.

After grabbing a hoodie and slipping on shoes, Katie slid the door open. Cisco pushed at her.

"No, stay here," she said.

The dog gave two distinct whines and spun around in anticipation.

Katie stepped outside, readying her weapon as a precaution. She inched along the side of the house, making her way to the far side of the yard. She had a feeling of déjà vu. She had done this before when someone had come inside her yard, leaving a note attached to her gate with a knife. Incidents such as that made it more and more difficult to not become suspicious when her alarm was triggered. And tonight, she couldn't shake the feeling that someone had been there—watching.

Katie slowed her breathing and calmed her heart rate. The cold night air chilled her, filtering through her nightshirt and hoodie. As she crept around the corner of her home, her gun guiding her direction, she moved to the yard zone. Nothing. Noiseless. Nighttime quiet. The wind had died down and the area was undisturbed.

Katie continued to walk the property one section at a time until she was satisfied nothing was out of place and there wasn't anything or anyone lying in wait. However, she didn't breathe a sigh of relief as she walked back toward the sliding door as Cisco interrupted the quiet. It wasn't just a couple of woofs, but a barrage of serious barks.

Katie ran to the kitchen. Cisco was at the front door, still barking, and jumping high to the top of the frame.

She cautiously moved to the entrance and sidled up next to the windows, peering out. There was nothing, no sign of anyone or anything that would send Cisco into an alert.

Had there been someone there?

Katie decided to open the front door with her weapon trained ahead. No one was there and there was no indication that there ever had been. She surveyed her driveway and the Jeep, but there was nothing. No movement. No sound.

Cisco jetted out and immediately poked his long nose along the foundation on the porch.

"What's up?" Katie bent down and looked everywhere but could see nothing. She slowly stood up and scanned her front yard before she went back inside, secured the doors, and double-checked the security system.

It was after midnight, but she couldn't get back to sleep. For Cisco to take notice the way he did, for the scent to be strong enough at the front, there had to have been someone close to the house, but strangely, the video didn't record it.

EIGHTEEN

Thursday 0655 hours

Katie had arrived at the sheriff's department almost two hours before she was to meet McGaven. As she couldn't sleep, she had readied herself and gone to work instead. She spent the time going over everything they had on Abigail's disappearance and studying the map—and waiting for information about Anthony Drake's murder inside the prison. There wasn't much to go on until they uncovered more information. The fact that Abigail had had some intermittent car trouble, and her car had been found where it was, Katie thought it was likely that someone on one of the nearby properties would have some new information for them. Or at least give some indication of what could happen to someone if their car broke down in the vicinity.

McGaven had discovered that the property that had been foreclosed more than a decade earlier had been last owned by a Thomas Harland Dayton, though there wasn't any more information about him, other occupants, or where he was currently. In fact, they couldn't find any basic information on Dayton at all.

Katie focused on Detective Jamison's notes from the original missing person's case. She then read McGaven's interview with the detective, but it didn't seem to give anything new.

She sighed. It was indeed going to be a tough case.

Katie looked up at the board, which was now empty. She would usually have lists of the killer's behavior, crime-scene characteristics, and a number of people of interest. It wasn't that they didn't have any information, just nothing substantial enough to begin a killer profile and a victimology. She didn't want to make random lists. She needed new clues and forensic evidence. Frustration nagged at her. It felt almost as if she wasn't doing her job. It wasn't just the Abigail Andrews case. She knew what was bothering her. It was Chad's plans to leave Pine Valley to stay with his mom in Florida in order to get his thoughts together—and not staying here to work it out with her.

"Hey, partner," said McGaven as he entered the room.

"Morning."

"I know that tone. What's up? And why are you here so early?" He set down his jacket and laptop.

"How do you know I've been here for a while?" she said.

"By that," he said, pointing at several empty Styrofoam coffee cups.

"Oh."

"Did you forget that I'm a detective?" He laughed. McGaven was always chipper and positive, even in the early mornings. But he'd noticed the stricken look on his partner's face and softened his tone. "How's Chad?" he asked.

"He's... he's doing better. But..."

"But what?" McGaven sat down next to Katie. "What's going on?"

Katie didn't want to get into a personal conversation when they had a case, but she knew she should get it off her chest. "Chad and his doctors, even the fire department, have decided that he needs to go to Florida to stay with his mom and sister to sort things out. To have a rest away from here."

"Okay. I can see their point. He has been through a lot."

"I know. Maybe I'm just being selfish, but I want him to be here—with me. Is that wrong?"

"No, it's not. Did he say how long he'd be gone?"

Katie shook her head. "Maybe a couple of weeks."

"You know he's safe and if he needs time away from everything that reminds him of his ordeal, then maybe it's for the best."

"I know you're right, but it feels so personal... I feel very vulnerable for some reason."

McGaven sighed. "I don't claim to know what he's been through, but this has been tough for you too. Maybe taking a breather is best for both of you."

Katie didn't want to talk about it anymore. "Well," she said abruptly, changing the subject. "This property isn't going to search itself."

McGaven started to say something but decided not to. "Is Cisco ready?" he said instead.

"We just need to pick him up at the PVSO kennels."

"I miss that guy," he said, smiling.

"When was the last time you saw Cisco?"

"A few days ago." He laughed.

"He has that effect on people. I'll be ready in a moment."

"Okay. I brought some things that I need to transfer to the sedan. I'll do that now."

Katie raised an eyebrow in question.

"We don't know how rundown the property is," explained McGaven. "I have some tools and gardening things. It looks completely overrun and jungle-like from the aerial views."

"Good idea. Always prepared." She looked back at the blank board. "I'll meet you out there."

"See you in a few."

Katie quickly skimmed through the rest of the paperwork and loaded the aerial map on her tablet.

Her cell phone buzzed with a text.

Katie, just heard about Chad. How are you holding up?

Katie stopped and reread the message. It was from Evan Daniels, or more specifically, Detective Evan Daniels from the Sacramento Police Department. He had been her supervisor briefly when she was a patrol officer, and after Katie enlisted in the Army to be in an explosives K9 team, he had been her K9 trainer. He was instrumental in solving their last case and had assisted with the investigation into Chad's abduction. There'd been the possibility for things between the old colleagues to become complicated as they worked together, but they parted ways on good terms after the investigation had ended. It was nice that he was checking in.

Katie was about to send a reply but decided she would do it later. She gathered her things, including a pair of hiking boots, and left to meet McGaven and pick up Cisco. She didn't want anything, or anyone, to distract her from Abigail's case.

NINETEEN

Sometimes places can be abandoned, long forgotten, but still full of truths. It's up to you to find those truths through persistence, awareness, and understanding. Learning how to read the signs, the history, and walk the paths of those who were once there will open more possibilities. Retracing the past will only strengthen the outcome of the present and help solve the case.

Thursday 0845 hours

Katie and McGaven arrived at the property once owned by Thomas Dayton, which consisted of twenty-five acres including a house, guesthouse, stables, various animal pens, and two barns. It had been a working farm with horses and several head of cattle. There was no doubt the place had been picturesque, but now it was severely neglected and overgrown. The farm fencing was barely visible, even nonexistent in places, as Katie navigated the car along what she thought was the drive leading into the property, the sedan bumping and bouncing as they approached.

"This is fun," said McGaven as he held on to the handle above the door.

Cisco stayed stationary behind Katie, keeping watch through the windshield. The movement didn't bother him as he had been in Army convoys before.

"I can't tell if we're on the right drive," Katie said, fighting the steering. The ground and vegetation crunched underneath the tires. Low brush scraped across the car doors.

"Just take it slow."

"It's not like I can speed through here. I'm concerned that we might hit a ditch or hole that we can't see."

"It looks like there's a gate up there," said McGaven.

Half the gate was gone, but it was clear that it was the way in. After entering through what was left of it, Katie pulled the vehicle to the right in an area that was mostly cleared and where the vegetation had been flattened.

"We should park here. I don't trust not getting stuck if we go any farther."

"That's fine by me."

Cisco pushed his large head forward as his ears perked, listening, and his wolf-like yellow eyes watched for anything that moved. He was on high alert.

"You sure you want to check out this place?" said McGaven. "It looks like no one has been here in years. We would see signs if they had."

Katie looked at her partner. "We can't turn back now. It was a working farm when Abigail went missing. What's on your mind?"

"Oh, I don't know. This place reminds me of a horror film where the protagonist's car breaks down... and then you know the rest."

Katie laughed. "Gav, you have quite the imagination."

"Just saying... look around."

"It's abandoned, not possessed."

"You're right." He referred to notes from Detective Jamison. "It looks like back when Abigail's car was found two uniforms talked to a Mr. Dayton along with a farmhand, Ferris, and they looked around the property. Nothing seemed out of place, and no one had seen anything—no car, or Abigail Andrews."

Katie opened the car door and stepped out. She shed her nice work jacket, opting for a hoodie, and then changed into hiking boots.

Cisco whined, wanting to get out.

Gray clouds moved in and obscured the sun, making it seem later in the day instead of the morning. Katie took a couple of steps and stood still. Her usual practice of assessing a new area, especially outdoors, was to take a moment, close her eyes and listen. It seemed silly to some, but it allowed her to gain perspective and be in the moment. It was a time when everything else in her mind took a back seat so that she could completely concentrate on where they were going and the next step in the investigation.

There was a slight breeze, but there was no sound of it filtering through the trees. It was an area that had been cleared for a farm so there were very few trees except around the perimeter. The birds were quiet. No sounds of cars or people. It was completely silent—and secluded.

Katie opened her eyes. The overrun landscape and dense area did resemble something from a horror movie. But one thing stood out to her. Even if it was cleared and looked how it did fifteen years ago, the property would still be isolated.

"Where do you want to check out first?" said McGaven. He knew her habit of listening to the area and had kept quiet until she opened her eyes again.

"Are the structures still standing?" she said.

"From what I could see from the satellite photos, they seem to be."

"Okay, let's start with the house and the guesthouse... then spread out from there."

"What are you looking for?" he said.

"That is a good question. We'll know it when we see it."

Cisco barked.

"You want to bring him?"

Katie hesitated. She didn't like the fact that they were going into the unknown, but having the senses of a canine would be beneficial. It was clear that no one had been there in ages, and they didn't know what they were going to find.

She nodded and turned back to the sedan. She let Cisco out, who was extremely happy at the decision. He bounced up to Katie, did a couple of spins, and decided to check out some of the dried brush before returning to her side.

It was difficult for the detectives to navigate the property with the uneven ground, dried brush, and high weeds, and it was a struggle to try to stay on some type of path. Even Cisco stayed close and slowed his happy pace to be with them. Katie didn't like that the weeds were almost four-foot tall and extremely thick. It bothered her that something could be hidden until they were on top of it. From the experience of their last case where they dealt with explosive traps, she was nervous about not seeing what was beneath her feet. About the only things she could see were the water tanks, which were once used for watering the fields and taking care of livestock.

McGaven varied his path, looking around carefully as he did so. He appeared to have the same thoughts as Katie about the area—and potential surprises.

Katie finally saw the outline of a farmhouse. It had once been yellow with white trim, but now it was badly faded with remnants of peeling paint revealing the bare wood underneath. The windows were mostly broken, and the roof sagged. The corners were missing, allowing the weather easy access.

"Wow. The house looks really old," said Katie.

"It does." McGaven looked concerned. His eyebrows furrowed and his mouth turned down, which was uncharacteristic.

As they neared the house, they could see the porch had almost completely rotted away and what was left was dilapidated. The front door drooped cockeyed, hanging by one of the barely attached hinges.

Katie forged ahead. She carefully tested a few of the planks to make sure they would hold her weight. When she was satisfied, she climbed up and made her way into the house. She pushed the door aside as it swung out of the way. Cisco easily navigated the entrance with expertise, hopping up, balancing, jumping inside, and then he stayed close to Katie.

Katie didn't need to turn on a flashlight. The daylight streamed in through the broken windows. It seemed to have been an open and well-lit home, once. Heavy dust, scattered leaves, and broken floors were what was left of the living room and kitchen area. There were a few pieces of furniture—an old couch, a broken dining table missing two legs, and a few cheap knick-knacks that once sat on the built-in bookshelves.

"It looks like they didn't fully move out," said Katie as she carefully walked around. "There are too many personal items left behind."

"I've seen foreclosures before and many times people just take a few things and leave the rest," said McGaven.

Katie studied the shelves, noticing broken jars and vases, and seeing a teddy bear too. It sat staring at them with black button eyes. "Interesting."

"What is it?"

"These are canning jars—Mason jars—what you would use to preserve food like vegetables and fruit."

"And?"

"Well, they are all broken but there isn't any sign of what had been in them."

"We're talking years here. There wouldn't be anything left. Would there?"

"There would be *something*. And"—Katie watched Cisco casually sniff around the room—"Cisco would be interested where any food was involved, but he's oblivious."

"So, you think that whatever was in those jars was taken deliberately?"

She nodded. "And I'm betting it wasn't food."

"Then what?"

"I don't know."

"Maybe we can have one or two of them analyzed," said McGaven.

"Let's remember to grab them before we leave." She continued to look around, not knowing what they were looking for exactly, but knowing it would be something out of place. It was the only thing she could think of.

"I'll search this way," said McGaven indicating a part of the house.

"Okay," she said. "C'mon, Cisco."

Katie decided to check out the two bedrooms on the far side of the house. The inner hallway was intact and in fairly good condition, but the floor still creaked as she moved toward the bedrooms. She heard Cisco pad down the hallway as his nails clicked against the old wood floor.

The first bedroom was on the left, and when Katie opened the door it squeaked with a high-pitched sound, making her flinch and Cisco whine.

"Sorry, Cisco."

She pushed the door open, and the dog moved inside. To her surprise, the bedroom was still furnished. There were twin beds, but the covers and blankets were gone. A small desk and a bookshelf were in one corner, and one small red sneaker lay in another. A picture of dogs in the woods in a glass frame hung askew on the wall. The window was broken, and a tattered curtain fluttered against the opening.

Katie stood in the middle of the room. It told a story.

Cisco seemed interested in the sneaker.

"*Hier*," said Katie, instructing the dog to stay close to her.

She bent down and looked at the shoe. Nothing seemed unusual about it—it was just a discarded or lost shoe. It was clear the room had belonged to a child or children. By the style of desk, shoe, and picture, Katie would guess it had belonged to a preteen girl.

Katie spent a few more minutes there and then checked out the next bedroom, which was empty except for some trash. She wasn't sure why, but the bedrooms bothered her. Moreover, her gut instinct told her there was something that she was supposed to see. But what? She poked her head into the bathroom, but there wasn't anything inside but an old bathtub.

She walked back through the house and met up with McGaven. "Anything?" she said.

"Nope. Just an abandoned house that's deteriorating."

"Same with the bedrooms." She looked around once more, trying to imagine what it was like when a family had lived here. Was it cozy? Was it warm and inviting? Or was it something more sinister?

McGaven glanced at his watch. "Let's check out the guesthouse and the rest of the property."

Katie nodded. "Let's split up."

"So that means Cisco is with me?" He smiled. He never hid the way he felt about the dog.

"Nice try."

"Keep your walkie on," he said. "I'll take the guesthouse."

After they carefully exited the farmhouse, they stood out front surveying the property before them.

"I half expected there would be signs of vandalism or squatters," McGaven said.

"It's too remote here. No one would know about this place unless they knew about it."

"Okay, I'm off to check out the guesthouse—not quite sure what we're looking for."

"You'll know it when you see it," said Katie as she watched her tall partner walk across what was the front yard. She and Cisco waited until she saw McGaven disappear. "C'mon, Cisco."

Katie made her way to what used to be the animal pens where there was a large red and white barn. The two-story structure still seemed to be intact.

Katie continued to push her way through the weeds, careful not to step on anything. With a working farm, there might be remnants of tools, fencing, or something from the animal enclo-sures. Cisco kept close to her side keeping his tail down, but his ears and eyes were alert for anything moving or suspicious. The wind kicked up a little, swirling around the area, blowing leaves and pieces of trash. Cisco stopped, held his nose high, taking in the various scents blowing across the property.

Katie pulled the barn door open. A stench hit her senses, reminding her of old animal pens that hadn't been cleaned. She hesitated.

"Finding anything interesting?" said McGaven over the walkie attached to her hip. His voice sounded crackly and was fading in and out.

She pulled the walkie from her belt and said, "Just entered the barn. Nothing yet. Over."

Something shiny caught her attention as she hooked the walkie again. In a corner there was disturbed earth, as if someone had tried to dig up something, but there was nothing to see. Katie bent down and wiped dirt from several instruments. One was a cattle prod, another looked to be some type of meat hook.

Cisco pushed his nose toward her hands and the instruments.

As Katie tossed the tools back where she found them, she stood up to look around. She was beginning to think they were wasting their time searching an overgrown and long-forgotten piece of property when several gunshots rang out, followed by a second round of shots in response.

Cisco barked.

"Gav..." she whispered.

Several bullets suddenly peppered the barn doors behind her.

Katie dropped to the ground, taking cover under a work-bench with Cisco snug at her side. Like a camera flash, she recalled several occasions in Afghanistan when she and Cisco holed up during gunfire and explosions. She pulled her weapon and spoke over the walkie, "Gav, what's going on?" she said softly.

She waited.

Nothing.

"Gav? Gav, come back."

Still nothing.

Katie didn't want to leave her safe cover until she had more information, but she had to get to her partner. Anxiety crept through her body, causing her breath to tighten in her chest and a tingly sensation to run down her limbs. She tried not to think of the worst-case scenario, but it was clear what she had to do.

TWENTY

Thursday 1055 hours

Katie's time in the military out in the field, and how terrifying it was, instantly resurfaced at that moment, making it difficult to concentrate on what she needed to do. She had to get the upper hand, figure out who was shooting at them and why, instead of rushing into the gunfire. Thoughts flashed through her head, but maybe McGaven had to stay quiet in order not to give away his position. From the last walkie contact, he was most likely still in the guesthouse.

Katie kept low with Cisco at her side, and they moved cautiously toward the doors. Sitting with her back to the interior, she peered out with her gun trained in front of her. There was no movement or further gunshots so seeing any type of muzzle flash to find the exact location of the person firing wasn't likely.

Retreating inside, she looked around for another exit. Staying low, she crouched toward the back where there was another door leading out of the barn. Slowly and quietly, Katie disengaged the lock and opened the door. Surprisingly, the hinges were quiet. She peered out through a small opening. There were several trees behind the barn, which would make good cover. Listening intently, she deduced that no one was nearby, and she and Cisco made their way to the trees in unison, where Katie could re-evaluate their next move.

After they reached the trees, Katie crouched down and scanned the area around them. Even though she didn't have binoculars, she could still deduce if someone was nearby. Not only by sound, but also by any movement. It was easy to see weeds being pushed aside, or to hear someone walking, crushing brush, or the subtle crunching of gravel beneath foot-steps. She waited two minutes to see if anything moved. It remained silent.

There was something hard and metal-like beneath her knees. She quickly brushed away debris, revealing some type of heavy container. There wasn't time to investigate, but she made a mental note of the location.

"Cisco," she whispered. The dog was on high alert; she felt the heat from his panting breath on her thigh. "Let's go."

They moved in tandem around the trees, pausing at every trunk before moving on. Katie wanted to make a large circle before nearing the guesthouse in case there was someone still there. Her mind raced through scenarios of who was shooting and why. There wasn't anyone living nearby, and there was no indication of a caretaker. Who could it be?

She glanced at her cell phone to see if McGaven had sent a text but realized that there was no signal. She kept moving. Her breath was stilted. She felt the sun beat down, warming her back as the morning dwindled, leaving behind any shadows.

When Katie and Cisco reached the back of the guesthouse, she glanced in the window that looked into the kitchen area. The only remaining appliance was an old gas stove detached from the wall—everything else had been removed, leaving holes in the walls and the floor. She looked for the back door and it was in place, but the hardware had been removed, including the doorknob. It would be a quiet entry.

Katie put her left hand on Cisco's side, feeling his body tense, then used her right hand to push the door open. Again, it was whisper quiet as she pushed the door wide enough for them to get through.

"Gav?" she whispered. She moved cautiously across the room, staying away from the windows. Pausing at a wall, she said again, "Gav?" before continuing to edge her way to the other part of the small, one-bedroom house.

"Katie?"

She was relieved to hear her partner's voice. "Gav, where are you?"

"Living room," he replied. "Stay down."

Katie looked down and saw expelled shell casings, which must've been from McGaven's gun in return fire. She started to crawl toward him.

"Lower!" he yelled.

Instantly Katie dropped flat. Cisco mirrored her moves.

Gunfire blew through the only intact window in the house. Bullets hit the wall above Katie's head, chipping drywall and plaster. Bits and pieces of the interior of the small cottage showered down on her and Cisco.

In a panic, Katie wrapped her arm around the black dog, keeping him as close as possible to her. The two of them did an Army-crawl motion to get to McGaven.

As they did, several more shots whizzed through the room.

Katie managed to get to a safe position next to McGaven and Cisco hunkered between the detectives. They took cover behind a large cabinet that had been left behind.

"Hey," she said, winded.

"Having fun yet?" he said, trying to keep the mood calm.

"Where are the shots coming from?"

"Higher ground," he said. "At the west side of the property. By the sound, velocity, and impact, I'd say it's a rifle."

"Sharpshooter?" Katie hadn't expected someone with that expertise firing at them on an abandoned farm.

"Could be."

Katie looked at her partner and saw that his upper arm was injured. Blood seeped through the sleeve and trickled down his forearm. "You've been hit."

"It's okay. It just grazed me."

She looked closer at the wound and saw that it had already stopped bleeding, but it would still need some medical attention to prevent infection. Katie couldn't believe that her partner had been hit by someone who must've followed them to the property. But why? Why did someone not want them there? Was it a warning? Or was someone really wanting to hurt them?

The only people who knew about it were police personnel. They never mentioned it to Mrs. Andrews, so there would be no one outside the department who would know they would be there. She recalled that she did mention it to Chad in conversation. Maybe someone at the hospital overheard them. The more she thought about it, the more unlikely these theories became. Someone had to have followed them.

"Any ideas how to get out of here?" McGaven said, snapping Katie back to the present moment.

"Not anything you're going to like."

"I don't have a signal on my cell. Do you?"

"Nope."

"Now what?"

"We're going to have to flush them out," she said.

"Oh, that sounds easy."

"How many magazines do you have?" she said.

"One extra. And I fired several shots from the current one. I have three bullets left."

"Oh."

"Well, I wasn't planning on a gun battle," he said sourly.

Katie leaned back, contemplating the best way to get to safety. The only scenario she could think of would be to flush or scare the shooter out so that they could get back to their vehicle. Her thoughts kept returning to the same thing.

"We need to split up again if we want to take this person by surprise."

"They haven't fired in a bit. Maybe they're gone?"

"Let's see," she said.

Katie told Cisco to stay as she crawled toward the window. She fired two shots randomly and then took cover. Within seconds, bullets fired back.

"I guess they're just waiting," he said.

"It seems like it's one person."

"At least that's a good thing."

Katie made her way back to McGaven and Cisco. She sighed. "You and Cisco need to head back to the car and use the police radio."

"What about you?" McGaven asked.

"I'll flush this shooter out away from where we parked. I have a sense they accessed the property from somewhere else and not from the main entrance. It will be easier and safer for Cisco to be with you."

"So, you think it'll be like an ambush move?" he said.

"That's what I'm thinking."

"I don't know if—"

"We don't know anything about this person. Where they came from, why they're shooting at two cops. So, let's force him out."

"I'm good with that," he said. "I just don't like the unknown factors here."

Katie understood his point and that was what made this decision so difficult. "No one knows we're here and they won't come looking for us for a while. We have to get a call out."

Glancing at her watch, she said, "Give me five minutes to get into place and you and Cisco start heading back to the car. I'm going to go back to the barn area and come around, flanking them."

"What's the signal?"

"Two shots with a three-second pause in between."

He nodded.

Katie readied to leave. She didn't want to look at Cisco; otherwise, she might change her mind. McGaven had spent so much time with the dog, and he knew how to handle him.

"Katie," he said. His voice had a low tone of concern that she had rarely heard.

She turned and looked at her partner. They had been through so much together, dangerous situations, killers, yet they still continued to hunt down perps with little or no new clues. There was no other person she wanted to be her partner, especially in this type of situation. She trusted him with her life.

"I know," she said softly. There didn't need to be any explanation. Words weren't necessary between two people who knew each other so well. She synced her watch to his and left.

Katie crawled through the living room toward the kitchen and left out the back door she had entered through. Her heart pounded to an almost erratic level, making it difficult to concentrate. She could hear her ragged breathing. The stresses from her combat experience were never far from her mind when she was forced into a battle-like situation such as this, where she wasn't sure who the enemy was or why they were attacking them.

She moved easily back to the barn, weaving in and out with stealth. It was simpler without Cisco where she only had to worry about her own safety.

Katie forged on, the heat of the day pressing down on her. Sweat trickled down her back and forehead. Wiping her face with the back of her hand, she slowed her pace as she reached the tree line again. She began to have a better picture in her mind of the layout of the property.

Wishing she had binoculars to see farther, she surveyed the area on the opposite side of the property from the main entrance. She surmised that there had to be another access in addition to where they had entered. Because the property had been a working farm, larger vehicles needed to enter and exit for the cattle and horses—even deliveries of hay. The unknown shooter must've entered from that area. It made sense.

Katie decided to move inward, backtracking, to force the person toward their vehicle. She would then be able to follow them—at least she hoped so.

Feeling more comfortable with the terrain, Katie moved with ease and swiftness, which gave her more confidence. Her approach was almost silent. Someone could hear her light footsteps if they were listening for them, but she didn't think that would be the issue. Birds began to fly from the trees and chirped with their usual rapture.

There was a snap.

Katie stopped in her tracks, barely breathing. She knew exactly what that noise was and had heard it a million times in the military and her police career. It was the sound of a magazine being loaded into a gun, readying for fire.

She bit her lip, thinking that maybe shooting two warning shots might not be a great idea. Caught in the middle of the long-forgotten farm without backup or anyone knowing where they were made her vulnerabilities intensify. What if the shooter decided to return fire and charge? Katie decided to go with her gut along with a little bit of luck that the shooter would cut their losses and head for their vehicle to escape without being identified. She had the element of surprise and was going to use it to the full extent.

Katie raised her weapon and shot, counted in her head for three seconds... and fired again.

Almost instantly, heavy footsteps thrashed in the brush and moved away.

Katie took off after the sound. She ran effortlessly and hoped there was nothing she could stumble over or step in. She could see a brief outline of a person charging through the weeds, most likely a man by his stature and movement, heading for the back area, probably a gate.

Katie increased her pace but still kept her attention on her surroundings. She saw the trail the shooter left behind, bent weeds and bootprints. Breathless, she kept her pursuit.

The sound of an engine turning over filled the quiet of the farm. There was a gunning of a V-8 engine as tires spun, and pieces of debris showered over Katie, causing her to stop and cover her head, which was when she heard the engine moving away.

"No," she said.

Katie pushed herself and followed the noise. She finally reached the broken fence with barbwire protruding from various areas. She saw the dust still filtering in the air from the vehicle. Frustrated, she stopped her pursuit. She didn't get a make or model—and most important, she didn't see the shooter. It was back to square one.

Katie pulled her walkie-talkie. "Gav? Can you hear me?" She began to retrace her steps to their vehicle.

"Loud and clear." It was a crackly connection, but she could still hear him.

"He's gone." Her rapid breathing began to settle again. Relief filled her. "You okay?"

"Fine."

"You and Cisco?"

"We're fine. Your plan worked."

Still frustrated, Katie grimaced, watching the area around her in case there might be anyone else. She shivered, imagining that someone had their sights on her. Her plan had worked, flushing out the shooter, but they didn't have any answers and weren't any closer to finding out what had happened to Abigail. But whoever was shooting at them obviously didn't want them to pursue the case. And that meant they had to be close to finding out the truth.

TWENTY-ONE

Thursday 1345 hours

Katie and McGaven watched as the sheriff's department personnel arrived at the property. Several police cruisers, ambulance, fire truck, two SUVs, one older SUV from the police motor pool, forensic van, and a construction truck pulling a trailer with a backhoe.

"I'd say that would qualify as the cavalry coming to our rescue," said McGaven.

"I'm so glad that the radio worked. I wasn't looking forward to walking down the road until I could find a cell signal," said Katie.

Their sedan's front tires had been the victim of several bullets. They would have been stranded if the police radio had been sabotaged as well. There was no doubt to Katie that the shooter, whoever he was, intended on sending a strong message and was trying to scare them off the property. It just made Katie more determined to push forward to find out why.

Cisco barked and wagged his tail as he watched the parade of vehicles arrive.

Sheriff Scott was the first to park and hurry toward the detectives. "You both alright? McGaven?" he said looking at his arm.

"I'm fine," he said. "Just a scratch."

"I'm having you checked out." He gestured at the two EMTs approaching. Turning to Katie, "Catch me up. What were you two doing out here?"

Katie updated her uncle as McGaven was checked out and bandaged properly.

"You never saw anyone tailing you?" said the sheriff.

"No, but they already had their escape route planned. There's a back entrance on the property."

"And?"

"It seemed as if they wanted to make more of a presence."

One of the police officers approached quickly with a rolled-up map in their hands. A construction employee began to offload the backhoe.

"Sir," said the officer.

"Coordinate with John and Eva," he said to Katie as he moved away to manage the scene.

"On it." Katie secured Cisco in the car before she met up with John.

"So, looks like you found trouble," said the forensic supervisor. "I'm glad you're both okay." He searched Katie's face, concerned for her.

"Trouble actually found us," she said.

"Eva and I familiarized ourselves with the property." Looking around, he said, "It doesn't look like anyone has been out here in years."

The backhoe fired up its engine and slowly began to creep through the entrance to clear away weeds and debris. Two of the police officers took point ahead of the moving equipment to make sure there wasn't anything that would impede its job.

"The main house has some jars and other items that need to be dusted for prints," said Katie.

"Okay. It's possible to get prints after a long period of time," he said.

"I think someone has been here recently. Maybe we'll get lucky. Also, those jars had something in them, and I want to know what it was."

He looked at her curiously. "Okay."

A thin petite woman with spiky blonde hair walked up. "Hey, Katie. Glad you're okay."

"Yeah, we're fine, Eva."

"I need you to search, dust, and gather evidence at the main house," said John to his technician.

"I'm on it," Eva said, turning back to get everything she needed to document and process the scene.

"John," said Katie, "I need you to check out something I found when I was behind the barn area—after the shooting started."

"Let me grab some tools first."

Katie nodded. As she waited for John, she watched the entire property. It amazed her how after just a few minutes everything seemed to change. What had looked creepy and forgotten when she had first arrived now looked like the beginning of a construction project. As the area was being cleared, it seemed more like just a piece of property with an old farmhouse and barn.

McGaven joined her. "Everything okay?"

"Shouldn't I be asking you that?"

"You mean this?" he said, referring to his bandaged arm. "It'll just be another battle scar with a cool story behind it."

Katie couldn't help but chuckle. "Gav, you know how to make everything seem okay."

"It's part of my job."

"Can you assist Eva with areas of interest in the main house?" Katie said.

"Of course. Where are you going?"

"I'm going to show John that metal container I found."

"I'm on my way," he said.

Katie watched him walk off. She never wanted to take for granted what a great partner she had.

"You ready?" said John, holding a bag of tools.

She nodded then explained the circumstances about how and why she found the container.

They walked toward the trees behind the barn.

"So, do you have any idea who the shooter might've been?" said John.

"No. Just that they wanted to scare us away. If they were intent on killing us they could have well before we entered the buildings."

"That's pretty bold. They took a chance of being identified."

"I know."

They reached the trees that she and Cisco had hidden behind only hours before. Katie searched for the exact spot where she'd taken cover. The huge tree trunks were close in proximity and layers of pine needles had compacted, leaving the ground spongy—except for one area. She knelt, pushed the debris to the side, revealing the metal plate. She thumped her knuckles on it, making a dull ringing sound. "Here," she said. "I don't think it has to do with utilities or anything for the working farm."

"Let me take a look." John began scraping away the landscape layers, discovering two distinct round areas in the ground. "I think these are—"

"Metal drums—like oil drums," Katie said.

He looked at her with a serious expression. "This can't be good."

"Why would someone bury these here? Close to these huge trees?"

"Maybe they wanted to make sure they could find them again using the trees as a landmark," he said.

Dread crept in, causing her to hold her breath for a moment. Even though it was warm outside, her body felt cold and clammy. Katie's mind spun with possibilities, but none seemed to be innocent or part of the farm's life.

John unzipped his bag and retrieved a crowbar. "Let's see what we're dealing with first." After removing excess dirt, he began working to pry open one of the drums. His expression was solemn, and he seemed to steady himself for the worst-case scenario.

Katie leaned back in her kneeling position and let John work the metal lid. There wasn't much rust to indicate how old they were, but the condition of the ground and surrounding debris indicated that they had been buried for a while.

Finally, John wrenched off the casing of the metal top. He glanced at Katie before opening the top with another tool.

The smell hit them before the sight of the contents.

Katie gasped and stood up, unable to drag her eyes away.

A body had been stuffed into the drum. They could only see the head and shoulders, but it was clear it was a woman. Decomposition had been slow. There were still remnants of hair and skin on the bones.

John slowly stood up. "You were looking for a missing woman?"

"Yes. Abigail Andrews. Her car was found a couple of miles from here." Katie tried to ascertain if it could be Abigail or not. "It definitely could be her."

"We need to cordon off this entire area like any other crime scene."

"Of course. But what about—"

"We need to carefully document this area first and then

open the other drum." John retrieved his cell phone. "I have to have someone from the medical examiner's office come out." He began coordinating the situation.

Katie took a couple of steps away. Something still didn't sit well to her. The missing person's case for Abigail Andrews had become complicated with a layer of secrets and now it was most likely going to be ruled a homicide. If the woman in the drum was indeed Abigail, then the shooter today might be the killer and didn't want the body to be found. And the fact that the boyfriend, Anthony Drake, was murdered in prison made the case even more suspicious as well as dangerous. The prison investigation was closed, and the conclusion was that an inmate disagreement had led to the brutal attack. It was suspicious.

But one thing was definite. They were getting closer to finding out what had happened to Abigail and who had killed her.

TWENTY-TWO

Thursday 1830 hours

Katie and McGaven waited patiently in Sheriff Scott's conference room. They had been summoned to meet with him and Detective Hamilton. It had been a long day at the farm and Katie wondered why this meeting couldn't wait at least until the morning. She glanced at her partner who also had a curious expression on his face.

The sheriff and Hamilton walked in.

"Thank you both for meeting us here," said the sheriff.

"Of course," she said.

Katie expected Hamilton to have a smugness about him, but he looked sincere and relaxed. He wore a hint of a smile, which seemed odd to her.

The men sat down, facing the detectives. Hamilton opened a couple of files of reports, photographs, and maps. Katie recognized the information immediately. She knew she wasn't going to like what the meeting was about.

"Let's get started so we can all get home." The sheriff shuffled the paperwork before he began. "We could have just sent you the final reports, but since these cases were the last ones you worked on, I wanted you both to hear from us what has transpired." Turning to the detective, he said, "Detective Hamilton will fill you in."

"First, I want to thank you both for the detailed reports and investigative work for the Lane/Hyde case."

Katie thought he was trying too hard and would piggyback on their case to get credit. She had to almost bite her lip to keep from saying something she shouldn't. It should have been their case to complete, but since Chad had been part of the investigation she had to back down. It made sense. But it didn't mean she had to like it.

"We've officially closed the cases."

"What about the heavy plastic found inside the wall at the bunker?" said Katie.

"We're having it analyzed in case it's connected to any other missing person's case," said Hamilton. "So far, there aren't any connections to other cases."

"How can you close the cases so quickly?" she said.

Hamilton looked to the sheriff before he answered. "Terrance Lane decided to cooperate for a deal."

"Deal?" she repeated.

"He provided information about everything his bodyguard, Sean Hyde, had done. He had records, dates, places, and names."

Katie couldn't believe that the murders had been catalogued and organized on paper. She shook her head. "What if there are more victims?"

"Not according to the records."

"So... he made a deal for himself, am I right?"

Hamilton nodded but didn't verbally say that was true.

Katie tried to keep her temper in check. "Okay, so what was the motive? Why bring Chad into everything? I'd say there are definitely more questions that need to be answered." She looked from the detective to the sheriff.

"What about the guy who held Chad hostage?" said McGaven.

"We have identified him as Roland Danner. He had been one of Terrance Lane's security guards. It's only a matter of time before we pick him up." The sheriff watched Katie and McGaven. "You have to understand that these murders have been going on for two decades."

"So let me get this straight," she said, trying to keep her simmering anger in check. "Hyde, with the assistance of Lane, was this prolific serial killer who manipulated Simon Holden—who's still in prison—to be the fall guy for his crimes, and you don't have more questions to continue the investigation? What's going to happen to Holden? Will it change the charges? What was his connection?" Katie leaned back in her chair. She didn't know if it was the fact that Chad was leaving town for a while, or the twisty turn the Abigail Andrews investigation was taking, but she was losing her patience.

"Detective," began the sheriff, "I know you have a lot of questions, but there are circumstances you don't know about."

"Please tell us then."

"Terrance Lane not only gave us the proof of the serial killings, with all the related information, but he also had information pertaining to two currently sitting senators."

Katie raised her eyebrows in disbelief. She recalled watching Lane talk about running for office and his entourage following his every word. "Such as?"

"I'm sorry, but I'm not at liberty to discuss it," said the sheriff.

"Oh, I get it. So now a man who helped a serial killer for the last twenty years is—what—in witness protection?"

The sheriff nodded.

"And that's why this case has to be closed. Because two

senators' misconduct is more important than those women's lives over two decades? Politics at its best..."

McGaven put his hand on his partner's arm to calm her.

"It's not like that," said Hamilton.

"Then what is it like? With all due respect—"

"We wanted to talk to you in person instead of sending you a report."

"Why thank you. I'm very disappointed," she said. "We uphold the law, we investigate, and we bring criminals to justice... not coddle senator wannabes. I apologize for my outburst, but out of everything that I could imagine about those cases, I never would have predicted anything like this as the outcome." She looked away. "What about Chad? Was that some kind of bonus for them?"

"From everything we, and you both, have gathered," said Hamilton, "it seems you popped up on his radar and Hyde wanted to make things interesting by bringing you in as an adversary."

"Adversary? Really? You don't seem to understand. Those killings were some of the most horrific we've ever seen, and he basically gets to walk. There's a lot of collateral damage here."

"We are confident that everything related to those other cases has been closed. There's nothing that would indicate either one of you is in any danger due to them. I'll have Hamilton send you both the report. Redacted, of course," said the sheriff.

"Of course." Katie stood up. "What about Chad? What if there's someone else who helped to facilitate his kidnapping? It was an intricate orchestration so it's not a difficult conclusion to come to. They had to know that we were staying at that particular cabin, the drugging, and the fact it left me..." She couldn't finish her sentence. The room was unnaturally silent as the three men watched her. She wasn't going to rant or whine, but the entire situation was infuriating.

McGaven joined his partner, standing next to her.

"Is there anything else you need about our serial cases so you can put a bow on it?" she said, making sure her point was clear about the cases first being investigated by her and McGaven. She had lost a part of herself and maybe her relationship with Chad over those cases. She wasn't okay with it, but she had to take what was dealt her and somehow make peace with it.

"You and Detective McGaven are dismissed," said the sheriff. He was professional and stern, but his eyes told another story, that he was deeply concerned about his niece.

"Thank you," said Katie as she turned to leave.

"Thank you, sir... Hamilton," said McGaven.

They left the conference room and headed out of the building to the parking lot before either said anything. During that time, Katie tried to calm the anger welling up inside her. She couldn't get her mind to stop spinning in disbelief, disappointment, and simmering anger. She walked to her Jeep, looking forward to going home to escape from thoughts she didn't want to process—just yet.

"Hey," said McGaven. "You doing okay?"

"Not really. What about you?"

"This is BS and I'm not onboard with it in the least, but it is part of the darker side of the criminal justice system."

"That's one way of putting it. Gav, when things like this happen, how do you go on with future investigations when they can be derailed this easily? Almost like an afterthought."

"You can't fixate on one experience. You have to put everything into perspective. Look at our record. We've solved all our cold cases to date... and we have another one that we need to concentrate on. Every case is important."

Katie was about to say something, but she hesitated and sighed. "I know you're right. You are definitely the calm, intelligent one between us." She smiled at her partner. "Go home to Denise and try to put this day behind you."

He nodded. "I'm worried about you. Are you going to visit Chad?"

She took a deep breath. "Not this evening. He has a meeting with his psychologist." Holding back her urge to break down, she felt her world slowly eroding.

"Katie," he said. "Go home, take care of yourself, and we'll get a fresh start and a new perspective in the morning. Maybe we'll have some information from John. I'm going to try to dig up more about Thomas Dayton, the farm's owner."

She nodded.

"And Katie? If you need anything, you call me. Anytime. Denise and I can be there in less than ten minutes."

"Thank you, Gav. I appreciate that." She didn't know why she deserved someone like McGaven in her life—her partner who always had her back. She opened her door to the Jeep. "I'll be fine. See you tomorrow morning."

McGaven waited a moment, watching his partner as she started her SUV and drove out of the parking lot.

TWENTY-THREE

Thursday 2210 hours

Katie sat on her back porch in a comfortable swing as she had on so many occasions—too many to count. Whenever she had something difficult to process or figure out, she would sit on her back porch. It was late, but that didn't matter. The outdoors was quiet, making it easier for her to think without distractions.

The same things kept rattling around in her mind. How it seemed that everything she loved, everything that she believed in, and everything that mattered seemed to be slipping through her fingers. Driving home, she fought the urge to go to her uncle's condo and wait for him. After thinking about it, she knew she would be unsuccessful in trying to change the outcome of the Lane/Hyde cases. What was done, was done. She had to live with it and move on. Abigail needed their attention now.

She'd left the outside lights off and as her eyes had adjusted to the darkness, she watched the dark outline of Cisco: tall, pointed ears; poised tail; trotting from one tree or bush to another. It made her smile. Just the simplicity of watching the dog frolic in the darkness taking in scents made her stresses calm.

When Cisco had had enough of his yard and made sure everything was as it should be according to him, he returned to Katie. The dog made himself comfortable and nestled close to her side. They both swayed slightly in the swing in the darkness.

The evening was cool, but not cold. She had a quilt wrapped around her to stay warm and she could almost sleep outside. It gave her the feeling of freedom, being with nature and relaxation. Memories flooded back from when she was growing up in the farmhouse with her parents. How she wished she could talk to them now. She needed advice. She needed a sounding board. She needed family.

Looking down at the dog, she said, "Oh, Cisco. What are we going to do?" Chad was leaving. No matter how much she wanted to convince him to stay and recover in Pine Valley, she knew it would be best for him to go home to his family for a while. Even though he was safe, and she knew what had happened to him, she still felt like he was gone.

The loneliness crept in as it had on so many occasions. The questions still nagged at her. What was she going to do? How was she going to cope? She knew that she had to wait things out.

And though she was feeling sorry for herself, Abigail was still on her mind. She felt in her gut that the woman in the drum was Abigail. But she had to wait until an official confirmation of identity was made. She thought of Mrs. Andrews who had already lost her husband and had had her daughter missing for more than a decade. Now she would have to identify Abigail's body, knowing that she had been murdered and stuffed into a metal drum—left buried at a farm where no one was likely to ever find her. Was it the previous owner? One of the Daytons? A neighbor? Or someone else after the property had been vacated? It would have seemed like a perfect place to bury a body.

Katie watched the darkness. Shadows seemed to move. The outline of the beautiful trees looked more ominous than during the daytime.

She petted Cisco as she listened to his relaxed breathing. It had been a long day for both of them. Katie had rehashed the events many times in her mind. She had been rash in her plan at the farm. What if McGaven had been seriously hurt instead of a bullet graze? What if Cisco had been hurt, or worse? These thoughts repeated in her mind over and over.

Before Katie couldn't sleep at all from her thoughts, she decided to go to bed. Tomorrow was going to be another busy day and she had to be present and rested. Hopefully they would find a new lead about Abigail.

She soon drifted off to sleep in her comfortable bed as her sweet dreams were filled with love... and Chad... at the cabin...

Katie moved closer, wanting only to feel his warmth and heartbeat next to her.

Chad held her tight.

Finally releasing his embrace to look at him, Katie said, "What would I do without you?" Her voice was almost a whisper as she fought back tears—not for sadness but joy.

"Hopefully you'll never have to find out," he said lightly. He kissed her and then rose to refill their glasses.

Katie turned her attention back to the fire, watching the flames lap up the oxygen. What Chad had said was true. Her last cases had been brutal on her psyche, not to mention on her perspective on life. It was fragile. Her experiences had made her feel vulnerable, but as though she didn't want to miss anything. And now, being here with Chad without all the distractions and urgencies of everyday life, she felt free but somehow strangely helpless at the same time. Life could prepare her for the day-to-day stuff of work, but not how to decompress and enjoy all the important moments in between.

"I love you, Katie. And nothing is ever going to change that," he said sitting next to her again.

Katie knew Chad loved her but hearing him say those words now meant more than before. She felt a shift, a kind of change that was coming. They were going to build a married life together. It was probably her imagination, but the feeling was strong. "Love you more..." She leaned into him, connecting her lips with his in a slow passionate kiss.

TWENTY-FOUR

Friday 0730 hours

Katie managed to get several hours of sleep but woke up just before daylight. She decided to go on a five-mile run to clear her head and to get everything straight in her mind. She wouldn't do anyone any good if she couldn't concentrate on the case, the investigation, the profile, and Abigail Andrews.

Katie sat in the investigation room in the forensic division at the Pine Valley Sheriff's Department. When she had arrived, she noticed that the forensic examination room doors were closed, and she didn't want to bother John or Eva as they were working hard on the cases. She hoped that they would learn some news soon. Instead, she moved into her and McGaven's area.

She studied all the reports from Detective Jamison's investigation into Abigail again. This time, she began a profile for the killer, under the assumption that it was Abigail's body in the fifty-five-gallon drum. Everything seemed to convince Katie that Abigail's disappearance and murder weren't planned but rather an opportunity. Was it an accident? Was it a killer's fantasy and she fit the profile? Everything seemed to point to the farm and the Dayton residents.

It occurred to Katie that the only real information they had about Abigail's missing person's case was from the initial investigation. Now, a body had been found, and the boyfriend murdered. Things were complex, but the information they had told a story and pointed to a direction to go in. *What was she missing? If that was Abigail's body in the drum, why was she at the Dayton property? Did she know someone there? Was there another body in the other drum?*

Katie pulled up information about fifty-five-gallon drums. They were primarily used to store bulk items, like liquids, chemicals, powders, and animal food used on the farm. It made sense. So, it was consistent that someone who resided at the farm or worked at the farm, or even visited, would have access to these types of drums. She wanted to see the inventory of what was left at the farm and the results from the Mason jars. At first glance, Mason jars and drums could be easily explained, especially on a working farm. But why were the jars all broken? Were they used for more sinister reasons? Most likely, during the move out they were discarded and left behind as trash.

Katie opened a file where McGaven had made notes on trying to find Mr. Dayton and there seemed to be nothing. No credit report. No homeownership. No Social Security number. She decided to check obituaries, beginning with the local area of Pine Valley, and then making the search wider. She began her search for Thomas Harland Dayton, between thirty and sixty years old.

An hour passed and she came up with nothing—no family references. Katie sat back and thought, *What if Mr. Dayton was in a type of witness protection program? It was possible. Maybe there was something sinister going on at the property. How would she be able to find out?*

"Hey, partner," said McGaven, coming in. He slung his briefcase on the table and set down his laptop.

"Morning," she said.

"You look like you're really into something. Care to share?"

"Trying to find Mr. Dayton or anyone related to him."

"I see that great minds think alike."

Katie turned to her partner. "What's that look?" She tried not to smile, but when McGaven found out something new he always had a grin on his face.

He opened his computer. "Well, I came up empty like you. But I thought where would someone go after their property and home went into foreclosure? They would either have to stay with family or friends... or rent a house, right?"

Katie realized where her partner was going.

"So, I started searching databases for rental properties in this area and made some calls to property managers. And guess what?"

"You have a lead?"

"Yes and no."

Katie was excited, but then deflated.

"Don't worry. I went back eleven years to when the property had first gone into foreclosure and searched from there."

"That would mean that Abigail would have already been buried for almost four years by then. If our timeline is correct."

"And if the body is indeed Abigail. Which would be almost ninety percent likely."

"Where did you get that percentage?"

"Just sounds good."

She laughed. "What did you find?"

"A couple of things." He keyed up information.

Katie moved closer to view the computer screen.

McGaven showed a listing from eleven years ago. "Okay, I searched specifically for places that could house some animals... and then narrowed my search."

Katie scanned the listing and agreed with what McGaven had indicated.

"And I made a few calls this morning. Luckily I got a hold of someone who was able to access a database and found the name Dayton. He had rented a house in the rural area southwest of the foreclosed property."

"With his family?"

"It was noted that it was just him and his daughter, Desiree. He rented the house at 1720 Redfield Road for four years and then moved."

"That would be seven years ago. Any forwarding address?"

"Just a PO box in Evergreen."

"Anything else?"

"No, not yet."

"Anything about the daughter, Desiree?"

"Nope."

Katie sighed. "It's a start." She glanced at the clock. "Haven't heard back from John yet, so let's take a drive until we hear from him. Let's head to the rental and see if any neighbors knew Mr. Dayton."

"You read my mind, partner."

TWENTY-FIVE

Friday 1045 hours

Katie followed the GPS instructions to get to 1720 Redfield Road. It was still considered Pine Valley, but on the border edge inside the Sequoia Forest area. One of the densest forests around, even more so than the area where Chad had been found.

McGaven was still searching through databases to find anything more about Thomas Dayton—taking Katie's advice about searching death certificates as well as marriage licenses. His phone chimed with a text. Katie was hopeful that it might be John or the medical examiner's office.

McGaven grimaced as he read the message. "It's the Pine Valley Psychiatric Hospital requesting that I come and meet with Lara Fontaine at four p.m."

"Why?"

"It seems that she requested me to sit in on her meeting for discharge."

Katie didn't say anything, but she could tell that her partner was torn, and it bothered him. It was unclear if he was going to accommodate the request.

"Would you come with me?" he said.

Katie didn't want to, but she saw how much her partner needed it. "Of course. Whatever you need me to do. We should be done with our running around by then," she said, trying to sound positive.

McGaven text messaged back.

Can we push the meeting until 5 p.m.?

It took a few minutes before he got a reply.

Katie slowed the sedan as they headed onto a winding road. She patiently waited for her partner to tell her what was said.

"Good. They said five p.m. would be fine."

Katie nodded then decided to change the subject. "It looks like the rental house is only a few minutes away."

McGaven closed his phone and stared out at the landscape and trees until Katie turned onto Redfield Road. The detectives kept an eagle eye out for the property. It wasn't like a regular neighborhood where the addresses counted along in odd and even increments. The properties were larger than the average, with some houses close to the road while others were set back within the trees with dirt driveways winding up to the residences. The mailboxes weren't in typical places either, which might answer the question why Mr. Dayton had a PO box.

Katie slowed their speed to a crawl, trying to find number 1720.

"There," said McGaven. He pointed at an unkempt property with an old mailbox missing the closure, but the numbers were 1720.

Katie pulled over and parked in a shady area. She leaned forward, craning her neck at the small blue house. "What do you think?"

"I'd say the owner should take better care of the property."

Katie opened the car door and was immediately struck by the smell of something burning. "What is that?"

McGaven joined her outside. "It smells like someone is burning tree limbs and brush."

Katie looked around and was skeptical. "I hope so." She looked around the vicinity. There was a neighbor directly across the street with a manufactured home, with hanging pots and various plants alongside it, and a freshly painted white fence. It was difficult to tell whether the neighborhood would be close-knit, but the detectives would make some inquiries and see if anyone remembered or was around when Mr. Dayton lived here.

They decided to walk across the front to get a better view of the property. The small blue house looked to be a two bedroom with a large storage barn next to it, which doubled as a garage. An old white pickup truck and a small SUV were parked inside. Two small animal trailers were parked on the opposite side of the storage area.

"I can see why Mr. Dayton rented this place," she said. "There's plenty of property behind the house for some livestock."

McGaven nodded. "He probably kept some and sold the rest."

"Let's go see who's home," she said.

They walked on the uneven steppingstones through the unkempt front yard to the front door. Katie knocked. A dog immediately barked from inside, sounding like a medium to large pet.

They waited, but no one answered, and the dog quieted down. There were two vehicles, so it was likely the occupants were home but not inside.

"Let's go around back," she said.

The detectives walked around the small home keeping an eye on their surroundings.

Katie suddenly realized that the smoke they smelled when they arrived had become stronger. She slowed her pace. The backyard was large with pens and enclosures for animals. She saw several dogs and puppies in one pen and there were goats in another. As much as she didn't like what she saw, which resembled a forced breeding area or a puppy mill, she kept moving. At least everything was clean, organized, and fully stocked with feed.

"What do you think?" said McGaven quietly.

"Not sure." She looked around and then saw smoke coming from the outer part of the property. "Over there."

They walked toward the smoke along the side of the property. The terrain was level but there were signs of tire marks. An older man with grayish hair and a bushy beard wearing overalls and a T-shirt was throwing dead branches onto the growing pile of brush. He waited until the flames receded until he added more to the mound.

"Excuse me," said Katie. "Hello?"

The man turned and saw the detectives approach. It was difficult to read his reaction to them, but he nodded his greeting and slowly walked toward them.

The man glanced at their badges and guns. "What can I do for you?" he said. There was no inflection in his voice. He didn't seem mad or annoyed.

"Hi, we're Detectives Scott and McGaven from Pine Valley Sheriff's Department," said Katie.

"I'm Buck. What brings detectives out here?" he said.

"We are actually working a missing person's case. We're looking for any information on a tenant who used to live here—Thomas Dayton and his daughter, Desiree."

"That name doesn't ring a bell. I'm sorry."

"They moved about six years ago."

Buck shook his head. "I'm sorry, Detectives, but I moved in about that time and I never saw the previous tenant."

Katie was disappointed, but she hadn't been expecting much. "Thank you for your time, Buck. We appreciate it."

They turned to leave.

"There are some crates in the corner of the garage that were here when I moved in. I think they belonged to the previous tenant. You're welcome to them. Whatever you want," he said.

Katie's hope rose. "Thank you. We'll check them out."

Katie and McGaven hurried back to the garage. They passed the old pickup and followed the path to the back of the garage. There were two windows letting light in and fans rotating above moving the stagnant air that smelled of hay, cleaners, and engine oil.

Katie spotted three wooden crates in the corner. "There they are," she said hurrying to them.

Spray-painted in black on the sides was THD.

"Thomas Harland Dayton?" said McGaven.

The crates were heavily encrusted with dust. It was clear they hadn't been opened in years. If they did belong to Dayton, then he must've forgotten them when he moved out.

Katie found a rag and began clearing the dirt and grime from the boxes. She carefully opened the first one, not touching the contents or the box with her hands.

"I'll get us some gloves," said McGaven as he left to grab them from the car.

Katie knew it was likely that the contents would be considered evidence. She peered inside the container and found there were towels, clothes, and more of those Mason jars. "Bingo," she said, realizing that Dayton had been at the residence for certain.

Then she noticed the clothing. There were two women's shirts, a hat, and a dog leash. It wasn't unusual because he had a daughter and probably a dog, but... something seemed familiar about the clothes.

Katie moved the first crate and looked inside the second; it contained mostly clothes apart from some jewelry at the bottom. She carefully pulled it out. She stared at it, remembering all the butterfly jewelry in the box at Mrs. Andrews's house.

McGaven joined her and stared at the jewelry. "Is that...?"

"Maybe." Katie opened it and saw a pair of butterfly earrings. "But it could belong to Dayton's daughter, Desiree."

"Still."

"We need to get these crates to forensics. There could be something that identifies the contents as belonging to Abigail—some biological or possibly fingerprint evidence."

"Okay," said McGaven. He picked up one of the crates and headed out to the car.

Katie was still holding the jewelry. Her mind wandered and she questioned why Dayton would have Abigail's things. But why would he keep the items? She picked up a crate and followed her partner.

Once the crates had been loaded into the trunk of the sedan, the detectives readied to leave.

Katie looked across the street at the nicely manicured property and wondered how long the residents had lived there. Then her cell phone chimed. She looked at a text from John.

Body has been identified as Abigail Andrews. Second drum had a dead Labrador retriever. More info soon.

"The body in the drum has been officially identified as Abigail and the second drum had her dog," she said.

"You don't seem happy about that."

"I'm not surprised, but this case seems to be a lot of loose ends we can't connect."

"What do you mean?"

"Well, everything points to Mr. Dayton, but we can't find him. Or his current ID."

"Not yet."

Katie let her gaze settle on the house across the street as she saw someone moving around inside. "I want to talk to the neighbors across the street."

"Let's split up then," he said. "I'll go to the next-door neighbor's, and we'll meet back here."

She nodded, her mind still reeling from the identification of Abigail and their challenge to discover how and why she ended up at the Dayton farm buried in a fifty-five-gallon drum.

TWENTY-SIX

Friday 1200 hours

Katie walked across the street still thinking about the clothes and the butterfly jewelry. She also thought about what Buck had had to say, but she believed him and there was no need to pursue the man further.

As Katie neared the tidy home, she saw some canes at the front door. One of them had a red section on the bottom, indicating that it was for a person with limited vision. She noticed how neat the flower beds were. The colorful flowers, pansies and petunias, had been planted recently. The pots, garden figurines, and the front door mat were also brightly colored and extremely well-ordered.

She stepped in front of the door and knocked. Waiting patiently, Katie couldn't hear anything from inside. There was no one moving around and no sounds of a dog barking. She looked back to see where McGaven was headed but couldn't see him anymore due to the trees and heavily filled-in hedges.

She turned as the door slowly opened. A thin older woman wearing a jogging suit poked her head out. "Hello?" She didn't focus directly on Katie, her pale blue eyes seemed to be gazing across the street. It was clear the woman was blind.

"Hi. I'm Detective Scott from the Pine Valley Sheriff's Department."

"Oh, a detective? Is everything okay?"

"Yes, it is. I'm sorry to disturb you," said Katie. "My partner and I are investigating a cold case of a missing woman. And we wanted to talk to a previous tenant who lived across the street."

"Previous tenant?" she said.

"Yes, ma'am. Mr. Thomas Dayton."

"Yes... Mr. Dayton. I remember him and his daughter."

Katie was encouraged that someone remembered the man. "What can you tell me about him?"

"Well, why don't you come inside?" She opened the door wider.

"Thank you," said Katie as she entered the house. She pulled out her badge to identify herself.

"Oh, no, dear, you don't need to show me your identification. I can't read the small print anyway."

Katie smiled. "Okay." She was amazed how the older woman seemed at ease with her impaired vision and even a bit lighthearted.

"I have just made some tea. Would you like some?"

Katie thought for a moment. "Yes, that would be nice."

"Please, have a seat," the woman said as she disappeared into the kitchen.

Katie looked around the living room. Everything was decorated in monochrome colors, beige, tan, white, and brown. There were no colorful pillows or artwork like the outside landscaping exhibited. There was an orange tabby cat curled up in a chair in the corner.

Even though she knew the woman couldn't see well, it struck Katie as unusual that there were no photographs, knick-knacks, or any of the usual personal things most people displayed. There were no magazines or books on the coffee table. She didn't see a computer, TV, phone, or any other technology.

"Here we are," said the woman, carrying a tray with two cups of tea and sides of sugar and cream. She set it down on the coffee table.

"You can call me Katie."

"I'm Bess Trainer. Please call me Bess."

Katie watched the woman as she moved, seemingly counting paces and making distinct turns. It was clear she always kept her home the exact same way—never moving the furniture and keeping surfaces clear.

"Bess, you said that you knew Mr. Dayton."

"Yes, they lived across the street for about four years or so."

"Did you talk to him?"

"Of course. He was very nice, but he could be..." She stopped midsentence.

"Bess?"

"Well, I don't like to speak ill of anyone, you know."

"It's okay. Did you witness something or hear something that didn't seem usual?" asked Katie, trying to carefully form her words. Her curiosity was heightened as she drank some of her tea. Maybe Bess could help fill in the blanks in the case.

Bess took a breath. "The first year or so, Mr. Dayton was really nice. He would send Desiree over with casseroles or chocolate chip cookies. I knew that they weren't home baked, but it's the thought that counts." She picked up her teacup. "They seemed kind and caring. My husband died almost ten years ago, and we never had any children, so it was nice that one of the neighbors cared about my well-being."

"Was he ever mean to you?"

"To me? No, nothing like that. But he could be abusive to his daughter, yelling and scolding."

"I see. Did he have any visitors? Was there a Mrs. Dayton?"

"No, I never noticed or heard any visitors. Not even friends for Desiree. And..." She took a sip of tea. "And I never heard about a Mrs. Dayton. I just assumed she had left or died, or maybe they were divorced."

"Can you recall anything that seemed out of place about him?"

"I'm not entirely sure what you mean, but I never saw or heard anything that needed me to call the police."

"Do you happen to know where they moved?"

"No. They didn't say anything and the next thing I knew they were moving out. I thought they might come over to say goodbye, but they never did. They seemed to be in a hurry."

"I noticed the property is set up for animals."

"Yes. Many renters over the years have had cattle, horses, goats, chickens, and of course dogs. Actually, quite a few dogs."

"Bess, how long have you lived here?"

"Let's see... it's been more than twenty years."

Katie thought about the neighborhood and the people who might live in such an out-of-the-way place. There were other rental properties out here, which meant that there would be all kinds of people with a wide range of backgrounds and reasons for renting a house.

"Is there anything else about this street and the neighborhood that might be helpful for me to know?" Katie didn't want to sound like she was profiling the area, but she did want to know if there were any other issues. "You can tell me anything. If there's a problem, I will do everything I can to remedy it. If you need anything, I would like to help you."

"You're very kind, Detective, but I can't think of anything."

"Were there any other neighbors who Mr. Dayton seemed to be friends with?"

"He spent time over at the Wills house."

"The Wills house?"

"Yes, they have the stables. They rent out stalls for horses that are moving or for horse shows during certain times of the year—I think in the spring and fall."

"Do they live here?"

"Not all the time. I think they have a home in Southern California."

Katie pondered this information. She didn't know if it meant anything to their investigation, but she would make sure to stop by before they left. "Was it a family?"

"No, it was a couple. David and Veronica. I'm not really sure if they were married or not."

"Would you say they were good friends with Mr. Dayton?"

"I guess so. I never heard their conversations, but they seemed to talk a lot."

"Was there any other neighbor who seemed friendly with the Daytons?"

"Not that I could tell. And I spend as much time outside as I can. It makes me feel useful working in the garden and planting flowers."

Katie smiled. The front yard was indeed beautiful and all of Bess's hard work showed. "Bess, thank you for the tea. You've been helpful and I appreciate your time."

TWENTY-SEVEN

Friday 1335 hours

Katie left Bess's house with their conversation still rolling through her mind as she walked across the street to the police sedan where McGaven waited. The woman had provided new information, but again, Katie wasn't sure if it would push the investigation forward.

"I can tell by the look on your face, you didn't get the information that you wanted," he said.

She walked up to her partner. "Yes and no."

"I learned from the neighbor that the Daytons seemed to strike up a friendship with the Wills," said McGaven.

"Bess said the same thing."

Katie and McGaven updated each other, both neighbors seemed to corroborate the other's statements.

"I want to check out the Wills stables," she said.

"Lead the way."

Katie decided to walk to the residence, which was only a few houses away. She noticed that the smoke from the burning brush had subsided, clearing the air. It made the walk that much more pleasant, and Katie could understand the appeal of the area.

The stables appeared to be vacant. There were storm windows in place, which helped with security. The front of the home was almost completely hidden by a large hedge and a grouping of pine trees.

Katie took inventory of the standard places where security cameras would be located and was surprised by the fact she didn't see any. It seemed odd if someone wasn't a full-time resident not to have any cameras set up.

"What's the matter?" asked McGaven.

"I find it strange that there are no cameras."

"Maybe they're more camouflaged than the ordinary ones."

"Maybe," she said. Katie had that feeling that something was odd about the house. At times it seemed like an irrational emotion, but it had steered her in the right direction on more occasions than she could count.

There was large well-established fencing—part wood and part metal. With no locks, the detectives easily walked through and made their way to the backyard and stables. The acreage was immense, much larger than the neighboring properties. There were at least a dozen stalls, indoor and outdoor yards, two riding rings, several storage areas, and a modest house. It was clear that there weren't any horses boarded and the place was definitely unoccupied.

The clouds covered the sun for a moment and made the place dark, forming strange shadows. There was almost a supernatural atmosphere, in that way only an abandoned or a vacant area can match.

Katie slowed her pace, taking in the landscape and the buildings. "I didn't see any no trespassing signs, did you?"

"No, I didn't."

"So, if you were going to be staying at a property part-time wouldn't you have cameras and signs?" she said.

"Maybe they did, and someone removed them."

Katie thought that was an interesting observation—they could've been torn down for many reasons. She wouldn't think that would be logical, but under the circumstances it might make sense. Everything they had seen and investigated had been strange.

"Where do you want to look?" said McGaven. He seemed extra cautious but wasn't saying if anything was bothering him. He absently touched his holster, making sure his gun was ready if he needed it.

"I'm not sure. Let's just take a quick look through the stables."

He nodded, but she could tell his senses were on high alert.

"It won't hurt to take a few extra minutes before we get back to the department. I want to drop off the crates for John and we need to fill out chain-of-custody forms as well." Katie was rambling, which was uncharacteristic of her.

As they checked the stables, Katie decided to go through to the storage and feeding areas. For some reason, her mind turned to Chad and the room where he was kept. A sudden sadness filled her about him leaving for Florida, so she pushed forward and continued to search, pushing the feeling down, trying hard to concentrate on their investigation.

As Katie walked through the back areas, she came across a cooler, which she found odd. The property appeared vacant—almost abandoned. Why would a new cooler be sitting there? She eased the lid open. Inside were some wrapped sandwiches and several cans of beer. Everything was chilled.

Katie turned to McGaven who had watched her open the cooler. Neither detective said a word. They knew each other's moves well—and they also knew there was someone at the property.

They could go left toward the stalls or right toward the storage areas. Katie pulled her weapon and gestured with her hand that she would go right. McGaven took her lead and went left.

As Katie quietly moved past the last stall, she glanced from left to right, and back again straight ahead. She wondered if the person or persons who were on the property heard them arrive and were hiding. Along the walk area, she saw a line of what looked like some type of kibble. She slowed her pace, thinking about the dogs at the rental house both inside and out back.

She stopped and listened. She'd heard a soft noise coming from one of the stalls behind her. She turned, expecting to see someone, but there was no one there, but in a quick flash of light she saw long scrape marks and dark spots in some of the stalls. Nothing seemed to indicate horses had been kept there recently.

Katie looked back to where she had come from, expecting to see McGaven appear, but it was quiet. He wasn't near. She didn't want to call out to her partner so instead she slowly back-tracked to the stall where the noise had come from. She had to keep moving.

The sigh sound became louder—almost like a snort or chuff. She took another step, crunching on more pieces of food that trailed into the stall. Katie put her hand on the latch and slowly lifted it. A squeak emitted. Katie paused. She slowly pulled the gate open just wide enough for her to squeeze through, and, keeping her weapon directed in front of her, she eased forward.

There was an empty duffel bag lying on the ground, but it was difficult to tell if it was new or old, especially as the large holding area was dark. Light shone along the other side where it led to the outdoors, but the corners of the interior were obscured. Katie stepped farther in and headed toward the outside enclosure. She noted that nothing had the smell of fresh hay or oats, another indication that the property hadn't had any animals inhabiting it for quite some time.

Katie kept moving. She didn't want to be a fixed target.

She did a 360-degree turn looking for the origin of the sound or whoever left their cooler at the entrance. Nothing caught her attention, but she couldn't shake the feeling of being watched. Maybe this case and its unusual circumstances were making her think there was someone hiding everywhere she went.

But then a small creak above her made her stop. Before she could look up, a person jumped down from the rafters, knocking Katie from her feet. She hit the concrete floor hard as her gun flew from her grip. She couldn't breathe; the wind had been knocked out of her. Panic set in but her adrenaline took over, giving her strength until she could catch her breath.

A man in his thirties to mid-forties, dark hair, beard, and a black ball cap, pushed her onto her back. He was medium build and thin, but extremely strong, and he was taking aim to begin punching her.

Katie's Army training kicked in—be proactive, not reactive, keep the assailant off balance. She brought her right knee up and blasted his groin. The man cried out in pain and Katie used her elbows to pummel his torso and face. He released his grip and his body weight moved to the side as he reacted to the pain inflicted.

Katie quickly crawled toward where she thought the gun had landed. She searched the area with her hands as if she was blind. The man behind her had recovered enough and was angry. His rage moved toward her as he grabbed her jacket trying to get a better grip.

Katie used everything she could, including stomp and roundhouse kicks, causing the man to retreat for a moment. She felt her moves make contact, but she kept working diligently to find her gun. It was going to be the only way to regain the upper hand on the unknown assailant.

The man stood up and pounced on her, throwing her head backward against the wall. His breath reeked of stale cigarette smoke. She looked into his dark, almost black eyes, and it was clear that he was intent on killing her.

It felt to Katie that she had been fighting with the man for a long time, when, in fact, it was only for a minute or two. As she tried to focus her eyes, the man pressed her against the wall. He wasn't going to stop. She was able to get her right arm free and reached down, finally touching the cool barrel of her Glock. She managed to wrap her finger around the handle and, breathless, she yelled, "Get up now!" She pulled the trigger, the bullet hitting the ceiling, causing the man to instantly stop. "Show me your hands! Get up now!"

McGaven appeared as if he was an apparition. He grabbed the man by his collar and yanked him to his feet. "Put your hands on your head," he demanded.

The man hesitantly followed orders and did so.

McGaven snapped a cuff on one hand and pulled the man's hands behind his back, securing the other handcuff. "Get down on your knees and on your face now!"

The man didn't hesitate this time and lay on the ground.

Katie's breathing returned to normal. She still clutched her gun.

McGaven leaned down. "You okay?"

"Yeah, I think so."

He helped his partner up. "Where did he come from?"

"Above."

"What?" he said, looking up and spying the rafters.

Katie slowly gained her bearings and her dizziness subsided. She walked up to the man. "Who are you?"

He grumbled something incoherent.

Katie knelt down and stared the man in the face. "What's your name?" She reached into his back pocket and retrieved a wallet. Opening it, she pulled out the driver's license. "You are Ferris Baldwin. Really? Ferris?"

"You got a problem with that?"

"Not really. But what I do have a problem with is you attacking a police officer."

Ferris didn't respond.

"So, tell me, Ferris... what are you doing here?"

"Nothing."

"C'mon, you can do better than that. We're going to find out anyway. Make it easier on yourself. We're going to run your license and your name. And I bet we're going to find some fun things about you," she said.

McGaven pulled Ferris up to his knees and pushed him against the wall and sat him down. "What made you think you could attack a cop?"

"I didn't know she was a cop."

"Okay, but you could've just stayed in your hiding position," she said.

"Yeah, that's twenty-twenty hindsight now."

McGaven was about to call for patrol to arrest him.

"Wait," she said. "Who did you think I was?"

"I thought you were with him, one of his crew."

"Who?"

He stopped talking as if he had already said too much.

"Look," said Katie. "We can make things easier on you, but you have to talk to us. Right now, you're looking at assaulting a police officer, impeding an investigation, and whatever we find when we run for warrants." She studied the man. He didn't seem as threatening now, sitting there in the natural light. "Who are you running from?"

"Harland," he said quietly.

"Harland? You mean Thomas Harland Dayton?"

"Yeah, he goes by Harland."

She looked up at McGaven who was already on his phone, searching.

"When was the last time you saw Harland?" Katie asked.

"Two months ago."

"Where?"

"Here."

"You mean here at this property?"

"Yeah."

"How often does he come here?"

"I don't know."

"Why would you be here if you're afraid of him?" she said.

"I was looking for something."

Katie looked at her partner. "Looking for what?"

"Something. Anything. He's dangerous and I wanted to find something I could give to the cops anonymously."

"Are you saying that you would give up something to get Harland arrested?"

"Yeah," he said, nodding.

"Say we believe you. What can you give us if we're going to help you?"

Ferris squirmed as he seemed to consider whether he should trust Katie and McGaven. "Look, he's eccentric. Even more than when I first met him when he had the farm."

"You mean the property that foreclosed?"

"Yeah."

"Tell us something about it," she said, hoping that he wasn't just jerking them around because he didn't want to get arrested.

"Have you found them yet?"

"Who?"

"The bodies."

He had Katie's undivided attention. "What *bodies*?"

"I don't know their names, but he hurt them and then buried them."

"Who were they?"

"I don't know. He would take them, or they would end up at the property lost or something, like this girl one time. I don't know a lot about it, but I do know that he buried them there."

"How many?"

"I only know of two. One of them had a dog. That's all I know. I swear."

"Do you know where they were buried?"

"Behind the barn."

It was as if electricity shot up Katie's spine. There was another body buried on the property.

"Where does Harland live now?" said McGaven.

"I don't know. No one knows. He just shows up from time to time."

Katie studied the man's body language and considered what he had told them. She believed he was telling mostly the truth, though there seemed to be some deception.

"Get up," said McGaven.

"What you going to do?" said Ferris.

"Our job." McGaven directed him out of the stalls and toward the front. To his partner, he said, "Patrol is on their way. We'll sort everything out in holding."

"Okay. First I'm going to do a quick search of the rest of the property, call the sheriff, and see what our options are," she said.

This was the first break in the case from firsthand information and she was going to get the answers they needed.

TWENTY-EIGHT

Friday 1650 hours

Katie sat in the waiting room at the Pine Valley Psychiatric Hospital. It was almost five p.m., the time for the appointment. She watched McGaven pace the small sterile waiting room without any décor or artwork on the walls and could see that the meeting with Lara Fontaine made him uncomfortable. Katie was there for support but there was a bit of curiosity on her part as well. She didn't know exactly when, but she knew that her partner would confide in her when he was ready.

Katie rehashed the incident on the bridge with Lara standing on the ledge. There had been something that almost seemed rehearsed about Lara's body language and her conversation. There was distress about her, absolutely, but there had seemed to be something else. Katie had seen only two other attempted jumpers in her career, but they weren't going to let anyone close—and the conversations with the cops had been different, more hostile and angry.

"Detective McGaven?" said a nurse as she approached them.

"Yes."

"Lara is in the conference room, and she is ready to speak with you."

"My partner will also join us," he said.

"I don't know…"

"If she doesn't like that, then I will leave," he said firmly.

This was completely out of character for McGaven. He was always kind and accommodating, even with criminals. His approach was that everyone needed to be heard and understood.

"Gav, that's okay," said Katie.

"No, I would like for you to be there."

The nurse hesitated, but she then nodded. "Follow me."

The detectives followed the nurse down two hallways and then went through a security checkpoint. They had already locked their weapons away when they had entered the hospital. They stopped at a door with a sign: Conference Room G.

"Please let us know when you're ready to leave," said the nurse, indicating the nurses' station across the hall.

"Thank you," said McGaven. He pushed open the door and Katie followed.

The room was just as sterile in décor as the rest of the place. There was a table with three plastic chairs and sitting across the table was Lara, patiently waiting. Her wide eyes seemed surprised that McGaven had brought Katie, but the woman smiled and seemed to be more excited that there were two detectives meeting her.

"Sean," she said. Her voice was sweet and chipper. She continued to smile at them. "Please sit down."

McGaven and Katie each took a chair across from Lara. Katie instantly felt uncomfortable. She had interviewed violent offenders, but sitting across from Lara made her take notice that she seemed relaxed but fragile—it was clear that she was wounded. She was dressed in aqua-colored scrubs, with her hair pulled back in a ponytail and her face washed clean of any makeup. Her skin was flawless, almost porcelain-like. Her eyes were dark with heavily dilated pupils, indicating that she was on some type of medication.

"Lara, how are you?" said McGaven with little inflection in his voice.

"I've missed you," she said, ignoring his question.

"Where have you been since school? I haven't seen you around."

"I've been around, and I've always loved Pine Valley. This is my home."

"Is there something you wanted to talk to me about?"

"I'm being discharged first thing in the morning."

"That's good. Do you have a place to go?"

"Yes. My apartment."

McGaven was taking everything in, but he seemed distant. Katie waited patiently and noticed that after their initial entry, Lara hadn't looked at her once. It seemed odd because Katie was the one who had talked to her on the bridge.

"Sean, I've never trusted anyone else but you," Lara then said, making small gestures that were more reminiscent of those of a young girl. She was acting cutesy, shifting in her seat, and cocking her head.

He shifted his weight. "We weren't even in the same class, Lara. You were three years behind me."

"Oh, yes. I know, Sean."

"Lara, I don't know what's happened in your life since I last saw you, but I hope that you're getting the help here that you need." McGaven took a breath, leaning slightly forward in his seat. "What made you get on the bridge? Why would you want to end your life?"

Lara began to fiddle with her ponytail. "It's all because of him. He's with me every day. I was trying to get rid of him... he's still out there, you know. Even when I close my eyes. But I want him to go away."

"Who?"

"The bad man."

McGaven didn't blink or change his expression. "What bad man?"

"He killed her."

Katie raised her eyebrows in surprise but remained quiet. She wondered what this woman was talking about—and whether it was based in reality or her imagination.

"Lara, are you saying that you witnessed a murder?" McGaven asked.

"Uh-huh." She nodded.

"When?"

"When I was at my friend's house."

"What friend?" he said.

"Desi. We were best friends, and I don't know why she wouldn't help me. I've been trying to find her. Please... *you* have to find her." Lara became agitated.

Katie decided to interrupt. "Lara?"

For the first time, the young woman turned her attention from McGaven to Katie. Her eyes narrowed slightly as if she was unhappy about Katie's interruption. "Yes, Katie."

"How old were you when you saw this murder?" said Katie.

"Twelve. *Almost* thirteen, almost a teenager." She smiled.

"Do you know who the man was?" she said. Katie felt the tension from her partner, but he stayed silent, not interrupting her.

"Yes."

"Can you tell us who it was?"

"I... I... don't want to get in trouble."

"Lara, you won't get in trouble. We need to know to get the bad man off the streets."

"Lara," interrupted McGaven.

The young woman returned her gaze to him. She stared intently, leaving her hair alone. "Yes, Sean."

"Can you tell us the name of the man?" he said.

"Desi's dad."

"Do you have a last name?"

"Desi's last name is Dayton."

Katie almost sucked in a breath in complete amazement. Of course, Desi was Desiree Dayton. Lara wasn't making it up. Not wanting to interrupt what McGaven was doing, she stayed quiet as her mind ran through everything they knew about Dayton at this point.

"You mean Thomas Dayton?" asked McGaven. His voice and mannerisms were calm and balanced.

"I don't know. Just Desi's dad, Mr. Dayton. Please find her..."

"Desi? Is that short for Desiree?" he said.

"Yes, but she always liked Desi because it was cute."

For the first time since the detectives had sat down, McGaven turned to his partner. "What do you want to do?"

Katie was careful of how she answered in the presence of Lara. "We need to take her statement and follow up," she said quietly.

"Sean, I want to help. And I want the bad dreams to stop."

Katie quickly reviewed in her mind everything that happened since they'd reopened the case. They had found Abigail Andrews's body at the Dayton farm buried in a fifty-five-gallon drum, her dog killed, her boyfriend murdered in prison, an associate of Dayton hiding, and now someone who saw a murder committed by Dayton.

"Lara," said McGaven, "do you know where Desi is?"

"No. I've been trying to find her."

"When was the last time you spoke to her?"

"Um... we were in high school."

"And not since then?"

Her face turned sad. "No."

McGaven spoke with Lara a while longer trying to get more information, but they didn't glean much else. When the detectives left the psychiatric hospital it was dark outside, the dull parking lot lights casting an eerie glow and making everything they had just learned seem more like a spooky tale than reality.

"What do you think?" said McGaven finally.

"That was a lot to digest," she said. "But if you're asking... if I believe her. I believe that she thinks it's true, and there are too many things connected to Dayton that we already know to be true."

"I think maybe this is the first time where we have the key pieces of the puzzle. Looks like some big overtime coming up."

"True. But we don't know where Thomas Dayton is right now. That's the million-dollar question."

TWENTY-NINE

Friday 1930 hours

Katie had left the Pine Valley Psychiatric Hospital and driven to the Pine Valley Rehabilitation Center to spend time with Chad. Even as the new information fell into their laps about Abigail's case, her thoughts were still never far from Chad. Her emotions teetered between deep relief and deep despair every time she thought about him, everything he had been through, and where their relationship was going.

She was concerned when she reached his room and there were no more guards or security. She knew the Lane/Hyde cases were essentially closed, but they still hadn't arrested the man who had kidnapped and orchestrated Chad's abduction and imprisonment for Hyde. There was still one of the perps still on the loose.

Katie curled up in the comfortable chair next to Chad's bed. When she arrived, he was sleeping, and she didn't want to wake him. He needed to sleep. She hoped that he was beginning to filter through his emotions in order to begin to work through them.

As she watched him sleep, he was beginning to resemble more the Chad she had always known. He was beginning to put on weight, color had returned to his face, his hair had been cut, and he looked peaceful.

So many questions spun through her mind. *How was she going to go on without him? Would he be back? Would their relationship survive this trauma?* Between the cases and new developments and Chad, she didn't know how she was going get through the days ahead.

"Hey," said Chad as he sat up rubbing his eyes.

"Hi," she said and moved to the bed. She hugged him tightly. "I missed you."

"I missed you too."

"How you doing?" She searched his face for some type of indication if he was doing better or just being strong for her sake.

Holding her tightly, he said, "Doing better. I feel like I'm back in reality instead of being chained in a nightmare."

"I'm glad. Every day will be better, I promise."

"One day at a time," he said. "Katie, I love you so much."

Katie snuggled closer to him. "Love you more."

He kissed her.

Katie almost felt like nothing had changed in that instant, but everything had changed, and things wouldn't be the same. She wanted to be supportive and loving, but she still wanted him to stay so they could go through this together.

"I really need for you to understand something," Chad said quietly.

She sat up.

"I have to take this time away from here, from Pine Valley, from work, to get my thoughts together and to work through everything that happened. But I'm not leaving you. You understand that, right?"

"Of course," she said. Her heart was breaking, crushed into

a million pieces, but she wasn't going to let Chad know. He had so much to deal with already.

"We'll need to postpone wedding plans, just for a while."

"I understand," she said. Katie knew this was going to be the case, but hearing Chad say those words out loud was devastating.

"Katie, this isn't easy for me either. I don't want to be away from you, but it's the best thing right now. I want to get through this and heal, so that we can be together, strong and happy, without this unknown trauma hanging over my head."

"Whatever you need, I support you." She hoped and prayed that he would come back, and they could soon begin their married life together.

Chad hugged her, holding her tightly. "I heard those cases were closed after you found where I was held."

It surprised her that he knew about the Lane/Hyde investigations. "Yes, they closed it."

"I'm sure you're relieved."

Katie nodded. She really wasn't, but she had to make peace with it.

"You look tired. Are you working a new case?"

"Yes, it's complicated and even surprising." But she didn't want to discuss it with Chad. Not now.

He looked closely at her. "I've never heard you describe an investigation like that. It must be a heck of an investigation."

She laughed. "That's one way to describe it."

"Katie," he said. "I know more than anyone everything that you've been through over the past few years."

"That's all over now. We need to concentrate on you."

He smiled. It was something that she'd loved about him—his amazing, charming smile—ever since they were kids.

"Always looking out for others—that's my Katie."

She looked down.

"Hey," he said. "It's going to be okay. We'll get through this."

"What time are you leaving in the morning?"

"My plane takes off at six-thirty."

"Oh."

"And I have a friend from the firehouse who is going to stay at my place while I'm gone. I don't want it to be empty any longer." He looked at Katie. "It's going to be okay..."

Katie wasn't so sure.

THIRTY

Saturday 0815 hours

Katie had rushed to the sheriff's department as she was running a little bit late. She had decided to see Chad before he left the center, thinking it might make her feel better, but it made her heart break again. But she tried to push away her depression and ignore her shattered heart—once again. She knew it was best for Chad, but the unknown scared her.

Katie had been doing so well with her PTSD, physically, emotionally, and cognitively, before the last cases, but her anxiety could potentially paralyze her, making her unable to do her job. Chad leaving churned up all the feelings and emotions from the past, with the death of her parents and more recently the murder of her aunt. It was almost too much.

There was a tap on her window bringing her back to the present in her Jeep in the parking lot. John stood there waiting for her. He smiled and seemed to have something to tell her. She always felt at ease with the forensic supervisor and former Navy SEAL. There was something about people who had served in the military that connected them to each other.

Katie got out. "Hi, what are you doing here on the weekend?" She felt a bit embarrassed that she had been feeling sorry for herself when there was a killer on the loose and wondered how long John had been standing at her car window watching her wallow in her personal sadness.

"We have some things to report. Glad you're here today," said John.

"Great," she said. "This case finally seems to be growing with information and clues."

"Gav has already put in for a search of the Dayton property for another body. We're going to use GPR," he said, referring to ground-penetrating radar. John gave her a look. "You okay?"

"Sure." Katie gathered her briefcase and jacket. She followed the forensic supervisor into the building and through the secured entrance to the forensic division.

"I'll check in with Gav and we'll be right in," she said.

"Okay."

John went through to the examination area as Katie went to the working cold-case area. McGaven was standing at the board filling in information for the Abigail Andrews investigation.

"Hi," said Katie.

"Good morning," said McGaven. He seemed to be back to his usual positive self.

Katie put down her things. "I see you're filling in some of the gaps."

"You bet. It was an interesting day yesterday."

"To say the least," she said, not looking at her partner.

McGaven put down the pen. "You okay?"

"Sure."

"I'm not buying it."

Katie didn't want to rehash things at the moment. She didn't know if it was the right time—or if it ever would be. She said instead, "We need to see what John has for us. And I want to be at the property when they search for this other body that Ferris mentioned."

McGaven leaned against the worktable. "Nope. Not moving until you tell me what's going on."

"Gav."

"Nope. I'm not moving—not even an inch."

Katie knew her partner meant what he said. "Look, we have a job to do—"

"And, we need to be mentally healthy and ready to go."

"Point taken. Look... I just said goodbye to Chad before he left for the airport. I'm worried about what's going to happen now."

"He's not leaving forever. It's just a break to take a rest and get things straight in his mind. Right?"

"Yes, but—"

"Katie, I know you've been through a lot—more than most. But you need a break too. Just because Chad's leaving for a while doesn't mean he won't be back. His job is here... his life is here. And most important, you're here."

She knew he was right, but it still didn't change the fact that she was sad and insecure. "It's just tough right now."

"There," he said. "Was that so bad?"

Katie rolled her eyes and chuckled. "Gav, you're really something. You know that?"

"Sure," he said, smiling broadly.

"Thanks for your concern. I'm fine. Really."

"Good, because I need my brilliant partner to be at the top of her game."

Katie went to the door. "C'mon, partner, let's see what John has for us."

The main forensic examination area had been rearranged again. There were new computers with larger screens and worktables. She wondered if they were testing out more forensic software.

"You've cleaned house," said McGaven.

"Yeah, we received a grant and have new equipment. It's been long overdue," said John. "But better late than never."

"That's great," said Katie. She looked closer at some of the computers and was impressed. She didn't see Eva and assumed that she was working on something else.

"We have some preliminary results for you," said John.

Katie was hopeful as she focused her attention on what they were going to find out.

"First, Abigail Andrews was officially identified, and her mother came in to identify her jewelry and clothes—as well as... her dog."

"So..." said McGaven. "What about Abigail?"

John moved to one of the new computers and brought up images. "The medical examiner will give you a more detailed explanation of the injuries, but I wanted to give you something now."

Katie looked at the screen. The image of Abigail's body was difficult for her to see, but she had to focus on the evidence and not the reality of someone's loved one being dead.

Abigail's body had been broken and shoved into the fifty-five-gallon drum. There were numerous injuries on the body, some made before and some after death. Her neck was what stood out to Katie.

"Was her neck broken or cut?" she asked.

"The body had been sliced, cut, stabbed, and anything else that a knife or other sharp implement could accomplish."

"She was tortured," said Katie.

John nodded. "Yes. Most of the wounds were made when she was alive. Now, if you see here and here." He pointed on the computer screen. "These are injuries that happened when they were making her body fit into the drum."

"Did she die from all the wounds or the one that impacted her neck?" said McGaven.

"From what we can see, and Dr. Dean will give the final word, her throat was slit, and from the size and area, she would have bled out quickly."

"The body is so decomposed. Was there any evidence from her clothes, fingernails, or anything else?" Katie asked.

"Unfortunately, we weren't able to get anything like prints or any biological evidence. We have the remnants of her clothes and her personal things, but nothing has indicated anything about the killer."

John walked over to one of the large exam tables to show the detectives what he had recovered from the body for testing. What was left of Abigail's clothes in the drum had been carefully laid out, pieced together with what they already had from the hillside near where the car was found. It appeared she had been wearing blue jeans and a T-shirt that had a band name imprinted on it. There was a plain brown leather belt and the remnants of one sock. Alongside the clothing were two pieces of jewelry: a butterfly necklace and a thin leather bracelet.

Katie stared at the necklace.

"Mrs. Andrews identified the clothing she was wearing as well as her jewelry," said John.

"What about the dog?"

"The dog had a slashed throat as well."

That made Katie flinch. "What about the drums?"

"Unfortunately, they are extremely common. You can find them at any hardware or maintenance super store. You can also find them at feed stores."

"Do they have ID numbers or dates?" she said.

"They seemed to be from a decade ago."

"That would check with the timeline of when Abigail disappeared," said Katie. She had begun to profile the killer.

"I can see your mind is already steps ahead of us," said McGaven.

"I'm realizing that this Thomas Dayton is an extremely violent, sadistic killer. And this could work against him."

"How?"

"People who have these characteristics also have a tendency to think they are smarter than everyone, and that they can't make mistakes."

"And that's why it's easy to push their egocentricity. And that's when they *will* make a mistake," said McGaven.

Katie nodded.

John smiled. "Well, do you want to see what else we've found out? Even though watching you begin a profile is interesting." He kept the energy light, but he wanted to move forward with the evidence.

"I'm sorry, John. What else do you have?"

John moved across the room. "We couldn't get any prints that weren't smudged—only a few points. Nothing that would be useful, unless there were other prints to compare. And even still... it wouldn't hold up in court."

Katie's hopes began to fall.

"However, the Mason jar had some interesting remnants inside."

Katie and McGaven leaned toward the computer screen.

"We found residues of water, lipids, and proteins."

"And?" said Katie.

"Along with proteins from cells, keratin, and nucleic acid."

"Wait," said Katie thinking about the components.

"That's skin," said McGaven.

"You're right, Detective. Human skin, to be more exact."

"So, you're saying that inside those common Mason jars was human skin?"

"Yes."

"We're running more tests and DNA to see if there were human organs attached to them, but it will take some time."

The image of human organs in those jars in the living room

turned Katie's stomach. "The killer was saving trophies from his victims."

"Which he displayed in his living room," said McGaven, stunned.

"It seems like it. Maybe they were moved from another room." She thought a moment. "I think there was another location we didn't see."

"We were in both houses, and you were at the barn. What else would there be?"

"A basement." She thought again. "John, is there a way to trace the jars? Like dates or places of manufacturing?"

John went to the computer where he had photographs of the jars from the farmhouse taken from all angles. "If you look here," he indicated, "it reads eight and fourteen, which means the mold numbers. But check around the side where it says Eclipse."

"What does that mean?" she said.

"It basically means that these jars are from 1926 to 1952."

"Like antiques?"

"Not really. Jars that are older would have the wording Improved, which were from the late 1800s through 1933."

Katie thought about it. "That doesn't tell us much, but that they seemed to be from an earlier time. It's interesting but makes it impossible to tell who owned or bought them."

"Another dead end," said John.

"I'm not sure. It tells us that the farm is older and there have been things that have been recycled and passed down," she said. "Makes me wonder what else we're going to find out there. If we find jars at any other location with similar numbers or identifications, it might be helpful."

"But they won't tell us where to find Dayton," said McGaven.

John looked away from the computer. "We're going out

today to search for any other drums or bodies. I assume you two are joining us."

"What time?" she asked.

"Two hours," said John looking at his watch.

"Do you have anything else?" said Katie.

"Nothing concrete. I'll email you guys the reports of what we have right now."

"Thanks, John. We'll meet you at the farm."

"I would be very careful. Even though the area is cleared now, and you can see anyone coming, still be alert. We'll be right behind you," said McGaven.

"I can handle it," said John with a smile.

Katie knew that the forensic supervisor carried a weapon when he was in the field.

The detectives left the forensic examination room, returning to their office. Katie grabbed her jacket and keys. "I think we should take my Jeep and bring Cisco."

"Instead of the police sedan," said McGaven. "Good idea. It's too easy to follow."

She nodded. "See you in a few."

THIRTY-ONE

Saturday 1200 hours

Katie pulled the Jeep into the long driveway at the property on the farm and immediately spotted the CSU van. They must've just arrived, as there was still some dust floating in the air from the tires throwing up gravel.

"Looks like John is right on time," said McGaven.

Cisco let out a whine as if he knew that he was going to get to run around and search.

During the entire drive, Katie thought about Thomas Dayton and his victims. She thought about Lara and what she must've gone through if she had indeed witnessed the murder. Even though there wasn't direct proof yet, she knew that they were uncovering the works of a monster. Every day seemed to confirm it.

McGaven was still searching for any more information about Thomas Dayton. Everything he found was a dead end, like the rental house where there was no forwarding address. It seemed, from the rental agency, he had returned to collect his deposit in person instead of having it mailed. Dayton seemed to cover his tracks, which could mean that he had changed his name and was going by an alias. It also appeared that his daughter, Desiree Dayton, was a ghost. There was no record of her after high school; it was as if she'd vanished into thin air.

Katie drove the Jeep closer to the house and parked. She saw John and Eva emptying containers, suitcases, and then the GPR device. It was a laptop computer attached to a long loop—similar to an oversize metal detector but with greater technology and capabilities. They were setting up prior to searching the terrain. John waved at the detectives.

"Let's go formulate a plan," she said.

"Let's do it," said McGaven as he got out of the Jeep.

"*Bleib,*" said Katie to Cisco, telling him to stay. The dog whined and did two fast turns in the back seat, wanting to join the detectives.

It was a much different atmosphere around the farm than it was the last time they were there. It was cleared and looked more like the neglected and abandoned property that it was. Katie was still on high alert as she surveyed the area, including the back entrance leading out to the utility road. It was all clear. She glanced at the farmhouse, and it seemed to beckon her. Had they missed something the first time? The feeling lodged in Katie's gut, not letting her forget about it.

"Hi, guys," said Eva. Her intense energy matched her spiky blonde hair. She carried the GPR and was ready for work.

"Hi, Eva," said Katie. As she was getting to know the forensic tech, Katie really was beginning to like her.

McGaven went up to the technician and they gave each other a high-five.

John faced Katie. "There is so much ground to cover. We did a preliminary search when we recovered the two drums, but everything has been massively overgrown, making it difficult to see if anything has been disturbed."

"I can run Cisco in quadrants and anything that he seems

interested in would be a good starting point for the GPR," said Katie.

"Did your witness have any other observations that might be useful?" said John.

"She's pretty messed up from her experiences as a kid," said McGaven. "But I do believe that she's telling the truth—at least what she believes to be true."

"She definitely witnessed something," said Katie.

"Great. We'll let you two search," said John.

Katie went back to the Jeep where Cisco waited anxiously. As she walked toward the car, she turned her head and looked at the farmhouse. What was making her so obsessive about the house? She would check it out again after Cisco's search.

Katie opened the SUV door and let Cisco out. He did his usual doggie happy dance and took a few circles. She geared him with his tracking harness and long lead. The area was slightly uneven, but there wasn't anything about the landscape that indicated potential dangers or hazards to either one of them.

Katie and Cisco made their way across the property and headed to the barn. Cisco zigzagged as they went, picking up all kinds of odors. She noticed that the barn door was wide open and remembered that when they had left it was closed. Maybe one of the first responders had left it open. She would run Cisco throughout that area just in case bodies were buried inside the barn.

McGaven, John, and Eva waited a short distance away as the K9 team began the search, making sure they weren't in the way of the direction of the wind, complicating the dog's nose work.

Katie calmed her nerves and put her entire attention on Cisco and the task ahead of them. She watched for any behavioral change, which was usually a change in the dog's body language. He would stiffen his torso, tail placed firmly downward, and nose funneling in the direction of the scent before homing in on the exact location. It could be one change or a combination of changes.

Katie wanted to begin at the tree line west of the property and begin a strip search formation in that area. She kept her pace at a slow to medium speed, allowing Cisco to freely move back and forth.

"Cisco, *such*," she said, telling the dog to search.

Cisco let out a quick bark and began working the area at the end of the ten-foot leash.

Katie didn't want to stop and check anything out until Cisco pointed at something specific. She trailed the dog for ten minutes when he slowed his pace and stopped around the area where Abigail had been located. The two holes were now filled in but there was quite a bit of scent left of the victims and from people trampling around the location.

Cisco finally continued and moved around bushes and another set of large trees. He stopped, keeping his nose high as if there was something in the trees that interested him.

Katie knew to trust the dog's scenting ability. She followed Cisco as he turned and doubled back. He seemed interested in a spot near the other set of pine trees. There was a slight breeze coming from the east, so it was blowing toward them. Katie thought it might be an issue, but the dog had learned instinctively how to compensate for the wind.

Cisco took another minute and then came back to the area near the trees. He downed and stayed in the position.

"Good boy, Cisco," she said and marked the area with a small red flag, sticking it into the ground. "Let's go."

The dog continued searching. This time he headed to another grouping of trees, slowing his pace. He took a few moments of interest until he downed at the location.

Katie took another flag and stuck it into the ground. She kept moving in strategic sections, including inside the barn.

Another fifteen minutes went by, and she marked another area before returning to the group.

"Well...?" said McGaven.

"No doubt there's something in that grouping of trees where I've placed the flags. That would be my best guess to begin your GPR in those sections. The terrain is fairly level, but the overgrowth and dead layer is thick," she said. "Be careful."

"That's why we brought garden tools," said Eva.

"We're going to get started," said John.

"Gav and I are going back to the farmhouse to have a look around," she said. "And to give Cisco a break."

Before they did, Katie walked closer to the areas she'd flagged. She ran scenarios through her mind of how and where the victims were killed, and then when they were buried. The mind of the killer was important. Why these particular women? Did he actively search for them? Who were they? A type? Or were they merely a convenience? From cases she had worked previously, killers generally had something that drove them. A fantasy. An obsessive need that was never quenched, which was why they kept searching for more victims.

Katie put Cisco back in the Jeep, after giving him water, under a nice tree to keep him cool. She also affixed the remote to the back door of her car that would spring it open if she needed the dog. It was general practice for her, but she hadn't been as diligent lately. Because the farmhouse property gave her pause and feelings of being uncomfortable, she decided to always have the remote whenever Cisco was with them.

"Do you know what you're looking for?" asked McGaven

"Exactly? No. But I have an idea that this type of killer would have some secrets."

"You mean like a horror torture chamber?"

The detectives stepped onto the wobbly porch.

"That's a very good description," she said. It never ceased to amaze her how McGaven always got her, never disregarded her theories and profiles, and was a supportive detective partner. "Let's find out."

They entered the farmhouse once again. There were signs that the forensic team had been there. Black fingerprint powder still stained the walls, windowsills, and various places around the rooms. There were imprints in the substantial dust of the heavy containers and briefcases John and Eva carried.

"This isn't a big house," said McGaven. "We should be able to find something."

Katie nodded and began looking at the walls, ceiling, and even the built-in shelving unit. "It's not that we haven't found secret rooms before."

"So true," he said.

"If Dayton killed several people here then he would have to have an area where he worked or stored his trophies—or even kept the victims to torture them. I did find some tools in the barn, but I don't think that there was a room there. It would be too visible. The house would make it more intimate and easier to keep victims quiet."

Katie walked through the living room leaving McGaven behind to take a closer look at everything. She looked at the kitchen. She almost bypassed the area, but at the last moment noticed unusual markings on the wall and floor. None of the appliances were still there, leaving behind the typical outline where a stove and refrigerator would sit. The old, yellowed linoleum peeled back along the edges of the room from age. It had once had a small square pattern, but now it was a muddled conglomeration of dirt, grime, and concentrated wear.

Katie remembered a previous case where a cabin kitchen had areas in the ceiling where items could be hidden. But the more she studied the ceiling, the more it didn't seem to be the case at this farmhouse.

Instead, she concentrated on the floor. She bent down and chipped away at some of the cracked flooring, revealing the subfloor. It was intact and built well. She carefully ran her fingers along the breaks in the linoleum where there might be some other type of opening. As she moved to the middle of the floor, where it was the most stable, there seemed to be a square outline.

Katie stood in the middle of the kitchen looking at all four corners. She realized that this would be where a table would most likely be located. She stomped her feet a few times, noticing there seemed to be a different sound than the rest of the room. She imagined a table and four chairs with a rug underneath. It would certainly hide any access.

"Hey, what's all the racket?" said McGaven, entering the room.

"I think there's some type of access here, but it's sealed."

"I'll be right back." McGaven left. When he returned he had John's toolbox, which included smashing and prying implements. He held up a sledgehammer. "Shall I?" he said with a smile.

"Wait. Maybe something less demolishing, like a crowbar to run along the perimeter of the opening," she said.

McGaven looked disappointed but got the crowbar. He began running it around where Katie had instructed. The hooked end slid along the areas where the indentation seemed to be more pronounced, and the floor suddenly popped a little. There was a three-foot square outline.

"Look at that," said McGaven. "It's a perfect square, but how would you know that?"

"This floor seemed wrong."

"Meaning?"

"Look at how wear and time has discolored and damaged it. But here, it seemed to be protected, like with a rug from above and reinforced beneath."

McGaven ran his hand along the floor. He tried to pull back the plastic floor covering, but it was glued solid. "Seems like it's secured with a strong glue or epoxy." He sorted through John's toolbox and pulled out a scraper. "Maybe this will help." He began running the blunt part along the outline and then slowly chipped away at the linoleum. Slowly, some of the flooring began to splinter.

Katie grabbed hold of the pieces and pulled them away. "It has been reinforced, that's for sure."

The detectives spent almost twenty minutes working at the entry.

"It better not just be access to underneath the house," she said, slightly winded.

McGaven then pried the subflooring and it easily loosened, allowing him to pull up the opening.

Katie leaned over and peered down. She flipped on a flashlight, shining it into the hole. The light beam flowed across steps and walls that led into another room. She leaned farther into the opening. Stale moldy air leaked from the underground space.

"Wait," said McGaven. "Make sure there aren't any booby traps or anything that would hurt someone trying to get into the room."

"From outside the house, it doesn't seem like there could be a room like this. There are walls, bricks, and reinforcements." Her voice sounded hollow and eerily echoing. She started to ready herself to climb down.

"You want to wait for John?"

"Why?"

"Because he's the forensic guy. Maybe there's something down there you don't want to disturb."

Katie knew McGaven was right. There could be chemicals or decaying things. Her thoughts turned to the macabre where Dayton might have kept body parts, at least it seemed so. She pulled gloves from her pocket, then shed her jacket, so her clothing wouldn't catch on anything.

"Of course, you're still going down there," he said sarcastically.

"I have to do a recce to see what we're dealing with."

Her partner stared at her because he knew that he couldn't stop her from entering.

A slight breeze blew up and around the kitchen with perfect timing, clearing the air of its moldy quality.

Katie hesitated, reassessing that it might not be a good idea to lower her body under the house, but it would be a tight fit for her six-foot, six-inch partner. It looked sound. In fact, the basement area, for lack of a better description, seemed to be in better structural condition than the house and the guesthouse combined.

"Just a quick look around," said McGaven with a sternness to his voice.

Katie put her flashlight in her mouth as she lowered herself onto the first stair. It seemed solid underneath her feet and was made of large rock pieces arranged as a steppingstone. She looked up and saw McGaven's face peering down at her.

"Everything okay?" he said.

"Fine." She turned and began to descend the stairs. No windows or doors. There was a light switch on the side. She quickly flipped the toggle, but nothing happened. No sound. No light.

Keeping the flashlight in front of her, Katie continued to step downward. She didn't know if it was her imagination, but she felt a heaviness in her head, making it difficult to focus. Taking a moment to breathe, she realized that she had been holding her breath in anticipation. Part of her thoughts reflected that it was some type of torture chamber. The investigation wasn't far from her mind—the photographs from the scenes, her firsthand viewing of Abigail's body in the drum, the horse stables, and the room where Chad had been held captive. Her pulse quickened.

Katie reached the bottom. Her footing was strong, the ground compacted dirt. There was no concrete, which would help if they had to gather any evidence.

"Anything?" said McGaven from above. His voice sounded distant and there was a dream-like and strange haunting quality to it as if she was lost in an abyss.

"Nothing yet," she hollered up to him. She stood still, just as she did when she was at a new place outside. There was a dripping sound. She hadn't noticed it before, but it had to be close to the outdoors. Maybe there was an outside door.

Katie opened her eyes, and she could see much clearer. The walls had been carefully built with bricks and concrete. That was after the hole had been dug to accommodate the room. It was about twelve feet by sixteen feet. It surprised her that the walls didn't have shelving or storage, or anything that would explain a room like this underneath a kitchen.

Why? What was the purpose of the room?

Katie remembered the chamber where Chad had been held and the secret wall. Maybe there was the same type of application to this underground chamber. She began looking at the bricks closer, shining the light directly on them.

"Take some photos and come back up," said McGaven. He sounded impatient.

Katie had been so intent on searching the underground room, she hadn't taken any preliminary photos. Pulling her cell phone from her pocket, she stood in the middle of the room and took photographs, panning her view as she clicked. The flash bounced light all over the room. For a moment, Katie had to readjust her eyes.

There appeared to be an entrance in the far wall. It was cracked open by a few inches and on investigating she saw it led to a long tunnel. Katie noticed footprints from heavy work boots —they gave a clear impression and appeared to be recent.

Katie carefully followed the bootprints and began walking

through the tunnel. When she reached the end some minutes later she saw it exited onto the farm.

"Katie!" yelled McGaven. He had been calling her name, but she had been too far away. She heard his heavy footsteps coming up behind her. "Katie!"

She turned and saw light moving erratically and approaching fast.

McGaven emerged, breathless. He had a look of relief on his face. "Katie, you're okay."

"I'm okay."

McGaven looked around outside. It was difficult to see where someone might've run to with the tall weeds, which seemed to go on forever, surrounding them.

"Well, we've discovered one thing for sure," she said.

McGaven faced his partner.

"It seems that someone is watching us investigate this property."

"And they know a lot about this location," he said.

THIRTY-TWO

Peel away the layers of the past and you will see the present more clearly. Every person has a story to tell whether living or dead—and it's up to you to find out the facts and accuracy. When a life is lost, it's tragic—but when it's taken by force, it's a travesty. It is left to those who will not stop until the culprit is tracked down, caught, and forced to take responsibility.

Saturday 1515 hours

Katie stood at the site on the Dayton farm. Several large holes had been dug near the trees where Cisco had alerted. The dirt had been carefully stacked in several neat piles for sifting through. Barriers and crime scene tape cordoned off the area as police cruisers arrived.

Katie stared at all three locations with a total of seven holes dug—some holes had more fifty-five-gallon drums and others had pine coffins. It was like a nightmare seeing the hidden graveyard scattered around the back of the property. It was difficult to tear her eyes away from the pits. It seemed almost impossible, questionable, or improbable, but the proof stared her in the face.

It was clear to her that the killer had made plans, carried out his violence, and kept the bodies nearby. It made him feel in control and powerful, in the same way he was following their investigation and keeping one step ahead. For Katie had no doubts that was who had been tailing them and firing at them. She could also see that the killer cleared his way, making sure that no victims would ever be allowed to tell their story. It bothered Katie. How long was it going to be before she or McGaven were in the way?

Still spinning from what they had discovered in the farmhouse, Katie now looked into the first grave where a body had been placed in a makeshift coffin made of sheets of pine wood. Inside appeared to be a young woman wrapped in a blanket. Based on the body condition and decomposition, it was likely that she had been buried for several years. There were visible long jagged wounds on what was left of her leathery neck, consistent with having her throat cut. The exact answers would have to come from the medical examiner's office. The makeshift coffin indicated that the killer either didn't have time to use a fifty-five-gallon drum or he used leftover sheets of pine that were hanging around the farm. After he killed the victim, he didn't seem to care whether she was stuffed into a drum or enclosed in a box.

Katie felt sick to her stomach looking around. How many more bodies were there? Her fears were rising to the surface. That woman's body was definitely after the foreclosure and there were more victims yet to be uncovered. It would take some time to recover them and for forensic evidence to be discovered.

She looked at two uniformed officers walking up. "John, make sure you have officers with you when you search and collect the evidence."

He nodded as he sent Eva with the officers to secure and document the farmhouse kitchen and the underground room as well as the tunnel. More officers spread out to search the rest of the land in hopes of finding the exit where the man had disappeared.

"Someone from the coroner's office will be arriving within the hour," said John.

"Here we go again," she said.

"Meaning?"

"More bodies... and little evidence. If those bodies are years or decades old, it's going to be a problem."

"This time seems different," said John. "The makeshift coffin. The body doesn't seem to have any other injuries or torture like Abigail Andrews, apart from the cut to the throat. I haven't checked the other pine boxes yet."

"Thanks, John. Let me know." She looked at the body again before she walked away. It was going to be a huge undertaking for the recovery process. Not to mention scouring through missing persons' cases. The victims might not all be from the area, making the process even more difficult.

She saw McGaven waiting at the Jeep, coordinating things on the phone.

Katie opened the back door and let Cisco out. The dog was happy to run around and relieve himself. He was still excited from the earlier search and no doubt was ready to go again.

McGaven ended his call. "Now what?"

"We need to do some serious digging ourselves if we're going to find Dayton," she said.

"On it."

"We also need to talk to Ferris Baldwin again... and... Lara Fontaine."

He nodded. "And maybe we need to do a deep dive on the background of this property," he said.

"That's a great idea. I'll set up a meeting with the county

archivist and see what else we can find out about the farm." She glanced over at the forensic area and watched John coordinate and take photos. Abigail Andrews's cold case had just become exponentially bigger.

THIRTY-THREE

Saturday 2045 hours

Katie and Cisco finally headed home after she'd spent a couple of hours at the office. She'd tried to search for Thomas Dayton and Desiree Dayton using every database available to the Pine Valley Sheriff's Department. Tired of hitting a dead end at every turn, she decided to call it a night and begin again in the morning.

She had added to the board preliminary photos of all seven buried bodies in order at the farm—more information would be added later. Again, the reality of the murders stared back at her. It was going to take time to receive all the forensic and autopsy results.

Katie tried to keep her mind occupied with the investigation instead of letting her thoughts drift to Chad and what he was doing. He had sent her a text saying that he made it to Florida as the plane landed. There was no other information or pleasantries, just a message of news to that effect.

She drove and glanced in the back and Cisco was snoozing soundly. He had definitely had a long day and could relax and sleep. Katie wished that she could do the same, but somehow, she knew that she would toss and turn when she tried to sleep with everything running through her mind in sequence.

Katie took her favorite route home along the less traveled road. She paid close attention to the roadway and felt more comfortable and at ease. Hopefully she would begin to decompress from her day and the events of the week. She flipped on her high beams to be able to see a wider view of the road because deer were known to jet across the area.

Her cell phone reported that she had two messages from a number she knew, but she didn't want to return the call. Evan Daniels had sent her a text earlier. There was no doubt that she had felt an attraction to him, but under the circumstances she didn't want more complications in her life.

Katie's mind pushed her thoughts to the Dayton property as she drove not far from another way to enter the acreage. She wondered if there were even more bodies than they'd found. It was a large property and there could definitely be more. She shuddered at the thought.

Suddenly, bright lights blasted her Jeep from behind, blinding her in the rearview mirror. An engine gunned. Katie couldn't be sure, but the vehicle looked like a large four-wheel-drive truck, and it was inching dangerously close to her bumper.

Cisco stood up and barked rapidly.

Katie tried to increase her speed to outrun the truck, but it kept close. The road was winding, and both vehicles sped over the lines into the oncoming lane. She hoped that no one was coming from the other direction. Katie wondered if the driver was someone who didn't want her conducting the investigation.

It was another two miles before Katie would be able to exit the road and drive to a more populated location. There were no driveways or side roads coming up.

The truck blasted its horn, flashing the headlights.

Cisco continued to bark.

Katie worried about the dog's safety. "Cisco, *verstecken!*" she said, meaning to hide. The dog obediently climbed in the passenger seat and tucked down on the floor. It was the safest place for him in case there was a collision or worse. There were many times where Katie and Cisco had to tuck into places on the battlefield or in villages during their tours.

Katie held tight to the steering wheel. "Call McGaven," she said to her onboard cell phone connection.

The phone rang and after two rings, "Hello... Katie?" said a sleepy-sounding McGaven.

"I'm on my way home on Pine Valley Road. There is a large, dark-colored truck behind us. Aggressive."

"Where's your exact location?"

"About two miles before Tarrant Lane. I don't know how long I can keep them off my tail."

Katie watched the truck attempt to drive alongside her. She dared to press the accelerator harder. "Gav, I need backup. We need to identify the truck..."

The connection filled with static.

"Katie, I can't..." McGaven's voice cut off.

Cisco whined but stayed in his location.

"Gav! Can you hear me?"

There was nothing.

The truck made its move and passed the Jeep, speeding away.

Katie slowed and took a breath. Maybe she had been too quick to think it was about the case. The stress was getting to her. She had been in situations before where the killer had followed her and made threats, even at her own house, so it wasn't a stretch of the imagination.

She slowed even more, wanting to pull over, but there wasn't a place to move safely off the road. As she made a tight half-circle turn on the roadway, she saw the dark, pickup truck ahead, stopped, and a man dressed in dark clothing with a mask covering his face standing with a rifle aimed at them.

The only thing that Katie could do was swerve to avoid the truck and gunfire. But it was too late. Two bullets pierced her windshield—one barely missed her head and the other on the passenger side. She glanced down at the passenger floorboard; Cisco stayed in place.

As Katie tried to avoid the gunfire, she skidded off the road on the opposite side of the street. Miraculously she managed to keep the Jeep on its wheels and continued down the hillside, bouncing and weaving around trees. There was no trail, or even the hint of a trail, but she kept the SUV moving. She knew it was the only way that she could get some distance between them and the unknown shooter.

Low-lying branches and dead brush scraped the sides of the Jeep, making an orchestra of high-pitched noises. Other branches pounded the Jeep's roof and windshield, causing more spiderweb cracks across her view.

The path narrowed and Katie knew that her escape route was going to end—abruptly. She estimated that she had driven about one hundred feet, giving her some distance from the shooter.

The Jeep drastically slowed and the gears ground. Katie didn't have a choice but to stop. It was as good a place as any. She quickly checked her gun and extra magazine. Grabbing her flashlight from the glovebox, she prepared herself. Cisco already had his harness on, so he was equipped to go.

Katie tried to open her door, which had something obstructing it. She realized that she had stopped the Jeep in a high pile of forest debris. She managed to squeeze through the opening followed closely by Cisco. She checked her cell phone again. There was barely a bar visible—it wavered in and out of range.

As she moved through the thickets to get to more of a clearing, Katie thought there would be bullets ricocheting off the trees—but it was strangely quiet. She prepared for the hike and thought she would move north and then backtrack south to her off-road location. It was the last thing she thought she would be doing that night, but maybe she could glean something from her encounter.

Katie and Cisco moved slowly and with stealth. Even the dog knew that something was up because he stayed in position next to Katie when the terrain allowed. The waist-high and hip-deep forest-floor debris began to decline and the area became more manageable to navigate as Katie forged on.

She was hesitant to turn on the flashlight for fear of giving away her position. It was fortunate that there was some moonlight and it filtered through the trees with the clarity of light fog. It was enough to see but still allowed for cover if she needed it to be. The available illumination helped her to make her way north.

Her legs were becoming weary. She didn't realize how tired she was until she slowed down. She was now hiking through heavily wooded areas, and her physical and mental faculties were taxed. She wondered if McGaven would have any luck getting the police to the location quickly.

That's when she heard it—what she feared the most since she had abandoned the Jeep. Several bullets ricocheted off the massive tree trunks high above her head. At least that meant that the shooter wasn't sure where they were and was shooting at a higher elevation to flush them out or force her to make a move. Katie wasn't going to play his game, so she and Cisco kept moving according to her plan.

She wasn't sure how, but soon the bullets seemed to be getting closer to them. Her growing fears were fast becoming a reality. The only choice was to move deeper into the forest and wait out the shooter until McGaven and the police arrived.

Moving as a well-seasoned K9 team, Katie and Cisco went

west quickly. Katie wasn't sure if she should stop and find a hiding area or keep going until she reached an adjacent road.

There was a loud rustling in the brush.

Katie stopped with Cisco flush against her leg. Both remained motionless.

Grunting and more rustling.

Katie knew the sound. Her body stiffened as she slowly retrieved her weapon. It was the distinct movement of a wild pig. They were extremely common and could be aggressive if people disturbed their habitat, feeding, and mating areas. The last thing she wanted to do was fire her gun—but she might not have a choice.

She waited for a full two minutes until the pig seemed to move away from them. They were upwind of the wild animal, which worked in their favor. Waiting a further two minutes, Katie then moved forward.

The moon seemed to brighten, making the forest glow, and it was easy to see where she was going. There was a crashing behind her, but she knew that it wasn't a wild pig. It was caused by human steps. The shooter was coming after them.

Bullets peppered the area on either side of them. How had he found them?

Katie thought it was going to continue, but instead the steps moved back toward the road. She thought it strange. Unless the shooter knew that police had been dispatched to the location...

She needed to know the license plate of the truck and a description of the shooter. Katie hated being in the dark and the investigation was too important to not pursue something as critical.

Only contemplating for a brief moment, Katie pushed back toward the road, running when she could, climbing over tree limbs when they impeded her path. This time, she and Cisco made noise as they approached the street. They made it close to the area where she'd had to leave her Jeep and there was a steep incline up to the road.

Katie heard the familiar sound of heavy footsteps—most likely from some type of combat or police boots. The steps were distant and moved with purpose. Suddenly they slowed and stopped.

Katie was halfway up the hill. She stopped as well, wondering if the shooter had heard her approach. She clung to Cisco's harness, holding him next to her. The dog was warm; he panted lightly with little sound, and she could feel his heartbeat against her ribs. His eyes were amber and reflected in the moon-light, making him resemble a black wolf.

She held her position.

Finally, the shooter moved again, and Katie heard a car door shut, an engine rev and race away.

Katie clawed her way to the street, part on her hands and knees, and lastly, running. Her breath ragged with exhaustion. Standing on the street looking in the direction of where the shooter drove, she heard in the distance the engine rev again and waited until it faded away.

"No!" Katie was frustrated and angry that she didn't see the truck, first following her and then that she didn't get the license plate number.

Cisco barked, staying close to her side.

Sirens rapidly approached.

THIRTY-FOUR

Saturday 2245 hours

Katie and McGaven stood at the roadside looking down the hill where workers from ACE Towing were connecting cables to the Jeep and getting ready to pull it out of the ravine.

"You were lucky," said McGaven.

"Don't worry. You don't have to lecture me. I know I was lucky. I wasn't paying attention to the vehicles that could be following me." She sighed. She was tired but didn't want to complain.

"Good news. They said that there isn't any real damage to your Jeep," said McGaven still watching the towing crew.

"Besides the bullet holes through the windshield," she said.

"Replacing the windshield is an easy fix."

She let out a breath.

"How many vehicles have you totaled since I've been partnered with you?" he said with a smile.

"I'm not counting."

"Three?"

She tried not to smile. "I'm not counting."

"Okay, I'm just saying what your uncle is going to say."

"Let's hear it." Katie was surprised that the sheriff wasn't at the scene, but that was just as well. She didn't need to hear lectures from him too.

"You take too many chances. You push too hard. You need to be more careful... shall I go on?"

"No," she said. Then she changed tack. "I've been thinking."

"About?"

"Maybe we're looking at Thomas Dayton the wrong way."

"Meaning?"

"Well, we're trying to find where he went after the rental, right?"

"Yeah."

"What about working backward?"

"You mean like... checking backward from the foreclosed house?"

"Yeah. And we need to try to figure out what type of alias or moniker he is using. Is he calling himself Harland, like Ferris Baldwin said? People are creatures of habit. They generally pick something that reminds them of a favorite person, favorite character, or a combination of their first, middle, and last names."

"Did you bump your head?"

"No. What makes you say that?"

"Because that's a great idea. Let's brainstorm some of these. I bet between the two of us we can come up with his fictional name that will give up more information," he said.

"And cross-reference with what we know. I'm very concerned about his daughter, Desiree. We can't locate her." Katie didn't want to think the worst, but it could be that Dayton's daughter was dead.

"I had a message from Mrs. Andrews that she wants to see us," he said.

"I wonder what she's going to tell us." Would it be more butterflies or information that could lead them to Abigail's killer? "I really want to talk to Lara again too."

McGaven tensed.

"I think she might know more than she's saying. There's something missing in her account of the murder she witnessed when she was a child. I know she's having some mental health issues but I think she's our best lead right now." She watched her partner closely and still couldn't pinpoint what bothered him about Lara. "How well did you know Lara in school?" She spoke softly, not wanting to push.

"She was just a girl who was three years younger. I really didn't know her well. She was a loner, and she attracted some bullying from other students. I couldn't just stand back and let them pick on her."

It became clear why McGaven had a connection with the woman. Katie knew her partner was good kid and that's why he was such a good man. It made her smile.

"What?" he said, staring at Katie.

"I can see you being that good kid doing the right thing, even if some of your classmates thought otherwise."

He smiled at her.

They watched Katie's Jeep slowly rise toward the road.

There were several uniformed officers measuring the area where the truck had stopped. There was a partial tire impression. John would be arriving shortly to photograph and take the impression for potential evidence.

"You need to call it a day," said McGaven looking at Katie with concern. "Cisco is waiting in my truck. I'll take you both home."

"Is that an order?" she said, trying to add some humor to a difficult day.

"You bet it is," he said lightly.

"Why don't you come over for breakfast... well, actually, bring brunch and we can go over our next moves."

"You had me at breakfast."

"Bring Denise and Lizzie. It will be fun," she said. Denise worked in the records division and was McGaven's girlfriend. Lizzie was her daughter and loved to play with Cisco.

"I think that can be arranged," he said. "Lizzie won't turn it down with Cisco involved."

"Good."

"C'mon, let's go." He began walking toward his truck where Cisco was patiently waiting in the passenger seat.

THIRTY-FIVE

Sunday 1005 hours

Katie slept well, which surprised her considering her day yesterday was hectic and harrowing. She had pushed her energy level to almost zero, and her body and mind needed a brief reprieve.

She had invited her previous Army sergeant, Nick Haines, to come over for brunch as well. He had been honorably discharged after a bombing incident overseas that resulted in the loss of one leg. He lived a couple of towns away and they made sure to get together frequently. He had helped Katie on several cases in the past, and now he was in the process of getting a private investigator's license. Katie thought he would be able to add to the investigative process.

"I think we've made enough food for an army," said Nick, chuckling to himself. He was scrambling eggs and bacon with well-orchestrated precision.

Katie grabbed some bread, orange juice, and plates. She made coffee—they were going to need lots of coffee.

Cisco waited patiently in the area where his bowl was

located. He knew that there would be some tasty treat dropping into it soon.

There was a loud knock at the front door.

Cisco abandoned his bowl and ran to the living room barking and wagging his tail. Katie opened the door to McGaven, Denise, and Lizzie. Before Katie could say hello, Lizzie jetted inside and dropped to her knees to pet Cisco.

"Hi, come in," Katie said.

Her partner gave her a quick hug followed by Denise who carried a bowl of mixed fruit and yogurt.

"Oh, your Jeep should be ready in a couple of days," said McGaven.

Katie was relieved. "That's great news."

"Good to see you," said Denise hugging Katie. "Wow, it smells great. I'm starving."

Everyone came inside and filtered into the kitchen.

"Need any help?" said McGaven.

"I've got everything under control, thanks," said Nick. "Start grabbing some plates and fill 'em up."

"I need coffee," said McGaven. "Strong coffee and keep it flowing."

Everyone served themselves and sat outside at a table Katie had set up. It was festive and high energy. It was what Katie needed after Chad had left. She loved everyone around her; it meant so much. Every single person was important and held a special place in her heart. Even though they weren't family, in the blood relative sense, they were still a family.

They talked about other things besides the investigation. There was plenty of laughter and upbeat conversations. Cisco and Lizzie were running around the yard—the little girl squealed with glee as Cisco played ball with her.

Katie smiled more than she had in a long time. They continued to eat and have a lively conversation for more than an hour.

. . .

While her guests continued to enjoy themselves, Katie decided to use her smallest second bedroom to brainstorm the Dayton case; it was her office and study area. She had brought home several copies of the files. On one wall, there was a large whiteboard.

Katie tried to separate the fact that they couldn't find Dayton and decided to focus on the evidence from the killer: behavioral evidence, MO, and signature. She was worried that she was muddling the two into an obsessive quest to find Dayton. She had to stay objective.

Katie began her killer profile as objectively as she could.

- *Violent acts to the point of sadistic—more violence necessary to kill victims (signature)*
- *Power/control killer*
- *Organized/disorganized? Some areas show organization with burying the bodies on the property and disorganized where all injuries aren't the same/not all containment is the same. Calm/frenzy?*
- *Buries bodies in drums or makeshift pine boxes— seems to keep them in close areas. Visits them? Has his own private graveyard? Is that what drives him? Keeping trophies in jars? Staying in control? Obsessive?*
- *Prefers torture to other means of killing.*
- *Appears to pick same type of victims—young women, possibly dark hair, were they alone or need of assistance?*
- *Stays close to investigation. Why?*
- *What drives him?*
- *What shapes his fantasies?*

- *Did he live through emotional or physical abuse? Environmental?*
- *Are there more victims? Victims in other areas?*
- *Will he continue?*

Katie stepped back, looking at her list. It wasn't the best start to profiling a case she had ever done. There was so much more she wanted to write, but it was coming from her personal feelings about the case and not from an objective standpoint. Her obsession to find Dayton had clouded her objectivity and she was going to correct that. She had to take a step back. If she just knew about the bodies and other circumstances—but not that Dayton was most likely involved—how would she describe the behavioral evidence? That was what she had to ask herself. She needed to search current missing persons' cases that potentially fit the profile.

Katie began making lists and questions. It was a little bit different from what she did at her work office, but she wanted to keep things more casual and to keep the flow moving. She could hear McGaven and Nick laughing about something that was said. It made her smile that her military sergeant and her detective partner were getting along.

She heard Cisco playfully bark in the backyard and knew that Denise and Lizzie were enjoying the dog. Cisco was going to be nicely worn out and tired by evening.

Katie moved some books aside and pulled out a couple of folding chairs from the closet. She saw a dark blue photo album that had been buried underneath a pile of magazines and books.

She held her breath and took a moment.

It was a special album that Katie had put together from when she was in school. All types of things were affixed to the pages, from photos and awards to letters from colleges and pressed flowers from her prom. The memories flooded back. It seemed like a lifetime ago, but she realized that there were few memories that didn't include Chad.

"Hey, Scotty," said Nick, studying her for a moment. He had always called her that ever since the Army days. He walked into the room, immediately reading the board. "Very interesting. Never been part of a brainstorming process with the cops before."

"Well, you should be," she said, trying to shake off the lonely feeling without Chad. "At this point, we need all views and perspectives. This is an unusual situation."

"Is this legal?" he said. "For me to know about the case that isn't public knowledge."

"Of course. Police always seek information from experts on any subject that might help with an investigation."

"You better believe it," said McGaven as he entered.

"You're fine and we appreciate your input," she said.

"I'm not sure what I can do," said Denise following McGaven. "Oh, don't worry, Lizzie is reading one of her favorite books to Cisco on the porch swing."

"Oh, he'll love that." Katie laughed. "A mystery, I hope."

"I think so. And I took a quick photo of them and sent it in a text to you," she said.

"Cisco will definitely watch over her," said Katie.

McGaven took a seat in the large leather office chair while Nick and Denise sat in the two extra folding chairs.

"Thank you for taking the time to come over here on a Sunday," said Katie.

"Just feed us and we're yours," said McGaven.

"Okay, I don't have to tell you, Nick, and Denise, that whatever is talked about in this room stays between us and the official investigation."

Everyone nodded in agreement.

Katie turned and began reading down the list of what they had so far. "We have a person of interest. Actually, a serious person of interest who owned the property where there have been seven bodies found. I think I've run into him twice now; first the shooter when Gav and I first visited the abandoned farm, and finally when I was run off the road."

"Geez, Scotty," said Nick.

"You know how she is," said McGaven.

"Our main suspect is Thomas Harland Dayton," said Katie, ignoring her friends. "He's forty-five years old. His last driver's license photo we were able to find makes him look average. Brown hair, brown eyes, no facial hair, medium build. I'm betting that he's changed his appearance like having a beard, a shaved head, or different hair color. Everything regarding this name has stopped. It's like he's a ghost, but I know he's still around. I just need to prove it."

"People will pick some form of these names. I see it all the time in records. Like Harland Thomas, Harland Dayton, Tom, Harley, Day, Dey," said Denise.

"Exactly," said Katie. She loved hearing other ideas from a trusted group of professionals and friends. "Ferris Baldwin told us he was going by the name of Harland, but he might use others."

"And I like crosswords and word games. I'm sure I can come up with some alternatives."

"That's my girl," said McGaven.

"What about things the guy likes? Cars? Equipment? Bar hangouts?" said Nick. "Do you know anything about where he hung out?"

"When we talked to neighbors, they basically said he was nice, but he didn't really offer any personal information. There was nothing they could add," she said.

"I reached out to the rental agency, but those records were incomplete. There was a forwarding address that proved to be basically an empty lot east of Pine Valley," said McGaven.

On the board, Katie added variations to his names, first,

middle, and last. McGaven used his iPad and read over things they knew about Dayton, which wasn't much.

"Okay, there's a listing for farm equipment. The usual, Deere, Champion, and looks like Caterpillar." He frowned. "I don't have names of his animals or Desiree's middle name."

"What's worse is that we can't find birth certificates for either one or a marriage license for Dayton." Katie made more notes on the board.

"Any PO box?" said Nick. He was searching on his phone. "Or organizations he might have joined?"

"There was a PO box listed for the rental after the foreclosure," she said.

"It was..." McGaven looked through some notes. "Box 1761, Springfield."

"That's almost an hour from here," said Denise. "Seems odd."

"Maybe he has some history there," said Nick.

Katie was thrilled that her friends were contributing great ideas. She filled in more information and realized that they needed to search surrounding, unincorporated towns. "Gav, were there any other real estate listings for Dayton?"

"No, not under that name."

"Let's get a list of the property owners surrounding Springfield and go back before he took ownership of the foreclosed farm."

"I can do that," said Denise.

"And cross-reference any combination of names that might indicate it was Dayton," said McGaven.

"To save time, I can check out any of the properties," said Nick.

Katie looked at McGaven and raised her eyebrows, asking what her partner thought about that.

"That would be helpful," said McGaven. "We'll get a list to you with potential names. Most likely two or three."

"Sure. Let me know."

Katie was beginning to feel that they were coming up with constructive ideas to help breathe new life into the investigation to find Dayton. They had their work cut out for them, but she wanted to stay a step ahead. Her thoughts kept circling back to the potential witnesses—meaning that Mrs. Andrews, Lara Fontaine, and Ferris Baldwin were all people who had information that could pose a liability to Dayton. Her own safety as well as McGaven was also in the spotlight because of the information coming to light. She needed to be more aware of the surroundings anywhere they were going.

"Why wouldn't Dayton just leave the area?" said Nick.

"Good question," said Katie. "My suspicion, not facts at the moment, is that he has something keeping him here."

"Like his daughter?" said Denise.

"Yes, but I was also thinking that he's one of those people who are extremely narcissistic and sociopathic making him high-minded and thinking he is smarter than everyone—especially the police," she said.

"That's why he is staying close to you and watching the investigation," said McGaven.

"Arrogance? Or curiosity?" said Nick.

"I'm hoping his curiosity will turn into fear and that's when he'll make a mistake, hopefully a big one," she said.

"You better watch your back, Scotty."

"I know." Katie stared at the board and was amazed how much information there was to look into. "You guys are great—look at all this."

They conferred a while longer as Katie and McGaven gathered more places they could check out. Katie didn't want to make them work too much on a Sunday, so she gently urged everyone to relax and eat more, before it was time to leave.

When McGaven, Denise, and Lizzie left, Cisco took his

place on the couch and within a few minutes he was snoozing—
tired from playing with Lizzie.

Nick stayed behind to talk to Katie. "I was serious, Scotty,
you're taking too many chances. You have to be careful and
strategic. Got me?" he said.

"I hear you, Sarge, loud and clear," she said with a smile. He
meant well and she understood why he felt that way.

"I mean it," he said. "You be safe and keep me in the loop of
what you need me to do."

"I will." She hugged Nick. "Thank you."

After Nick left and Katie closed the door, she realized that
she was alone again. Cisco was sound asleep, and she didn't
fully appreciate how important her friends were until they had
left. Without Chad, she felt strangely lost and wasn't sure if she
would be able to find her way again.

THIRTY-SIX

Monday 0915 hours

Katie pulled up to Mrs. Andrews's house and cut the engine of the small white Ford SUV. McGaven had permission to take a car from police impound to drive for the day. The detectives thought using a different car each day would make it more difficult for anyone to follow them.

"What's up?" said McGaven looking at his partner.

"I don't know. Do you know what Mrs. Andrews has for us?" She wanted to continue their search for Dayton and start forming a criminal profile from the victims.

"She didn't say specifically, but that she had something for us that might help in the investigation."

"Okay, let's go," she said.

They exited the vehicle and walked toward the home once again. Katie noticed that there had been some minor gardening work. The yard looked clean and freshly raked. There were some new colorful flowers and plants.

They reached the door and Katie knocked.

Within a minute, Mrs. Andrews opened the door. She

didn't smile, but cordially invited them inside. "Please come in, Detectives."

This time, Abigail's mother didn't offer any coffee or ask them to sit down in the living room. Instead, she walked to the counter and picked up a stack of envelopes with a pink ribbon tied around them. They were cards and letters. She handed the stack to Katie.

"From?" said Katie.

"They belonged to Abigail and she had them hidden in her bedroom. I read them, but I didn't have the heart to throw them away. I thought they might help you in finding her killer." Her face was drawn and her mouth downturned. It was clear that the woman was devastated by the reality that Abigail had been murdered—and the surrounding circumstances were that much more horrific than she'd ever imagined.

"Thank you," said Katie. "We'll return them when we've completed the investigation."

"No need," she said. "Just throw them away."

Katie wasn't going to do that, but she politely nodded at the grieving woman. "If you remember anything else, please don't hesitate to call us."

"Of course. I have a funeral to plan..." The woman's voice faded away.

"We won't take up any more of your time, Mrs. Andrews," said McGaven.

Walking back to the car, Katie turned to her partner. "Do you think she was holding back these letters for a reason?"

"Not sure."

"And now since Abigail's body has been found and the case is officially a homicide, she came clean." Katie contemplated the situation and decided that by keeping the letters, the woman was somehow keeping Abigail alive. And now, it didn't matter anymore.

They reached the SUV.

"Let's see if we can find out anything more from Lara."

McGaven tensed again but nodded before getting into the car.

The address for Lara Fontaine on 212 Spring Street was in the older downtown area of Pine Valley, which was still quaint and showed what the area was like before all the housing developments were constructed. More pedestrians meandered along the charming sidewalks where small restaurants and specialty gift stores spilled onto the walking areas.

"I forget how cute this area is," said Katie. "I rarely come here."

"I don't think I've ever heard you use the word cute before."

"Funny guy," she said. She found a parking place near a bakery, which was below Lara's apartment. "What did Lara say when you called her?"

"Not much."

"Do you think she'll be more open with us?" she said.

"As much as she can."

"Well, now that she's home from the hospital, it might make a difference." Katie glanced at her partner and realized that he was very uncomfortable. "Do you want to sit this one out?"

"No, I'm fine."

Katie wasn't so sure but respected his choice.

They went to a door that had four apartments: A, B, C, and D. Lara's was apartment A. They quickly walked up the stairs and found the apartment easily. The incredible aroma of baking bread hit their senses.

"Wow, I don't know if I could live here with that amazing smell of bread baking all day," she said.

"It's pretty intense."

Katie knocked on the door. They waited. She knocked again with no response.

"Did you tell her when we would be here?"

"Yes, and she said that she was going to be home all day."

"Lara, it's Detectives Scott and McGaven."

Still no response.

Katie looked at McGaven with a questioning expression.

"Maybe she stepped out for a moment," he said looking through his phone for her number. He called it. They immediately heard ringing inside the apartment.

Katie knocked again. She then tried the doorknob and discovered it was unlocked. Pushing the door open a bit, she said, "Lara, are you home?"

Again, there was no response.

Katie opened the door wider and stepped inside followed closely by McGaven.

"Lara?" said McGaven.

Katie looked around and noticed that things seemed to be out of place. Not just messy, but as if someone had been looking for something. She walked around the small living room, which had two comfortable-looking overstuffed chairs with pink pillows and a throw blanket. There were small tables cluttered with knick-knacks and framed photos everywhere in all types of frames—wooden, silver, gold, and even seashells glued together.

"Where do you think she is?" said Katie.

"Don't know," he said flatly. "I'll go back downstairs and see if she went inside one of the stores."

Katie looked around the room and saw that in the kitchen there was a mug of tea sitting on the counter. She touched it and it was still warm, not hot, but definitely not room temperature. There were small white bags, which had the remnants of bread and pastries inside them. There were two medication bottles: Zoloft for anxiety and some type of pain medication she couldn't pronounce.

Katie continued to walk around. There was something odd about the apartment—something that she had seen before at crime scenes. It wasn't just messy, with maybe dirty dishes and books and DVDs not put away. Things were tossed around, and pillows were lying on the floor but it appeared that it had been made to look this way, as if someone had searched it recklessly, but there wasn't an organic quality to it.

She continued to wait until McGaven returned. That's when she heard a faint sound of water.

Katie walked toward an open door that was the bedroom. Everything was tidy, the bed made, and laundry neatly folded. There was another door that was closed. She assumed it was the bathroom.

As she walked toward the door, she stepped in something. Realizing it was water, Katie immediately opened the door, entered, and that was where she found a flooded bathroom and Lara's body submerged in the bathtub.

Katie ran to Lara and dropped to her knees. Gently pulling Lara to the surface, she checked for a pulse. It was faint and she was barely breathing. There were two cutting marks on her inner arms, but they were superficial, and the bleeding had stopped. Katie carefully pulled the young woman out of the tub, laying her on the floor. She then covered her with a robe.

Katie retrieved her phone and called police dispatch. "This is Detective Katie Scott, badge number 3692. I'm at 212 Spring Street, apartment A. It appears to be a suicide attempt. Female. Late twenties. She has a pulse, but it's faint. Need an ambulance."

"Ten-four, Detective," said dispatch.

"What happened?" said McGaven as he stood at the doorway, his expression grim.

"Looks like a suicide attempt."

Lara began to mumble.

"Lara, can you hear me?" said Katie.

"I... I..." was the only thing the woman could say.

"Lara, just stay still. Okay? Help is on the way."

Katie looked up at McGaven. He still stood in the doorway. It was unclear if he was stunned, upset, or frustrated, which seemed strange to her. He was always caring and prepared.

Lara tried to sit up.

"No, stay down and don't move," said Katie. She examined the cut marks, and they didn't seem to be deep. There were other faint lines next to the fresh ones—Lara had tried this before. "Lara, it's okay. You don't have to be alone. There are people to help you. We're here with you until they arrive."

Katie stayed at Lara's side until voices and footsteps were heard coming up the staircase.

Lara grabbed Katie's hand. "Please... help me..."

The EMTs rushed inside to take over. Immediately checking vitals and giving her oxygen, they stabilized her.

Katie moved out of the way and joined her partner. "She should be fine."

McGaven remained quiet, watching the scene in the bathroom.

They brought in the gurney and carefully put Lara onto it, strapping her tightly. As they wheeled her through the living room and out the front door, her pale skin and delicate features made her seem so fragile.

Katie wondered how she had survived all these years after seeing a murder and what she was going to be able to mentally give the investigation so that they would be able to find Dayton.

McGaven checked the apartment and then went to the front door. "Let's lock it up."

"Okay," she said. "You okay?"

"Fine."

Katie stared at him with concern.

"I just don't think she's going to be able to help us. She's unstable—at least at this point."

"She might remember something that would be helpful," she said.

"Maybe. The hospital will update us."

Katie still felt that there was something that McGaven wasn't telling her, but she'd let him work it out and didn't push. She knew that he would talk to her when it was time.

They walked back down the stairs toward the car.

A text came in on Katie's cell from Dr. Dean.

3 victims IDed—come to ME office.

She turned to McGaven. "I just received a text from the medical examiner's office saying three victims have been identified, but not saying who they are and to come to the office."

"Let's go."

THIRTY-SEVEN

Monday 1145 hours

The drive to the medical examiner's office was quiet. Katie and McGaven both were lost in their thoughts about the case and how it was going. There were so many details and possibilities to contemplate but the biggest question was to figure out which direction to take.

Katie replayed what she'd seen in Lara's apartment and her condition in the bathroom. Was she unstable? Perhaps the demons had caught up with her, making her unable to focus and to come to terms with what had happened all those years ago. Had her condition made her ransack her apartment in a paranoid frenzy?

"Do you think Dr. Dean has some answers?" said McGaven.

Katie pulled the car into the parking lot. "Hope so. We need more solid clues to lead us to the killer, instead of more clues to add to the pile we already have."

"At times it feels like a merry-go-round."

"That's a good way of describing it," she said. Katie wasn't sure if he meant the investigation or having Lara pop back into his life. Possibly both.

They went inside the building. The temperature was especially cold—the air conditioner must have been set cooler than usual. She wondered if it was because there were more bodies than usual.

It amazed Katie that however many times they had gone to the morgue, it never got any easier. Three of the five senses were instantly triggered—smell, sound, and sight. The distinct cleaning solutions that at times overpowered the sense of smell, the sound of gurneys being wheeled into the exam room, and watching internal organs being extracted and weighed was always a stressful visit keeping the visitor in the moment.

The activity at the morgue seemed to be lighter than usual. There were only two technicians working and they didn't see Dr. Jeffrey Dean. It had always been the medical examiner's unusually chipper personality greeting the detectives. Katie and McGaven stopped and waited in the hallway, feeling a bit conspicuous.

"Does it seem a little bit vacant?" said Katie looking around.

"I was thinking the same thing," he said. "It's Monday and you would think it would be busy after the weekend. I read somewhere that more deaths, whether natural or not, happen on the weekends."

A young female technician with black hair, wearing a smock with a few blood spatters across the front, appeared from one of the smaller examination rooms.

"Excuse me," said Katie. "Is Dr. Dean here?"

"He's in his office I think." The technician barely slowed and continued on.

As the detectives neared his office, Dr. Dean appeared, in his usual festive attire, his personal signature of light khakis and a blue and yellow flower print Hawaiian shirt. Instead of his usual casual sandals, he wore sneakers without socks.

"Detectives," he said. "This way. Thanks for coming so quickly. And sorry for the cryptic text." He led them to the large exam area, which sometimes doubled as a training and observation room. There was another room leading off the main area.

Once inside the exam room, Katie saw the first three covered gurneys and four more in the side room. She knew that Abigail was one of them, but the others were unknown. She instantly felt colder thinking about the victims.

The medical examiner walked to the first gurney and stopped. He seemed to be hesitating, which was also odd. He flipped over a file and began his report. "Abigail Lynn Andrews, age twenty-one, death was hemorrhage from a deep laceration to the throat." He hesitated again. "It's inconclusive due to the decomposition, but there appeared to be many defensive wounds on her hands and arms, as well as more lacerations and punctures to her torso, neck, legs, and back. And of course, it's ruled a homicide."

"Dr. Dean, was there anything unusual about the body or worth noting?" said Katie. She had noticed that he seemed a bit vague, and she wanted to press him for an answer.

The medical examiner smiled faintly. "There were traces of a sedative in her organs."

"What kind?" she said.

"Diazepam."

"Isn't that like Valium?"

"Yes, it is from the benzodiazepine family, which is essentially valium. It can be a strong sedative depending on the dosages."

"Would it be fairly easy to get?" said McGaven.

"Definitely. It could be from a prescription or access to somebody's bottle of medication."

"You said there were punctures and cutting injuries. Is there any indication of what type of instruments would be consistent with these injuries?" she said.

"It's difficult to be precise," he began. "But the punctures were done with something thin and long."

"Could it be something from a farm, like various tools for caring for animals and building things?"

"It's possible. Definitely not to be ruled out. If you have something we can compare it to it would be helpful."

Katie thought about the farm.

"Now," said Dr. Dean. He carefully pulled back a portion of the sheet on Abigail's body.

Katie gasped. She couldn't help it. The condition of the body was horrifying. At the scene, she had seen only the top portion, which was just the head and shoulders. Now looking at the whole, broken, decomposed body was truly gruesome. She understood why the doctor was hesitant to show it to them.

Katie glanced at McGaven who was a bit pale, but he kept his usual stoic and professional demeanor. From his first visit to the morgue, he had a difficult time with viewing the bodies, especially children and women.

"It was difficult to separate which injuries were peri-mortem, at the time of death, and which injuries were post-mortem, after death," said the medical examiner.

Katie stared at the contorted body of the once beautiful young woman. The body that lay on the steel gurney was twisted and distorted. The arms and legs were broken at the joints, making them bend in the opposite direction in order to fit in the drum. The head and torso were the only parts that seemed to be in the correct positions.

"It's clear by these breaks," said the medical examiner indicating where the wrists, elbows, and knees were obliterated, "that the killer put the body in the drum by breaking any bones required for it to fit. Strength was definitely needed, and some type of hammer was also most likely used. You can see damage to the bones. There was no indication that the killer used any special tools, such as some type of cutting device. It was whatever got the job done."

Katie swallowed hard, still feeling a lump in her throat. This was one of the worst victims she had witnessed at the morgue. It was difficult to keep her eyes on Abigail.

"Was there any DNA on the victim or her clothing?" said McGaven. His voice was low and husky. It was clear that he was shocked by what he was seeing.

"No, there was nothing that was testable—everything seemed to be too degraded. She had been in the drum and buried for too long."

Katie sighed, gathering her thoughts.

"We did test her dog, specifically the collar, to find any biological evidence, but we didn't find anything." Dr. Dean covered the body and moved to the second gurney. "There is good news, though, we have identified the young woman's body in one of the pine coffins."

The medical examiner opened a file report. "This is seventeen- to eighteen-year-old Desiree Gayle Dayton. At least, that was what we were able to determine as her age. The estimation of how long she had been buried is six or seven years, approximately."

"What?" said Katie, barely believing what she had just heard the medical examiner say. "How do you know her identity so quickly? Did someone identify her?" The interview with Lana came rushing back. They needed to try to interview her again when she was lucid and able to talk about the incident.

"No, we were able to find her fingerprints in the system," said the medical examiner.

"For what?"

"According to the records, she had a background check for working at a stable in Springfield. There were some fingers still intact, and we managed to obtain prints by hydrating them. But we weren't able to find any family who could identify her body."

"What's the name of the stables?" she said.

"Uh, let's see," he said reading the report. "Capital Stables."

Katie looked at McGaven as he made a note. She was hopeful they were finally getting more information about the Daytons.

"I can see that this is a surprise to you," said Dr. Dean.

"Very much," Katie managed to say.

"Due to the body's condition," he said, "there was little to identify or look for in regard to forensic evidence. She was almost mummified by the conditions." He pulled back the sheet.

Katie didn't expect the body to be so dried and shriveled. The young victim's hands, arms, and legs had a distinct coiling of their shape, making her appear to have been caught in a fire. There was still some hair attached, along with dried skin on her face and patches on her arms. The rib cage protruded, and her jawline appeared to be dislocated.

"What was her cause of death?" said McGaven.

"I never want to give an 'undetermined' as the manner of death, but it's difficult to know for sure. There are broken bones, but not the usual, like the neck, to indicate homicide. There is no indication of any knife or bullet wounds on the bones and it's unclear, at this point, how she died."

Katie was once again surprised by these bodies and the outcome. She had never heard Dr. Dean say he ruled a death undetermined. It didn't necessarily mean that it was the official finding and couldn't be changed if other evidence came to light, but it was the verdict for now.

"Anything with toxicology?" she asked.

"Nothing at this point, but we're running more tests." He closed the files. "You'll be getting the reports and I'll update you when I know more."

Katie looked at the third covered body.

"Out of the seven bodies, we were able to identify three so far," said Dr. Dean. He moved to the gurney and uncovered the body.

The remains were similar to Abigail's. "Was this body in a drum?" she said.

"Indeed. The only way we could identify her was with her dental work. She had immaculate and extensive work done. It's something that a model or actor would have—or someone in the spotlight. Her name is Tina Evers, approximately twenty-nine years old, death by strangulation, and I've ruled it a homicide."

"Strangulation?"

"Her neck was broken in two places, namely her hyoid bone."

"Could it have been postmortem from being put into a drum?" said Katie.

"It's not consistent with the breakages of bones similar to Abigail Andrews. In my opinion, she was strangled before being put into the drum."

Katie was processing everything and her mind lunged warp speed ahead to missing persons' files that they needed to sift through.

"You'll find in the report that Ms. Evers was reported missing seven years ago."

Katie glanced at the other gurneys in the next room.

"You will have plenty of information to read through. We're still trying to identify the others, but their clothes and personal articles were sent to John in forensics. I'm sure he'll have more for you."

"Thank you, Dr. Dean," she said.

"Anytime. Call me if you have any more questions after you receive the reports."

Katie and McGaven left the medical examiner's office.

They were quiet, which wasn't unusual. They were lost in their own thoughts about everything they had learned and seen.

Once Katie was behind the wheel, she said to McGaven, "You're quiet."

"So are you."

"I don't know where to begin."

"That's a first."

"Seriously, we need to find Dayton ASAP."

"We have some more clues now."

"I want to scour missing persons with the information that John will have on the other victims. We might be able to connect something to Dayton."

"On it."

Katie glanced at her watch. "I have a meeting with Shane Kendall, the archivist, at the county courthouse in about an hour."

"I'll go see Lara at the hospital," he said.

"That would probably be best. She seems more comfortable with you."

"I'll do what I can." His tone wasn't reassuring.

"I'll meet you back at the office?" she said.

"You bet."

THIRTY-EIGHT

Monday 1415 hours

Katie jogged up the stairs outside the Sequoia County Courthouse, entering through the heavy wooden historical doors. The marble floors were impeccable as she hurried to the main lobby area.

She walked up to the clerk and said, "I'm Detective Scott here to see Shane Kendall."

"Of course, Detective," she said. "Follow me."

Katie followed the clerk toward the back of the building where there was a plain door. She remembered it well from her previous visits.

"Thank you," said Katie.

The clerk smiled and went back to her front desk.

Katie opened the door and entered. It was like being in the bowels of a historic building. The staircase and landing were metal as well as the handrail. As she moved forward, the steps moved slightly. It was a bit disconcerting, but she had walked them before. The basement space had been slightly updated for technology and storage. Unlike the stairs, the basement had modern lights, cabinets, two computers, and large worktables.

Katie immediately saw Shane Kendall. His shaggy brown hair and gold-rimmed glasses made him stand out. He was bent over several large blueprints, studying them under a bright light.

"Hi, Shane," said Katie.

The young man immediately stood up, first surprised, and then embarrassed. "Hi, Detective."

"I'm sorry, but we did have an appointment, right?"

"Yes, yes. I lost track of time. I just received these amazing old property blueprints from the Swanson family estate, but... I'm sorry, I'm rambling," he said, quickly moving to the next table where there were two sets of rolled-up blueprints. "I have the plans you requested. And I also ran a list of the previous owners. I know you didn't specifically request it, but I thought it might help in your investigation." He stood awkwardly.

Katie approached the table eyeing the list. "Wow, thank you. This will definitely be helpful."

"Okay," he said as he unrolled the blueprints. He switched on the table light, which illuminated the plans from beneath. "It shows the twenty-five acres and two structures."

"Would it show the barns?" she said.

"Not on these plans. A lot of times barns and other structures that aren't a residence aren't notated—unless there were architecture drawings that included all of them."

Katie familiarized herself with the property. She noticed the two houses and how they were situated. "Is there anything that shows the drainage?" she said. "That would be around here." She pointed to the area that exited east of the property.

"Let's see," he said, sorting through several sheets. "Here."

They both examined it.

"When was this put in?"

"It looks like somewhere in the 1970s."

"And was there any permit for a basement?"

He looked through a file folder. "No, but there's this."

Katie looked at the piece of paper. It was a request to add on an existing room. "What does this mean? No entry."

"I'm not entirely sure. It looks like someone notated that there wasn't access from the residence."

"That makes sense," she said.

"Did you see it?"

"Yeah, there's a crudely cut entrance on the floor in the kitchen. And the basement seems to have been reinforced."

"Interesting. Not legal though."

"When was the last time any type of inspection was done on that property?"

Shane went to one of the computers and typed in some information that Katie didn't see and pulled up material. He scanned the list. "Okay, seems like there was a building inspection on the barn about twenty years ago."

"Who was the owner?"

"It's listed as Thomas Dayton."

Katie wasn't surprised, but she wanted to know when and how the basement was fabricated.

"Something wrong?" he said.

"Well, how would I know when the basement had been reinforced? It's a large room about twelve-foot square and there's an exit to the drainage on the property. It was quite common on the older farms in case of flash floods."

"It's not easy to tell how old something like that is. A contractor who is experienced in building and reinforcing basements would know—it's kinda specialized."

"Why is that?"

"You have to know about grading, proper footings, soil inspection, underground piping, drainage, and structure reinforcement for historical farmhouses. It requires more than just adding another room to your house."

"I see."

"There's been nothing referring to what you've described."

Katie sighed.

"I'm taking it's not what you wanted to hear."

"I'm not sure what I was expecting, but thought I'd know when I saw it." She laughed. "I know that sounds crazy."

Shane went to the tall filing cabinet that housed blueprints lying flat. He rummaged through until he found what he was looking for. "I want to show you something. It's not the property you're asking about but check this out." He placed the old blueprints on the table. The edges were worn, and the printing was lighter and darker in different areas. It was clearly more than fifty years old. "This property is about the same age with a couple of structures. Look at this." He showed her lines that were drawn between the three houses.

"What is that?"

"Tunnels."

"Tunnels?" she said.

"They connect the houses. It was used during emergencies or for easy moving from one place to another without going outside—it was more popular in areas with severe winters and summers. Most places around here don't use this type of configuration anymore. It's old-fashioned and our weather conditions don't really call for it."

Katie was already thinking about possible tunnels from the houses and the barn area. That would make it easy for Dayton to move around and even hide victims. To her knowledge the GPR from forensics wasn't run in those areas.

"Detective?" said Shane. "What are you thinking?"

"I think you might have really helped in the investigation."

He smiled broadly.

"Can you send us the information?"

"Of course. I've already had them sent over."

"Thank you, Shane. You have once again proven how invaluable your skills are for our cold-case investigations."

Katie left the courthouse, excited by what she'd learned from Shane. She wanted to update McGaven. They needed to inspect the property again—this time with some new information behind them.

THIRTY-NINE

Monday 1600 hours

McGaven waited until the nurse called him to visit Lara. He had many conflicting feelings about seeing her again—he tried to push them aside while they investigated. He had watched over Lara in school. She was so frail, sweet, and innocent. And for some reason it had made her a target for some of the school's bullies. There was no way that McGaven wasn't going to step in and protect her. It was when he began to realize that he wanted to be a police officer to help and protect people. In a gut feeling, there was something that still seemed amiss about Lara's story.

McGaven wondered if Katie was finding anything useful at the county courthouse. He smiled slightly to himself because he knew that his partner was resourceful and wouldn't stop until the case was solved.

"Detective McGaven?" said the nurse.

He stood up.

"You can see her now."

McGaven followed the nurse and entered room 3104. The nurse smiled and left the room.

Lara was sitting up in the hospital bed looking as frail as he had remembered—maybe even more so. Her arms were bandaged, and she rested her hands on her lap. Her vitals were flashing on the digital monitor with her blood pressure and pulse, which seemed normal.

"Hi, Lara," said McGaven as he pulled a chair up near the bed.

"Hi, Sean." Her voice was stronger than before, and she kept his gaze. She seemed different somehow.

"Do you feel up to answering more questions?"

"Okay."

"These questions will be tough."

"It's okay, you're here with me." Her voice seemed lower and calmer. It must've been the medication she was taking.

"This hasn't been released in the news, but I feel you need to know."

"Of course. I won't tell anyone." Her eyes seemed to light up.

"We found another body at the Dayton farm."

She frowned, her eyebrows crinkling.

"She has been identified as Desiree Dayton." McGaven watched her expression and wasn't sure if she understood him. "Lara? Did you hear what I said?"

"She was my best friend. I never knew what happened to her after high school."

"The medical examiner estimated she was about seventeen or eighteen when she died."

"I guess I now know the answer."

"Lara," said McGaven. "Can you tell me anything that was going on at the time? Was Desiree having any problems at home?"

She shrugged. "Not that I know of."

"You said you were best friends."

She nodded. There were tears welling up in her eyes.

"What else happened that night?" McGaven tried to probe about the murder but wasn't sure if she was going to be able to answer.

Lara sighed and pushed back against the pillows. Her mouth tightened. "I don't know what else to tell you."

"We're up to three murders and counting, Lara. Do you understand how important this is?"

"I know..." Her voice faded and she seemed to go somewhere else in her mind.

"Can you tell me anything about Desi's farm and her family?"

"Like what?"

McGaven took a breath to slow down. He wanted to fire so many questions at her. "Did Desiree ever confide in you about anything?"

"She liked this boy at school."

"Anything about her dad?"

She thought about this. "No. I don't remember."

"What about her mom?" he said.

"Her mom was gone. I never knew her. And she never talked about her. It was just her and her dad."

The thought that Desiree's mom had never been present sent up a red flag. "Were there workers at the farm?"

"I think so."

"Do you remember anyone in particular?"

"Um, there was a guy who Desi's dad talked to a lot."

"What did he look like?"

She shrugged. "He was average, I guess. Brown hair. He was good with horses."

McGaven thought about finding Ferris Baldwin at the stables. "You said horses."

She nodded.

"Do you know Capital Stables?"

Her bright eyes darkened and her smile left her face. "Yes. They weren't nice."

"What do you mean?"

"Desi loved going there. She worked cleaning stables so that she could ride and exercise the horses."

"Did you ever go with her?"

"Once or twice. I'm not comfortable with horses."

"What do you mean *they* weren't nice?"

"They worked Desi hard and didn't always let her ride for all the work she did."

"Can you tell me again about the night you witnessed the murder?"

"I told you everything I could remember."

"Please, Lara. You could remember something else that might help us in the investigation."

"Okay, I'll try."

"Had you ever seen that woman before?"

"No." She shook her head adamantly.

"Did you ever see a dog?"

"A dog?"

"A golden Labrador?"

"No. Desi had a dog, but it was a smaller dog. A terrier, I think."

"Did the woman you saw ever say anything to you?"

"Um, no. But she was scared. I could tell. So was I."

"You had said it was in the barn, right?"

"Uh-huh."

"Why were you in the barn?"

Lara turned her head and tears flowed. "A noise woke me. I thought I heard something in the house. I got up and was dragged outside and to the barn. And that's... that's..." Her pulse rate skyrocketed, causing the alarm to beep louder.

"Lara, it's okay," said McGaven. He didn't like pushing her to remember such a horrible event in her life.

She began weeping and then wailing.

"Lara."

"I can't... don't make me... I just can't..."

The nurse arrived and began checking the vitals and then she adjusted Lara's IV. "It's okay. I'm giving you something to relax." The nurse turned to McGaven. "It's best that she rests."

"Would it be okay if I came back?" he said.

"Later. She needs her rest now."

"Thank you," said McGaven as he rose to leave.

Walking out the door and heading out of the hospital, McGaven ran through some of the new information in his mind. He wanted to share it with Katie. He knew that she most likely had some news for him as well.

FORTY

Katie sat in the office back at the Pine Valley Sheriff's Department going over the blueprints and permits for the Dayton property. She sifted through the lists all the way back to the 1960s. Nothing seemed to be jumping out at her.

Katie then took the time to read through the letters that Mrs. Andrews had given them. No matter how hard she tried to tie things into the investigation, the letters and cards were only short sentiments that Abigail had sent Tony Drake. There were no hidden agendas or ciphers she could uncover. It was just two kids sending thoughts and feelings to each other when Drake had been in jail for eighteen months for possession.

The door opened and McGaven entered. "Hey," he said.

"Hi. How'd it go?" She didn't expect a great deal, but she knew it had been better with McGaven going alone. Lara seemed still connected to him and trusted him.

He sat down. "Didn't get a lot but did get a bit more detail. When I pressed her about the murder she stressed out."

"That's understandable, witnessing something like that."

"But," he said, smiling, "I did find out that Capital Stables seemed to work Desiree hard and often reneged on the deal of her riding and exercising horses in return for cleaning the stables."

"It's been a while since Desiree was there, but let's pay them a visit tomorrow anyway."

"Absolutely."

Katie looked at her partner. "You seem like you have something else to share."

"You read me so well."

She halfway smiled. "Need I remind you of everything we've been through?"

"Nope. So, when I asked Lara about a Mrs. Dayton, she said that she never knew or saw her. Apparently Desiree's mom was just gone... if you know what I mean."

Katie thought about it. "Are you saying that no one has seen her? Like..."

"Like maybe she might've been another victim."

"It's something we need to factor in." She shuffled papers. "I don't recall seeing anything with Mrs. Dayton's name on it. No marriage license, driver's license, or deed for the property."

"I know. That does seem strange. Maybe she had another name. Maybe they weren't married," he said.

"It's possible, but we don't have anyone to ask."

"Lara said that a man who was good with horses was a friend of Dayton's. It made me think of Ferris Baldwin. Maybe he might know."

"He's on the list for tomorrow too."

"Busy day tomorrow."

"We're going to find Dayton."

McGaven smiled. "What makes you say that?"

"Because we are. If he's alive or dead, we're going to find him. We are going to get justice for the murders of Abigail and

Desiree and the others." She wished she knew more about the victims.

"Detective, I think those are fighting words."

"Ha!" She pulled up the copy of the property blueprints that showed tunnels between the buildings, and then those of the Dayton property. "Okay, these plans are from another property that has nothing to do with the Dayton property but is about the same age. Shane told me that some of these properties, a number of years back, had tunnels connecting the residences. Like for the weather or emergency situations."

"So, you're saying that there might be tunnels connecting the houses on the Dayton property?"

"It's very possible."

"But there's nothing on the old plans or deed records or tax records."

"No."

"But I guess that doesn't mean anything. Especially with everything that has gone on with that property."

"From what Shane told me and what I've seen on plans around the rural areas, tunnels and basements seem to be common."

McGaven studied the plans. "We need to check out the farm again."

"I'm not sure where to look. If there are tunnels, they could have been filled in or aren't accessible anymore."

Her partner leaned forward. "We'll find them if they're there."

"One more thing," she said.

"What's that?"

"I checked through our cold cases for any missing young women from ten to fifteen years ago who might meet the criteria of Dayton's victims but didn't find anything." She leaned back with some frustration.

"Wait a sec," said McGaven. He picked up the department

phone and punched in an extension. He waited. "Hey, it's McGaven. Are you here for a bit? Okay. We'll be right there." He hung up the phone.

"Who was that?"

"Detective Delgado. He's been working missing persons for the past year."

"Okay. Can we talk to him now?"

"Yep."

Katie and McGaven walked up the stairs to the detective division. She knew who Detective Delgado was, but she hadn't had any working relationship with him. He was very well liked around the department—but he was also known for being tough and opinionated. Ever since Katie had first worked with the department, there were some people who gave her the cold shoulder because she was the niece of the sheriff. But most had warmed up to her and respected the work that she and McGaven were able to accomplish.

The detectives walked through the main area and headed to Delgado's office. Most of the staff had already left for the day or were on assignment. To Katie's relief, it was practically deserted.

Detective Delgado's door was ajar. McGaven knocked twice and entered.

"Hey," said McGaven. "Thanks for taking the time today to see us."

"No problem," said the detective. "I have some reports to finish."

Delgado was an intense-looking man in his early forties with thick, jet-black hair, dark eyes, and he appeared to work out in the gym frequently. He had been a transfer from a Southern California department three years ago. He was dressed casually in a black polo shirt and light khaki pants. His usual turned-down expression lifted when he saw Katie enter behind her partner.

"Detective Scott," said Delgado. "Good to see you in person, instead of just sending you files for your cold cases."

"Detective," she said in greeting as she noticed files and paperwork neatly stacked.

"What can I do you for?"

"You know we're working the Andrews cold case? It's come to our attention that the killer had more bodies on the site," said McGaven.

"I heard that."

"We wanted to check with you about any missing person's case or cases that could be connected to our victims," she said.

Delgado quickly keyed up cases. "Time frame?"

"From the past year to see if he's still targeting victims," she said.

Delgado pulled up several files. "You looking for a certain type?"

Katie moved closer to the desk. "Young women, twenties, living alone, possibly brunette..."

"Okay. Are we talking Caucasian?"

"Yes."

"There are three who might fit the profile. I'll print out the reports and photos."

"Thanks. That would be great," said McGaven.

Delgado sent the files to the printer. The machine hummed and spit out several pages. He picked them up, shuffling through them. "All of these reports were within the last year. One was only a month ago." He showed the detectives the photograph of an attractive woman. "Here, her name is Theresa Simms, twenty-five-year-old, works nights at a twenty-four-hour diner. She was reported missing by her boss when she didn't show up. We went to her apartment, went by her work, and spoke with co-workers. No one has seen her. Her car was found at the local mall. Nothing to indicate anything violent. Also," he frowned, "there wasn't video footage."

"I see," said Katie. She realized that the woman was similar in appearance to Abigail. "Thank you, Detective. This is helpful."

"No problem. Let me know if you need anything else," he said. "And... you two be careful out there." He smiled, nodded his goodbye, and then went back to work.

Katie and McGaven left Detective Delgado's office and hurried back to their office to study the three missing women's reports.

Katie's growing concern for at least one of these women made her uneasy. She thought that Dayton might have her in his clutches right at that moment—and that's what she feared the most. Was Theresa Simms under Dayton's control?

FORTY-ONE

Katie had heard from her uncle that he had gone over to feed and let Cisco out. She was so grateful that she had him help with the dog when she had long days during the investigations where she couldn't bring Cisco.

Her mind wandered back to everything that she and McGaven had learned today. What shot to the top of her mind were the missing women who Detective Delgado had given them. Were they already victims? She contemplated back and forth the odds of the women falling prey to their killer. She was exhausted and looked forward to going to bed early—at least early for her.

As soon as Katie took the last turn on her road and was about one hundred feet away from her driveway, she saw a dark, four-door sedan with tinted windows parked on the street next to her driveway, the engine idling. It seemed odd because she knew what people in the neighborhood drove and when visitors would come over, no one parked in front of her place.

Katie's senses were heightened, partly due to the homicides, and also the fact she seemed to be being shadowed by an unknown individual driving a truck that had run her off the road. She slowed her rental Jeep, glancing in the rearview mirror, making sure she wasn't being followed. There were no head-lights or signs of any other car coming up or down the street.

She considered what to do—if she should confront the driver or wait to see if they would do anything. Opting for the latter, she pulled to the side of the road just before her driveway and waited.

The dark sedan stayed idling. The cool night air caused the tail pipe's exhaust to plume in small clouds. The windows were too dark to see the outline of who was in the car. Katie continued to watch the car, but it never moved.

Her cell phone rang, and it was Nick calling.

She answered. "Hi, Nick."

"Hey, Scotty. What's going on? I can hear there's something wrong in your voice. Not the truck guy again?"

"No. But..."

"But what? Where are you?"

"I'm actually on my street just before my driveway watching a dark sedan idling. I know it's no big deal, but..."

"I'm five minutes away," he said.

"Five minutes?"

"Yeah, I met with a potential client tonight in your area. Stay right where you are, and I'll be there in minutes." He disconnected the call.

Katie hoped she wasn't being paranoid. Gentle taps hit her car. It began to rain lightly, the drops pattering against her roof, windshield, and hood. She was simply being vigilant—all due to the job, but she could feel something was off and not just an innocent coincidence. As she thought about the killer who they couldn't catch up with, she was certain that if she stayed observant and steadily moved forward the killer would eventually make a mistake.

Katie continued to sit in the car. She wondered if Cisco was at the front door, aware of the unknown vehicle. Her uncle had left her house a little over an hour ago, according to his text. If the car had been there then, her uncle would have investigated it.

Katie was exhausted, her mind already filled with the many details of their case, but now watching the car idle made her even more fatigued.

Headlights lit up her car. A truck pulled up behind her and cut the engine. Katie knew it was Nick. He had made great time.

Her cell phone rang.

"Did you break the speed limit?" she said.

"I'm not answering on the grounds I may incriminate myself."

She smiled.

"What do you want to do?" he said.

"Well, now that I have backup I'm going to ask if they're lost."

"That's not a good idea, Scotty."

"I'm a cop, remember?" she said, still watching the vehicle.

"Is there a license plate?"

"No."

"Gee, that's not suspicious."

"I'm going to ask them if they need help. I have a responsibility to help and protect Pine Valley citizens and that includes my own neighborhood."

She could hear Nick sigh. "I got your six."

Katie slowly opened her car door and slipped out. She eased her Glock from the holster, keeping it down at her side. She heard the door latch open from Nick's truck and knew he was going to keep her in his sights.

Katie walked toward the vehicle. As she got closer, she saw two scrapes across the bumper, which meant that the plate had been removed quickly or forcefully. She could smell the pungent odor of gasoline, telling her the vehicle seemed to be out of timing and was in need of a tune-up.

Katie kept walking a steady pace toward the driver's door. She tapped on the window hoping that the driver would lower it, but they didn't.

"Excuse me," she said. "Are you lost? Do you need help?" She didn't know what else to say but wanted to sound legitimate and helpful. Glancing behind her she saw Nick staying back. She knew he carried a weapon.

She waited another minute but nothing happened.

"Hello?" she said. "Can you lower the window?"

Nothing.

Her instinct told her to try the door. Placing her hand on the door handle, she pulled. To her surprise it was unlocked. Usually a car's locking mechanisms engaged automatically when the key was initiated. The unlocked door meant it had been opened after the car was placed in drive.

Katie slowly pulled the door open.

Inside, there was a man slumped toward the passenger's side. He was dressed in jeans and a black hoodie. His dark brown hair was matted in blood and there was a gunshot wound to his temple.

Katie instinctively backed up, realizing she had touched the door handle of a potential crime scene. She quickly looked in the car, the seats, the floor, the back seat, but there was no weapon. She knew it wasn't self-inflicted by the position of the body. It appeared that the man had been trying to avoid the shot —to no avail.

The victim must've known the shooter.

"Scotty?" said Nick as he cautiously approached.

Katie shook her head. "The driver is dead. I'm calling it in."

She immediately called dispatch requesting police, ambulance, and forensics.

Katie and Nick watched as the police searched the area. She had already given her account of what had happened. The medical examiner's office was taking the body after Detective Hamilton gave consent to release it.

"Are you sure you don't recognize him?" said Detective Hamilton.

"No, never seen him or the car before," she said.

The detective stared at her for a moment before going and talking with patrol officers.

A big white SUV arrived, and Sheriff Scott stepped out and walked up to Katie.

"You didn't have to come out," she said.

"When there's a shooting in front of any of my officers' houses, I'm going to be there," he said. "I'm going to have patrol scheduled around the clock here."

"Wait," she said. "I don't need it. I have a new security system and Cisco. And do I need to keep reminding everyone that I'm a trained police officer and Army veteran? I can take care of myself."

The coroner technician wheeled the body toward the van.

Katie approached. "Wait." She unzipped the body bag and looked at the man. He wasn't familiar, but Katie wanted to remember his face. She wished she knew if it was the same person who had run her off the road. "Who are you?" she whispered.

"We'll find out," said Hamilton. He seemed to let down his stern exterior with Katie. "Believe me, we'll find out."

She nodded at the detective then walked back to the sheriff who had been talking with Nick. "I told you, I will be fine. Gav and I have a full day tomorrow."

"Well, the only reason I'm not calling in the cavalry is that Nick said he'd stay," said the sheriff.

The forensic van pulled up and John stepped out. Katie knew that if there was anything that was to be found, he would find it.

The sheriff went to talk with Detective Hamilton.

"Nick," said Katie. "You really don't have to stay. I'll be fine. I'm not going to hold you to it. Besides, you don't have anything with you."

"That's where you're wrong. I always carry an overnight bag," said Nick. "C'mon, Cisco has probably torn the door halfway off its hinges by now."

Katie watched the scene for a few more minutes. John was searching and documenting the car—he would soon be dusting for prints. Detective Hamilton would be taking the case, and she would have to wait to find out details, but that didn't mean she didn't have many questions about it all.

Why was that man at her house? Was he watching her? And who had killed him?

FORTY-TWO

Tuesday 0900 hours

McGaven drove their latest car from police impound. Today it was a tan four-door Toyota and actually had comfortable seats. He drove southeast toward Capital Stables to see what they could find out about Desiree Dayton.

Katie rode in silence as she gazed out the window watching the landscape speed by. In most cases she preferred to drive to the locations, but today she was content riding and thinking about everything. She had left a message with Detective Hamilton, but he hadn't returned her call. In any case, her mind was more concentrated on Chad and whoever was following her.

"How do you want to play this?" said McGaven.

"We need to check out the stables. Get a feel for it. According to Lara, they were tough and a little on the fraudulent side, but that was more than a decade ago," she said. The more she thought about it, the more she realized that they might be trying to revive something that had gone long cold.

"I know that look," he said.

"What do you mean?"

"Did you get much sleep last night?"

"Some. Actually, more than I thought I would." She shifted in her seat. "Every car I heard made me think of someone coming to take the place of the other car."

"That's to be expected. But anyone would have to be completely stupid to try to mess with you."

She laughed. "Glad you think so."

"You kidding? You're one of the most badass women I've ever met."

"Are you trying to make me feel better?"

"You know it."

"I'm sorry, I guess I haven't had enough coffee this morning. We need to see if we can get names of the people who used to work at the stables—and if they happen to know where the Daytons might have visited or moved."

"A little like grasping at straws."

"Afraid so. But we need to cross names off our list just the same." Her mind flooded through the leads they had. "And I really want to see if there are more tunnels at the property."

"What do you think we'll find?"

"Not sure. But I'm hoping we find something that will lead us to Dayton—or connect him to the victims. I just get this feeling that he's close—like he's watching our every move."

"It does feel like that." McGaven turned off onto a private, narrow, two-lane road. The gravel crunched under the tires making him slow the speed.

The landscape changed from the dense forest to an open meadow area. Horses grazed in the pastures. Brown, spotted, and black horses mingling.

"It's beautiful here. Peaceful," she said.

"I'm not a big horse fan."

"No?"

"They attract too many flies, the stalls always stink, and, well, they always seem like they want to kick me."

"You've thought a lot about this," she said. "I figured you for the ranch type."

"Nope. I mean I love animals, but there are some that I don't want at my house."

"But dogs?" she said smiling.

"Yeah, definitely dogs—tons of them." He smiled as they reached the main entrance to the stables. "Especially if the dogs are at all like Cisco." McGaven parked next to several pickup trucks and horse trailers.

They hadn't called ahead. They wanted their visit to be unexpected.

Katie stepped out, took a breath, and scanned the area as she always did. The warmth of the sun made her take off her jacket. Normally she didn't want to immediately expose her gun and badge, but in this case it would probably work for them. She tossed the jacket inside the car.

McGaven joined her. He paused and took a quick survey of the property as well.

There was a big wooden sign: Capital Stables, Inc. It had been freshly painted with white lettering against the dark wood. There were two holding areas where three horses were saddled and ready to go. An exercise ring as well as a large oval riding ring was located on the other side of the property. There were two large barns, which housed numerous stalls. Everything appeared to be well kept and the area surrounding the buildings was perfectly maintained. Freshly planted flowers in various pots made a favorable impression on new visitors. More lush woods were behind the stables, which led to acres of riding trails.

"Hello?" said a voice coming from one of the barns. A pretty woman in her mid to late forties with blonde hair pulled back in a ponytail appeared. She wore a pink cap with Capital Stables embroidered on the brim. She was dressed in tan riding pants and a T-shirt neatly tucked in.

"Hi," said Katie as she approached the woman. "I'm Detective Scott and this is my partner Detective McGaven. We're from the Pine Valley Sheriff's Department."

"Detectives?" she said.

"Yes. And you are?" said Katie.

"I'm Cece. Cece Taylor. I'm the general manager here."

"Nice to meet you, Ms. Taylor," she said.

"I'm sorry, but I'm confused. What is this all about?" She eyed them closely and seemed to not trust them.

"We are investigating two cold cases."

"And it brought you to the stables?"

"How long have you worked here?" said Katie.

"Eighteen years next month."

Katie was elated to learn the woman was there when Desiree was, but she kept her enthusiasm under wraps. She glanced at her partner who had also kept his poker face at hearing the news.

"Do you remember a Desiree Dayton?" said Katie.

Cece blinked in surprise and took a moment to respond. "Desi?"

Katie nodded.

"That's a name I haven't heard in a very long time. Is she...?"

"So, you knew her?"

"Yes, of course. Did something happen to her?"

"You knew her in what capacity?"

"Well, she loved it here. She would... help clean stalls and feed the horses."

"And?" said Katie as she watched the woman closely.

"She loved the horses and would help to exercise them."

"When was the last time you saw or heard from her?"

"It's been years. She just quit coming out here and I never

heard from her again. It was... about maybe six or seven years ago, I guess."

Katie believed Cece was telling the truth. She seemed genuinely surprised and upset by the question.

"I know it's been a long time, but you seem to remember her fairly well. Can you tell us anything that might have happened to cause her to stop coming? Trouble at home? Problems with her mom or dad?" Katie was nonchalantly inserting both parents to see if she could get an honest answer.

"No, not that I remember. But I do remember her dad."

"Thomas Dayton?"

"Yes."

McGaven stepped closer. "How would you describe Mr. Dayton?"

Cece stepped backward and glanced at the horses. "He was... I guess you would say controlling. He would show up sometimes and make sure that Desi was doing her work correctly."

"What about Mrs. Dayton?" he said.

"I never saw her or even heard about her. I was under the impression that Desi's mom was out of the picture."

"Dead?"

"No, just somewhere else. I don't know... maybe she was dead." She seemed troubled by the thought of Desi's mom.

"Can you tell us anything more about Mr. Dayton? Did you see him after Desi didn't come back to the stables?"

She shook her head. "No, I never saw either of them again. I thought maybe they had moved."

"You never went to their farm or called them?" she said.

"I did call Desi a couple of times but never got an answer."

"I know it's been some time, but could you give us any contact information or forwarding information for the Daytons?"

"Of course. I'll have to pull physical records. The computer doesn't go back that far. I'll find whatever I can."

McGaven gave her his card. "Just email this account."

She nodded.

"Anything else stand out about Mr. Dayton that you recall?" said Katie.

Cece thought about it as she looked around, avoiding eye contact with the detectives. "I had a conversation with him about the property once. He wanted to know if we would sell him twenty acres."

"This is a seventy-acre property, correct?" said McGaven.

"Actually, it's about sixty-five. The stables were originally twenty acres, but the rest of the parcel was acquired a couple of decades ago."

"And you are part owner?" he asked.

"Yes. I'm a partner in the business and the property. The owners, Mr. and Mrs. Compton, retired five years ago. Mr. Compton has since passed away and Mrs. Compton is ill, heart condition, requiring round-the-clock care."

Katie thought it was odd that Dayton wanted part of the property when he already had farm acreage. "Did Mr. Dayton want any twenty acres or a specific area?"

"That's what was strange. He wanted a very specific area of the property."

"Which is where?" said Katie.

"It's the back portion."

"Why do you think that is?"

"I don't know, he didn't say. But it's the most rural area. It's dense with trees and hasn't been cultivated in any way. We have a couple of overgrown horse trails that wind around the edge of it, but it isn't even good for hiking."

"Thank you, Ms. Taylor."

"Please, what happened to Desi?" She looked from one detective to another.

"We're not at liberty, at least at this point, to talk about details of an open investigation," said Katie.

"Please... is Desi dead?"

Katie looked at the woman and could feel her pain of not knowing. "Yes, I'm afraid Desiree Dayton is dead. That's all that I can tell you."

"Is... is that why she didn't come back to the stables?"

Katie wouldn't confirm or deny the question, but her expression told Cece what she needed to know.

Cece closed her eyes as they filled with tears. "Desi was just a wonderful girl, and she had such a bright future ahead of her. We had talks about horses so many times."

Katie wondered if Lara's story was true about how terribly the stables had treated Desiree. Before the detectives turned to leave, she turned to the woman. "Would it be okay if we quickly looked around?"

"Of course. Please."

Katie looked at McGaven, wondering how he felt about walking through a horse barn. "You can sit this one out if you want." She smiled.

"No way."

Katie wasn't sure what they were looking for, but she wanted to get a grip on how the stables were run and how well kept they were—even though it had been years since Desiree was last there.

The detectives walked through the barns, the storage and feed areas, and the outdoor exercise areas. They noted that there were two stall employees who cleaned up and fed the horses. There was one person who was in charge of exercise. Some horses were privately owned and were at livery, and the other horses were rented for trail rides.

Katie and McGaven walked back to the car.

"You know..."

"I know exactly what you're going to say."

"You do?" she said.

"Yes. You want to look at the parcel of property that Dayton was interested in."

"And the best way to see it—and the fastest—would be on horseback."

He sighed. "Okay, I did not see that coming."

FORTY-THREE

Tuesday 1115 hours

It only took a few minutes for Cece Taylor to saddle up two horses for Katie and McGaven to take the trail to view the back part of the property, which had interested Thomas Dayton.

"You sure you don't need a guide?" said Cece. "I'd be happy to take you. I have some time."

"No, we'll be fine. It's just a quick ride," said Katie. She didn't want anyone to know what was going on in the investigation. With just the two of them, it kept the confidentiality of the case.

McGaven had a blank stare on his face as he stood ten feet away from Wildfire, the dark mare he would be riding.

Katie petted the beautiful sorrel horse she'd been given. His name was Roger. "You're a beautiful boy. Just don't tell Cisco I said that." She smiled as she talked to the horse.

"He'll know you were on a horse," said McGaven.

"You okay?" said Katie as she eyed her partner.

"Sure," he said sarcastically. "I don't know where in the duty manual of a police detective it says I have to ride a horse."

Katie laughed. For some reason being around the horses had calmed her nerves somewhat. "You ready?"

"Yeah," he said, making a face as he approached Wildfire, ready to mount. "Ready when you are... partner. Why did I get the horse named Wildfire?"

Both detectives hoisted themselves up and into the saddles.

"You guys good?" said Cece.

"We're fine. We'll be back within the hour," said Katie.

Katie took the lead and headed out onto the trail. She glanced behind and saw that McGaven was keeping up, but his expression still didn't change from sour and uncomfortable.

Katie couldn't help but enjoy the ride. She hadn't been on a horse in years, but her skills came back quickly. She would have upped the pace if she was by herself, but with McGaven she decided to keep it to a nice walk, trotting here and there.

She followed the instructions that Cece had told them, and it was easy to stay on the trail heading north. Reflecting on why Dayton would want to buy the overgrown and dense part of the property didn't make any sense. What was his mindset?

Katie saw a sign that read: Do Not Go Behind This Point.

It was just a friendly warning for anyone going beyond the main riding trails. There was no danger, but it indicated the part of the acreage that Dayton was interested in.

"It's just up here," said Katie.

"Ten-four." McGaven's voice sounded grumpy.

Katie knew that if they had walked this trail it would take them more than an hour, not to mention it would be tiring fighting through the brush. She spotted a clearing that would be perfect to tie up the horses and take a look around.

"This is a good spot," she said and dismounted.

"How long do you want to search the area?" McGaven said.

"Eager to ride back?"

"Funny."

"Let's just check it out for the sake of new information."

McGaven went one way and Katie the other.

The terrain wasn't as dense and overgrown as the Dayton farm, so it was easy to see the ground and areas around the trees. After a few minutes, Katie realized that she might have been overly optimistic about what they might discover. She didn't see anything unusual or out of place. It didn't look as if anyone had walked around recently. There were no beaten-down paths or broken branches.

Katie thought they had better quit and get on with their next interview. She walked back around and saw that the horses were calmly waiting, swishing their tails, but she didn't see McGaven.

"Gav?" She looked around. "Gav? Where are you?"

There was nothing except the peaceful sounds of the forest with the wind and birds from above.

Katie didn't think much about it at first as she kept looking, retracing the tracks where McGaven had gone. She pulled her cell phone from her pocket and called her partner. There was a signal, and his phone rang.

After the fourth ring, Katie was going to hang up but instead she heard, "Hello."

"Gav?"

"Yeah," he said breathlessly.

"Where are you?"

"Not sure."

Katie didn't understand. "What happened?" she managed to say as her anxiety rose. She could hear him breathing hard. "Gav, tell me the last thing you remember."

"I walked away from the horses straight. Didn't see much… and then I looked up and then…" he said. "I don't remember."

"Okay, stay where you are. I'm coming to you. Stay on the line." She yelled out, "Gav!"

"I can hear you… keep coming."

Katie wasn't sure what had happened but her first thoughts were that he had fallen and hit his head. But she traced his obvious tracks cautiously. She kept her sight at her feet, stopping every so often, looking from side to side and then up. Whatever had happened to him was probably because he wasn't paying attention to his surroundings.

She stopped and looked around, completely perplexed. Where was he?

"Gav, do me a favor and yell so that I can find you."

"Okay."

She waited.

"Katie! I'm here!"

Katie heard him and it sounded strangely muffled, but it was coming from up ahead. She hurried as fast as she dared.

"Katie, I'm here!"

This time she definitely heard him close, but he wasn't anywhere she could see. That was until she looked down and saw his last footprints. The ground crumbled under her feet slightly and she took two steps backward. That was when she saw it. There was some type of hole. It had been camouflaged by years of forest debris.

Katie dropped to her knees and carefully crawled to the edge. She could see McGaven in the hole, approximately twelve feet down. She sucked in a breath. He was in a sitting position, leaning against the side of the hole. It was partially darkened, but she could still see his face. "Gav, are you okay?"

"Yeah, I think so. I hit my head and was disoriented for a bit."

"Are you injured?"

"I... I don't think so. Everything still works."

"Can you stand up?"

"Let me see..."

She watched as her tall partner got to his feet, but it was

clear that he was dizzy as he wavered a bit, using the sides to steady himself.

"I don't think I can climb out," he said.

"What do you see down there?" she said. "Anything that might help you boost yourself up? Roots? Indentations?"

He looked around, running his hands along the sides. "No, there's nothing. But…"

"But what?" She strained her eyes to observe what he was seeing.

"I don't know…" McGaven stopped and rubbed his forehead. He went back to the wall and began using his hands and fingers to remove dirt.

Katie surveyed the hole and noted that it seemed to be almost perfectly symmetrical. It didn't look recent—it appeared to be something that had been there for quite some time. She thought about the tunnels that Shane had brought to her attention. Could this have been one? Or had it simply been part of some drainage on the property?

"Katie," said McGaven.

She knew by the tone of his voice there was something very wrong. "What is it?" They didn't have a flashlight so she couldn't see what he was trying to show her. It looked like something whitish. "What is that?"

"It's part of a human skull." There was a flash from the cell phone camera. "I got a photo."

Katie sat back and reeled in the fact that they found another body on land that Dayton wanted to buy. That couldn't have been a coincidence. She crawled to the side again and leaned down. "Gav, it's a crime scene. We have to get you out of there now."

"What do you suggest?"

"I have an idea," she said. "I'll be right back." Katie ran back to the horses. Attached to one of the saddles there was a coiled rope. She quickly untied it and made a makeshift slipknot. She didn't think her light weight would be enough to pull out McGaven, so she untied her horse Roger and walked him toward the hole. She had him stop and then turned him in the opposite direction. The horse obeyed and gave a few snorts.

"What's going on up there?" he said.

"Wait for it," she said.

Katie tied the rope securely to the saddle horn and then took the length and dropped it into the hole. "Grab hold and I'll pull you out."

"Okay."

"Alright, Roger," she said, taking the reins and guiding the horse. "Ready, Gav?"

"I'm ready."

Katie made a clicking sound with her tongue. "C'mon, Roger, nice and easy."

The horse walked forward as Katie guided him, making sure that he wouldn't bolt. She kept control of the reins as the rope held taut.

"It's working," McGaven called. With a few more feet, he climbed out on his hands and knees. "I'm good." He looked at the horse. "I can't believe it. I was saved by a horse. Please do not tell anyone."

"Why not?"

"Trust me. Don't say anything."

"Okay," she said, removing the rope and securing the horse. Katie went to her partner. "You okay?" She looked McGaven over and at his forehead in particular. He seemed okay. "We still need you to be checked out."

McGaven pulled his phone from his pocket and turned it toward Katie. "Not before we call this in. That's a human skull."

Katie stared at the photo, which definitely showed the side

of a human skull with the jaw and teeth still intact. She couldn't look away from the distinctive dental work.

"This is now officially a crime scene," she said.

"Looks like we're following someone's killing spree, all this finding bodies buried at rural locations."

"That's what I'm afraid of."

FORTY-FOUR

Tuesday 1400 hours

Katie and McGaven watched as the emergency and forensic personnel descended on Capital Stables. Police officers were sent in to search and secure the area where the body was found.

John decided that he wanted to have his friend from the forensic osteology department at the university oversee the extraction due to the fact that they might be more ancient remains than modern. It was just a precaution. He also wanted to make sure they were careful and following every protocol.

Katie saw that Cece looked frightened and was unsure of everything that was going on since the detectives had arrived.

"I'm going to talk to Cece," said Katie to McGaven. "Get your head looked at too."

He nodded. "I'm fine. I have a hard head."

"Seriously, Gav. I will get the sheriff to order you to." She smiled, but she was still serious. She didn't want to take any chances on his health.

He pretended to salute her. "I will, I promise."

Katie joined Cece. "You doing okay?" She studied the

woman carefully and deduced that she was genuinely concerned and frightened at the thought of a body having been buried right under her nose.

"I guess so. I just can't believe there's a body buried on this property. I don't even know where to begin."

"It's okay. We don't know how long it's been here. It still could be ancient."

"You mean like Native American?"

"Maybe." Katie didn't think that would be the case, but she didn't want to alarm the woman any more than absolutely necessary.

"How do you do this?" the general manager asked.

"You mean investigating dead bodies?"

"Well, yeah. I couldn't do your job."

"It's not all about things like this. We help families get closure. We put bad people behind bars. But yes... it never gets easier when there are people who have died at the hands of another."

"Wow. I never think about things like this until..."

"I would be worried if you weren't upset by this." Katie looked around as more personnel arrived at the property. She wanted to ease Cece's mind. "By the way, Roger was awesome."

Cece nervously laughed. "He's such a great horse. I remember when we first got him. He was wild and a bit untamable."

"He stepped up and helped me pull my partner out of that hole."

"I could tell that he liked you when you approached him. Have you always ridden?"

"As a kid definitely, but I haven't in a while. I want to ride more."

"You are welcome here any time," she said.

"Thank you. I will take you up on that." Katie watched as Detective Hamilton arrived. "I need to ask some questions. Has there been anyone else interested in that back property area since Mr. Dayton?"

"No, not that I can remember."

"Has anyone ridden back there?"

"No, that sign stops them."

Katie remembered reading it and the area not looking like anyone had walked or ridden on it in a long time. "Yes, we saw that." She reached into her pocket and pulled out a card. "Please call me if you remember something or if you need to talk."

"Thank you, Detective."

"Please, call me Katie." Katie left Cece and met up with her partner who had an EMT tending to his head wound.

"See, I have a hard head. I'm fine," said McGaven. "Am I good?" he said to the EMT, who nodded.

"Let's go talk to Hamilton."

Katie and McGaven headed out toward the trail. Halfway to the site, Hamilton had a command center set up where everyone met back to re-evaluate. Forensics was excavating the body and any other pieces of evidence that might have been buried in the hole as well.

"Detectives," said Hamilton.

"Detective," said Katie.

"You two are giving me more work every time you go somewhere."

"What can I say?" said McGaven. "It's a job that keeps on giving."

"Is there anything else that you can add from your preliminary report?" said Hamilton.

"Not much to tell. We checked out the property because Thomas Dayton had wanted to buy it years back. And then Gav fell in the hole and that's when we discovered the remains."

"You said Mr. Dayton was interested in it?"

"Yes. We're trying to track him down. He's a person of interest—and he has a lot of explaining to do. We wanted to have a look around and see if there was a reason for his wanting to purchase the land," she said.

"I'd say there was a reason," said McGaven.

"Detective, everything here is under control. I'll update you if anything changes," said Hamilton.

Katie hesitated. She hated when any part of their investigations was handed over to another detective, but they had to talk to Ferris Baldwin and check out the Dayton farm again. "Any ID yet on the victim in front of my house?"

"Not yet, but I expect to hear something later today or first thing in the morning."

"Okay, looks like you have everything under control," she said.

"You sure you don't want to interrogate the horses we rode?" said McGaven with a smile.

Hamilton stared at him and then returned to the command center.

"Really? Was that necessary?" she said.

"What? I thought it was funny."

"It was but that's beside the point."

"Just keeping things real and letting him know that it's still on our investigation radar."

FORTY-FIVE

Tuesday 1645 hours

Katie and McGaven made their way toward the Pine Valley jail where they were holding Ferris Baldwin in protective custody until further notice—basically until they found Thomas Dayton or until the district attorney released him. The detectives had stopped for a quick bite to eat before heading in to question Ferris.

When they arrived at the jail, McGaven didn't get out of the car right away. He absently scratched his head where there was a bandage from his injury.

Katie looked at her partner, and saw he was struggling with something, so she waited for him to feel comfortable enough to share with her.

"I know you've been wondering why I've been grumpy," he started.

Katie waited.

"Ever since we responded to the jumper call, it's been digging up stuff from my past," he said.

"What do you mean?"

"I know this sounds silly."

"I don't believe that. Try me," she said.

"When I was in high school I realized I wanted to be a cop. And believe me I took a lot of heat for that, but I didn't let it get to me. I played football and baseball, and things were fine. But one day, I saw a couple of my teammates berating and teasing this girl. She was a loner, frail, and never bothered anyone." He stopped and took a breath.

Katie had never seen McGaven vulnerable like this before.

"I stepped in and stopped them. It didn't come to blows, but almost. There were a couple of other instances, but I stopped those too."

"You were a good kid and that's why you're a good man," she said.

"Well, that's when things got different."

"How?"

"Lara is one of those people who lives in a bit of a fantasy. Her way of thinking is different—even skewed."

"Are you saying she's delusional?"

"No, but I noticed some things about her during the two interviews."

Katie nodded for him to go on, listening intently.

"She still has this way of seeing things how she wants to see them. If something was terrifying, she would somehow rewrite it in her mind so that it wasn't anymore. Does that make sense?"

"After speaking with her—yeah, it does. But, Gav, why is this weighing so heavy on you?"

"I don't know. Maybe it's because now I know why she was the way she was after witnessing a brutal murder when she was twelve. Maybe I could have helped her more back then. Contacted someone. Anything."

"I saw in the file that she had no family. Do you remember her parents?"

"No, I don't recall. I did a background, and her parents are deceased."

"Gav, we were able to stop her from jumping off the bridge and taking her life in the tub. She is getting help now." Katie still had some reservations about Lara. Some things still didn't add up in her mind. The young woman was clearly distressed and even confused about facts, but she was a victim too.

"I know, you're right."

"The best thing we can do for Lara is to solve and close these cases. Maybe it will help her put those demons to sleep."

"If the body count slows down—and there's no more horse-back riding."

Katie smiled. She loved the way that McGaven could always find humor to relieve the pressures of the job. And her heart ached knowing that he was feeling a little bit responsible for a girl in school he wished he could have done more for.

Katie and McGaven walked into the jail and locked up their firearms. They were led into a holding area that was primarily used for special cases—inmates taken out of the general popula-tion, gang members testifying against their own, and any confi-dential informants.

Katie kept her focus straight ahead, but still couldn't help but feel the eyes of the prisoners staring at her. They kept walking until they came to a special meeting room and were directed inside.

The door shut immediately behind them. It wasn't like the holding cells they were used to at Mansfield Prison. The jail had a different dynamic to it, like a lower budget. It was a temporary place for short-timers, misdemeanor violators, or until the inmate was transferred to the prison.

As Katie moved farther into the cramped, stuffy room, she was going over in her head what questions she would ask Ferris

Baldwin. The smell of sweat and lack of filtered air made her a bit nauseous—she wanted to be back outside.

The other door opened and an officer showed Ferris Baldwin inside. He wasn't shackled or handcuffed and was dressed in regular clothing of jeans and a shirt.

"I was wondering when you two would show up. I need to get out of here," he said. His face was stressed, and he had grown a scraggly beard and mustache.

Katie almost didn't recognize him as the same man she had fought with at the rental stable property.

"Mr. Baldwin. You understand we brought you here for your own safety," said McGaven.

"I can't stay in here. I'm not under arrest."

Katie took a chair. "Sit down, Mr. Baldwin."

"I'm telling you—"

"Sit down... now," she said, never taking her eyes away from his. There wasn't time to appease him. They needed information that would be helpful to the investigation. Her mind flashed to the bodies at the Dayton farm and the skeletal remains at Capital Stables.

Baldwin kept scratching at his neck and behind his ears. "Fine." He finally sat down.

"We just have some questions. Some things have come to light, and we need to find Thomas Dayton immediately," said Katie.

"If he finds me, he'll kill me. You know that, right?"

"What makes you say that?" said McGaven.

"Look, I've had time to think about my situation and what I didn't disclose to you about Dayton."

"What do you mean?" she said as she watched his body language to ascertain if he was telling the truth. He kept his shoulders straight, maintained eye contact, and wasn't fidgety in his chair, which indicated a truthful person.

"I've known Dayton for a long time, and I would characterize our friendship as brothers. Know what I mean?"

"So you're saying you know what Dayton did?" said McGaven.

"Mr. Baldwin, do you need a lawyer?" she said.

"No, I want to be transparent with you. I don't trust lawyers anyway." He continued to scratch at his neck, causing it to turn red.

"Tell us what you know, if you want to help yourself by being honest with us. Don't forget attacking a law enforcement officer is still on the table if you lie to us," said McGaven.

Baldwin leaned back as if getting more relaxed before he told them about Dayton. It seemed somewhat out of character for a person to behave that way. Usually, most people became more intense wanting to confess or come clean about something —their body language was different, rigid, and or even fidgety. Though he seemed to be scratching a lot.

"First, I never saw him kill anybody." He looked at both detectives. "But there were things that didn't add up—like suspicious things."

"You never saw Abigail Andrews or Desiree?" said Katie.

"I never saw the person Abigail Andrews. What about Desiree?" He looked at each detective.

"When was the last time you saw her?"

"As soon as she graduated from high school, then she was out of there. Can you blame her? It was very tense. Why?" He leaned forward. "Did something happen to her?"

Katie didn't want to tell him details, but she said, "Her body was discovered."

"What? I had nothing to do with that. When? How?"

"That's all we can say right now. But it's imperative that we find Thomas Dayton."

He leaned back, rubbing his forehead and then scratching his beard. His expression softened. "What can I do?"

"Can you tell us where Dayton might go? What are his hobbies? Something he likes? Places he might visit? Where he would gravitate toward? Anything?" she said.

Baldwin thought a moment. "Even though he and I were friends, like brothers, and people even thought we were brothers, he was very private about some things... which makes sense about his fantasies with women and... he's good with stuff around the farm and firearms..."

"What about his wife?" said McGaven.

He shrugged. "I never knew her. Never knew her name or anything about her. I asked him about Desi's mom one time, and he blew up and said there was nothing to tell. So, I never brought it up again."

"Is there anything that you can think of that might be helpful in locating him?" she said. Katie's patience was waning, and she wanted answers.

"Well, he's comfortable roughing it. He could survive in the wilderness, no problem. He never let anything faze him when something went wrong. He's resourceful and quite a force to be reckoned with."

"Where would he go, in your opinion, if he knew we were looking for him?"

"He likes the area around Pine Valley, that's for sure, but if he was trying to stay low I would say he would be close. He loved that farm, more than you know. In fact, the bank would have foreclosed sooner, but he did everything he could to save it. It was just the way it was... he couldn't continue to pay the mortgage."

"What about in the surrounding areas? Would he stay close?" she said.

He nodded. "Most definitely."

"Would you say he would be brazen enough to intimidate anyone?" she said.

"I wouldn't be surprised, but I've never seen him do that to someone he didn't know."

"So, you've seen him intimidate someone?"

"Yeah. Workers. People at restaurants. Stuff like that."

Katie looked around the room. It felt as if the walls were closing in and it seemed to have increased in temperature. It was her imagination, she was sure, but there was something about Baldwin that made her cautious and even a bit suspicious.

"So, when can I get out of here?" he said. "You can't continue to hold me."

"We're still deciding whether to charge you. Don't worry, the time is running out and you'll be able to leave, but we can't guarantee your safety once you do," said McGaven.

"You still can't continue to hold me—you need to charge me or release me." He was becoming bolder, unlike how he was when they had entered.

"You're in a gray area right now. Do you want to take your chances of Dayton coming back to tie up loose ends?" she said.

Baldwin leaned back with a look of fear. He bit his lip, almost as if he wanted to say something he shouldn't.

"What about Dayton having girlfriends?" said McGaven.

"Nah. He always said he'd had it with women. He preferred hanging out drinking at a bar fondling women for a quickie than having any type of relationship."

Katie wasn't surprised by this description. She stood up to move to a different area of the small room. The walls still bothered her, and her arms were tingling.

"Why do I get the feeling you're holding out on us?" said McGaven.

"Hey, man, I've been honest with you. I don't know what else I can tell you. I want you to find Dayton as much as you do." He fidgeted with his hands. "I want to get out of here."

"Mr. Baldwin, we'll be in touch," said Katie. "In the meantime, we are going to have you moved to better conditions. You can come and go, but we'd really like you to be in protective custody. Would that be okay?"

"Okay," he reluctantly said.

"We can have someone bring things from your place," she said.

"No, that's okay. I'll just wait until I get to go home."

Katie studied him. She didn't know why he wouldn't want personal items.

McGaven rose to leave. "We expect to hear from you if you think of anything that might help us. Right?"

Baldwin nodded and appeared to be relieved.

The detectives left the jail facility. In the parking lot, Katie's cell phone alerted her to a text from John.

ID on shooting victim. Roland Danner.

He was the man they had been hunting down in relation to Chad's abduction.

"The guy out front of my house was identified as Roland Danner," she said, almost breathless. She hadn't seen that coming.

"The guy who held Chad hostage?" said McGaven.

"Yes." Katie couldn't believe it. Why was he at her house? Had he been following her? And was he the guy in the truck who had tried to shoot her? But who had shot him?

"You okay?" McGaven asked as he drove out onto the main road.

"I guess so. I actually don't know what to think." Things were adding up, or rather, becoming more convoluted and extremely problematic. "It doesn't make sense."

"No, it doesn't. It proposes more questions than answers."

FORTY-SIX

Tuesday 1945 hours

Katie was looking forward to relaxing when she got home. It was the first time since she had become a detective that she wanted to turn off the case and the day they had. She was afraid that every time she closed her eyes, she would see another buried body. Her stress levels were off the chart, and she needed to regain her sanity and not worry about Chad or her next move. She wanted to spend a quiet evening, grab a bite, and go on a walk with Cisco.

Instead, her phone rang. She saw it was Nick calling and accepted the call from her dash. "Hey, Nick," she said.

"Where are you?" he said quietly.

"Nick, what's going on?" She'd heard the urgency in his voice.

"Scotty, where are you?"

"I'm on my way home. Almost there in fact."

"How long would it take you to get to Springfield?"

"Uh." She glanced at the clock. "At this time, maybe twenty minutes, if I hurry."

"You said you're almost home?"

"Yeah."

"Bring Cisco and meet me at the post office parking lot on Park Street in twenty minutes. Text me when you're there and I'll update you on where to meet me. Okay?"

"Of course. I'll be there in fifteen."

"I'm sure you will. Oh, Scotty?"

"Yes?"

"Be careful and make sure you're not followed. I mean it. Be vigilant." He hung up.

Katie pressed the accelerator and hurried home. It only took her five minutes to change her clothes and grab Cisco. She was then back on the road heading to Springfield—it was a small unincorporated town. A million thoughts went through her mind—and none of them were good. She knew that Nick was going to check out the PO box for Thomas Dayton—and she also knew Nick. He had obviously found something of importance, otherwise he wouldn't have asked for her to join him. She wondered if she should have McGaven join them too. After thinking about it, she would assess the situation when she got there. If she needed to call McGaven or the Pine Valley Sheriff's Department for backup she would.

She glanced in her rearview mirror and could see that Cisco sat at attention in the back seat, ready to go, without his usual whines and spins. Instead, he waited for any command that Katie was going to give him.

Katie made great time. She didn't have to push the speed limit too much in order to get to Springfield. The town was located in an area that had been cleared many decades ago in order to build. The plan was to develop the town further, but it never came to fruition.

Katie turned off the main road onto a much less traveled road to get to the original downtown area, which consisted of a handful of buildings including the post office. The area was deserted due to the evening hour. She did as she was instructed and drove around behind the post office entrance on Park Street, where it was secluded and where she could also view the back door of the building. There were three large storage containers and as far as she could see, they were locked up tight. She was alone.

Katie called Nick and he picked up on the second ring.

"Scotty? You here?" he said.

"We're here. Why all the cloak-and-dagger stuff?"

"I'm on an adjacent street and didn't want you driving up because it might attract unnecessary attention."

"Okay." Katie tried to think what Nick had found out.

"I'll come to you."

"Okay," she said.

The call ended.

Katie kept an eye on her mirrors.

Cisco followed suit and watched out the windows, but he was still quiet.

Barely five minutes later, Nick appeared. He hurried, only slightly limping, but quickly made his way to Katie's car. He jumped into the passenger's seat and then quietly shut the door. His eyes were dark, intense, and he seemed to have been running for a ways. His body was tense, and his muscles were flexed. Katie knew this particular feeling well—it was like when they were on the battlefield just before a maneuver. The body went through chemical changes when it was in the fight-or-flight mode and afterward when the adrenaline still flowed.

"You okay?" she said.

"Yeah. Fine."

She watched her ex-Army sergeant and patiently waited.

"Okay," he said as he stared out the window. "I came out here to see what I could check out with box 1761 that belonged to Thomas Dayton." He turned to stare at Katie. "I went inside and there was this kid who was staffing the counter. It's pretty quiet around here. Anyway, I asked about box 1761 and he checked to see who the box belonged to—he said Harland Thomas, not Thomas Dayton. That ticked the list what we were talking about the other night."

Katie's interest was certainly piqued. With all the unusual happenings, she wanted to believe that maybe now they were going to get a break in the case.

"I asked how often this guy comes in to pick up mail and he said every Tuesday afternoon like clockwork."

"And?"

"And so, I waited and staked out the place to see who would show up."

"Did he?"

"You bet," he said. "At least I think it was him."

"Think?"

"You know that photo you have of Thomas Dayton is old, right?" He took a breath as he watched the area outside the car. "I saw a guy dressed in dark sweats with the hoodie pulled up. He had sunglasses and walked with his head down. But his build and general characteristics seemed to be Dayton."

"Did he go inside?"

"He did and then exited not even a minute later. I didn't see any mail in his hand, but it could've been in his pocket."

"So, did he have a car?" she said.

"No. And that's why I had to be careful to follow him. I called my guy inside and asked if the guy that came in had opened box 1761."

"It was him?"

"Affirmative. I drove out and didn't see him. I couldn't figure out where he had gone, so I had to get out and go on foot, which isn't the easiest thing."

Katie was thinking that Dayton must be close.

"I wanted to wait until I knew where he was before I contacted you. He's laying low in a studio apartment at one of the houses down the road. Actually, it's not a bad place to stay out of view."

"That makes sense," she said. "After talking with one of his ex-workers, he confirmed that Dayton would probably stay close and not completely leave the area."

"Why? It seems stupid."

"People who get away with things so long, like Dayton has, have this arrogance and high-mindedness that they like to sit back and watch the police—even clean up clues or people who might get in the way."

"Well, he's sitting back now."

"Take me to him," she said.

"I don't know. Shouldn't you call it in?"

"I'm not calling it in until I have proof. Then we would be bringing all the cops here attracting too much attention." Katie was ready to go, and she wanted to get her hands on Dayton. She could never get the images of those bodies out of her head. She wanted to get this guy no matter what it took.

Nick studied her for a moment. "We need to check things out, but you have to promise me that you will call in your troops."

"Of course."

"I mean it, Scotty."

"I will," she insisted. "I don't want anything to go wrong to make this guy walk."

"Okay."

"What about Cisco?"

"I wanted you to bring him so that you wouldn't be alone."

"You mean so I would have backup." She smiled.

"Something like that. Let's go out this way."

Katie started the engine, and she gradually eased the vehicle out the back parking lot onto an alley. She drove slowly. The houses were obscured by wooden privacy fences. Some had gates to the alley while others didn't.

"How far?" she said.

"Up here," he said and pointed.

Katie pulled into a parking area. She managed to squeeze the car off the roadway. There was an abandoned house with a red tag indicating it was going to be torn down. She cut the headlights.

"Where's your car?" she said.

"It's farther down the alley. Don't worry, no one will notice it."

Katie stared at the dilapidated structure in front of them. She imagined that the investigation was beginning to crumble too.

"I'll leave Cisco, but I always carry the remote for the automatic door release if there's a problem."

He smiled. "Always prepared."

"When it comes to Cisco—absolutely." She turned and looked at the black dog, then back at Nick. "Show me where this guy is at—let's go."

Katie opened the door and stepped out. She surveyed their surroundings and felt comfortable enough to leave Cisco behind. It was dark and there weren't any outside lights on, which seemed odd. She tried to listen for any type of noise— from anyone moving around or music or dogs.

There was nothing moving or making a sound.

She moved forward with caution.

They didn't speak. Nick made a gesture that they needed to go a certain direction. She nodded.

They entered through a six-foot wooden gate, which opened into a courtyard area. It wasn't nice, but neglected and overgrown. Weeds, old outdoor furniture turned over, and a stack of broken terra-cotta pots were strewn around. It must've once been a nice outdoor area shared by several of the residences.

Katie quickly inspected the area. Her usual cop instinct

made her not only curious but also vigilant. She knew that at a moment's notice, things could change or become dangerous. For some reason, the area reminded her of so many things that had happened on the job and in her private life. But she had a job to do, so she pushed away memories and fleeting thoughts.

Nick touched her arm. He must've sensed her momentary pause. Then he pointed. She saw the walkway that passed several apartments, which looked like an old single-level motel.

As Katie walked past one of the residences, she saw the flickering of a television from inside but still there was no sound. They continued to move by the apartments.

Nick suddenly stopped her and pointed at the last residence.

Katie nodded. She noticed that there was a single dim light inside. It was difficult to tell if it was in the living area or farther inside. They were fortunate that the night acted as a shield so that they weren't easily seen.

The entire area was still and quiet.

Katie could feel her pulse accelerate; she often used it as a means of knowing when danger was near. Her internal instincts were heightened, and it affected her heartbeat.

Nick moved slightly in front of her and then turned right. She followed, trying to see if she could hear anything from inside. The curtains were drawn, and the windows were shut.

The apartment was on the end, so they were able to move around toward the back to try to get a look inside a window. No luck. They moved almost silently around to the back of the building.

Goosebumps prickled her arms and down the back of her neck. She flashed on the tours she had been on with Nick in Afghanistan—and now being with him on this task in the dark, sneaking around brought up so many feelings. Even smells seemed to surface of what it was like on the battlefield. Gunfire. Smoke. Revving military vehicles. Being part of a tactical team.

They reached a small window and Nick peered inside. He nodded to her.

"Take a look," he whispered.

Katie cautiously peered into the small window, which was the bathroom. The door was open, and the view was the living room where a man was sitting in a leather chair smoking a cigarette watching television. She studied him. He appeared to be Thomas Dayton—with general features and body build, but she couldn't be a hundred percent sure. He wore gray sweatpants and a blue T-shirt. Smoke swirled around his head.

Katie ducked back down.

Nick eyed her.

"Is that the same guy you saw at the post office?" she whispered.

He nodded.

Katie wasn't sure. He looked like the photograph on his old driver's license. He seemed the right age, but still, she wasn't sure.

A strange thud caused both of them to react, ready for anything.

Katie mouthed the words, "What was that?"

Nick put his hand up to indicate to wait.

Katie peered back inside the window and the chair was empty. She grabbed Nick's arm and shook her head, pointing at the window, and indicating that the person of interest was not where he was when they had arrived. She thought it was probably a better idea if they retreated and figured out what to do in the morning. The man didn't appear to be going anywhere anytime soon. She didn't notice any bags packed or clothes and toiletries stacked up.

"Let's go back and Gav and I will come back in the morning," she said.

Katie and Nick retraced their steps. She wasn't sure how

she felt about the man inside the apartment—something didn't seem right.

As they rounded the corner, they walked right into the barrel of a shotgun.

"Who are you? Why are you following me?" The gun didn't waver, which indicated that he was familiar with a weapon.

That was all it took for Nick to use his quick hands of close hand-to-hand combat. Within seconds he was able to get the gun away from the man. With no other choice, the man turned and ran.

Katie gave chase, quickly catching up to the guy. As she ran, she thought about those bodies, the graves, the fifty-five-gallon drums. The torture signs. His own daughter. The anger made her run faster.

The man slammed a gate and threw various pieces of pots at her, trying to slow her down.

"Stop!" she yelled. "Police!"

The man turned the corner near her car. Katie pressed the remote on her belt. Just as he was about to pass the vehicle, the back door opened and a large black blur sprang out, knocking the man off his feet. He screamed as Cisco had the upper hand. The dog didn't attack but his rapid bark kept him on the ground.

Katie ran up. "Cisco, *hier*," she said, and the dog obediently trotted to her side. "*Bleib*." She wanted Cisco to stay in place.

"Who are you?" the man said, breathless. "I did what he asked."

"Who?" she said.

Nick joined her, still holding the shotgun.

As Katie studied the man, she realized he was younger than Thomas Dayton but there was a slight resemblance. If someone didn't know, they would have thought it was Dayton.

Cisco barked twice.

"I'm Detective Scott from the Pine Valley Sheriff's Department."

"Detective?"

"Why were you getting mail for Dayton?" she said.

"Dayton?"

"Harland Thomas," she said.

"Look, I don't know what you think you know, but I was given five hundred bucks to pick up this guy's mail. That's it."

"When did you meet with him?"

"I didn't."

"How did you get instructions and the money?"

"Look, I met a guy, Bambi, who said I could make some money."

"Bambi?" said Nick. "Haul this guy in."

"Wait. I'm telling you the truth. I received instructions in an envelope of money left for me behind the post office."

"You mean like a dead drop?" she said. Her mind reeled over the actions of this type of criminal-to-criminal contact.

"I receive a text telling me where to go. It's different every month, and then I follow the instructions. I pick up the money and I leave the mail where I'm told. Easy money."

"What phone number?"

"It's different every text. I guess they're from burner phones." He looked at the dog as he stayed sitting on the ground. "Can I go now?"

"Not yet," she said. She looked at Nick. "Great work."

"I'm sorry it isn't him."

"But I find it interesting that he chose someone who could pass for his brother," she said. She thought about the odds of finding someone who could do this. It would have taken some time to plan. "What's your name?"

"Chris."

"Chris what?"

"Chris Farrell."

"Well, Mr. Farrell, you work for us now," she said.

"What if I don't?"

She smiled. "Then you go to jail for impeding a homicide investigation and whatever else fits the crime."

His face turned sour.

"Look at this way. You work for us, and you'll be a part of getting a killer off the streets. Besides, when Dayton is done with you, I have a feeling your body would end up buried somewhere in Pine Valley." She stood over Farrell. "And Dayton is really good at making bodies disappear."

"Fine," he said with contempt.

"You have the mail, right?"

"Right."

"When do you drop it off and get your money?

"I... I don't know. I usually get a text with the place and time about midnight."

"Where were your other pickups?"

"Usually at an abandoned house or a park—one time behind a closed restaurant."

"Okay," she said.

Katie and Nick along with Cisco escorted Farrell back to his apartment. Katie called McGaven from her cell phone and the partners coordinated a plan.

After she finished, she ended the call and said, "Now we wait."

FORTY-SEVEN

Wednesday 0020 hours

The crew waited with Farrell inside his apartment and kept their voices low. There was only one light on in case anyone was watching or someone happened by. It wouldn't be obvious that there were several people and a dog inside. Farrell sat in his big chair, while Nick and Cisco watched him from an old worn sofa across the room. There was going to be a narrow window of time between the text and money/instructions left at a location.

McGaven hung up his phone. "Okay, two of Springfield's officers are going to stake out areas near the last drops and will wait until further notice."

Katie nodded. She never would have expected this. But the investigation had certainly taken them on wild goose chases. She hoped this wouldn't be another one.

"Is the department okay having two officers help us?" she asked.

"Nothing happens much around here and it's after midnight. The sergeant okayed it. He said Officers Wilson and

Hernandez are the best. Basically, not rookies. They know what they're doing."

"Okay." She thought about the two patrol cars sitting in the darkness waiting to get a visual on Dayton.

"Besides, if anything does happen, they can be taken off our watch any time."

"What's up, Scotty?" said Nick as he joined the detectives.

"Does this seem strange to you?" Katie asked them both.

"What do you mean? I'm still reeling over the fact I had to ride a horse," said McGaven.

"I guess I'm just saying it seems too easy. Dayton has always been ahead of us, even taking out possible witnesses. Why would he keep this PO box?"

"He's overconfident. Doesn't care. Or maybe he didn't think we would find the box," said McGaven.

"Maybe. We have to stay vigilant," she said. "Make sure to give the officers a heads-up to stay frosty. Okay?"

"On it," he said, and text messaged the officers.

Katie and McGaven had planned that one of them would follow Farrell and the other would shadow and stay back, so that there was someone watching the back of the other. Nick was to stay at the apartment with Cisco but be looped in on their cell phones for safety reasons. The two town police officers would be backups and ready to arrest Dayton.

Katie paced the room.

Cisco whined softly, watching her, sensing her energy and emotions.

Nick watched Katie and knew what she was feeling. It was similar to when they were waiting to go on maneuvers with the entire Army team.

Katie ran everything through her mind—the visit with Baldwin in protective custody; Capital Stables; Lara Fontaine; the stabbing of Abigail's boyfriend, Anthony Drake, in prison; and the bodies piling up. They still hadn't heard if the body at the stables had been identified. There was some connection that Katie was missing. What was it? She almost felt as if they were being fooled by a magician's sleight of hand—that they were being pushed in one direction in order to not see what was going on in the other.

"Hey," said Farrell. "Just got a text from an unknown number."

"What does it say?" said Katie.

Farrell read the text. "*210 Templeton Ct behind dumpster in back—under right side of wood pile.*"

"Do you know where that is?" she said.

"Yeah, it's not far from here. I usually walk to the spots."

"Let's go," she said. "I'll follow behind and Gav will shadow farther behind me."

McGaven checked the location from his phone and found it easily. "Is this an abandoned house or maybe a remodel?"

Farrell shrugged. "Don't know."

Heading to the door, Katie said, "Don't do anything different. Keep to your same routine as usual. Got it?"

"Yeah."

The detectives and Farrell headed out and shut the door behind them, leaving Nick and Cisco. Katie, McGaven, and Nick had synced their phones, able to know where one another was at any given time.

The temperature had dropped a few degrees since they had arrived. The coolness and blanket of nighttime made their cover that much more effective. There were no cars on the streets and most houses were dark as well. It was easy to stay in the shadows where no one would notice people out walking causing any type of concern or curiosity.

Katie felt her stomach tighten. Her muscles were also tense. She checked her firearm several times out of habit and from the uneasiness she felt.

Katie hung back, slowing her pace as she watched Farrell

walk at a normal pace toward the location—he casually walked past two fences and properties that were all dark. She kept her senses on high alert and watched every corner for anything suspicious. The night felt dead. Her wits seemed to bob and weave as she walked—she half expected the devil to jump out from the deep shadows. At this point where the investigation had taken them, it wouldn't have surprised her.

Farrell slowed his pace and took a left onto Templeton Court, at which point Katie couldn't see him anymore. She picked up her speed to a light jog until she reached the street and took a left. Looking at the addresses, she estimated that address 2 1 0 was about five houses ahead. Two of the homes had been demolished and another one had a small temporary manufactured home.

Katie stopped and stayed off the road in the shadows.

She looked behind her and didn't see her partner. He would have been easy to spot with his height, so he was hanging back and using the GPS application on his cell phone to track her and Farrell.

Katie looked ahead and still didn't see Farrell. Her thoughts were mixed that maybe they shouldn't have sent in Farrell but one of them instead. But she didn't want to raise any suspicions if Dayton was watching. They might not get another chance of finding and catching this guy. He could bolt and completely leave the area, forever.

She crept closer and saw the number 2 1 0 spray-painted on the curb. Not wanting to rush in too quickly, Katie studied the area, looking to see if anyone was watching or waiting in the darkness. When she was sure that she was alone, she proceeded and moved up the gravel driveway carefully, not wanting to make any sound. The small single-story house was dilapidated, windows and siding missing, and there was an abundant amount of caution tape wrapped around everything with a flimsy red fence attempting to keep people out.

Katie paused again. There was no noise filtering through the evening. No footsteps. No wind. No sound of anything or anyone moving in the night.

Taking a slow steadying breath, Katie moved cautiously around the house until she saw two large construction dumpsters. Still, she didn't see or hear anyone. That familiar prickly feeling began to rise up in her extremities and alert her to something that wasn't right.

Where was Farrell?

Why wasn't he leaving by now?

For some reason, the buried bodies on the farm surfaced vividly in her mind as if something unnatural had closed in around her at that moment.

Whenever she wasn't sure what was ahead or even around the corner, Katie always stopped to readjust her moves. Glancing at her phone, she saw that McGaven was still on the adjacent street and was obviously watching her position. They kept their communication quiet and didn't want to draw attention.

Katie kept against the side of the house as cover; she didn't want to walk into the light. She kept watch and listened, but there was only darkness and extreme quiet. She was cautious and made sure that if Dayton was watching, he wouldn't see her approach.

After a couple of minutes, still not seeing Farrell she decided to move in closer.

She approached the large construction dumpster, where the lid was closed and locked. Carefully walking around the metal container, she turned the corner and saw Farrell lying on the ground—there was an empty envelope next to him. Scanning around her first, she then dropped to her knees and could see that he was still breathing.

As Katie stood up to retrieve her cell phone, someone grabbed her from behind. She dropped her phone on the ground and began to struggle with her attacker. She was dragged backward but she managed to push her assailant against the wall of the building. She felt the outside wall of the house give beneath the force. The person spun her so that she faced the house and began to slam her against it. The flimsy construction began to give way—the lumber screeched and groaned beneath each hit.

Katie couldn't fight the man's strength and she began to gasp for air. She managed one last effort and put her feet against the wall so that she wouldn't take another impact against her body.

She could feel the man's strength tighten around her body and neck. His sour cigarette breath against her neck repulsed her.

After the next slam, the wall siding gave way, and they tumbled inside the house. It was dark, making it almost impossible to see what was around them. She turned toward her attacker but couldn't see him well enough. His build and the way he moved seemed consistent to Dayton, but she still wasn't sure.

Katie had reached for her gun, but it wasn't in the holster. With no other choice, she charged the man. They went down. She could smell sawdust and some type of lubricating grease. The man overpowered her, pinning her face down.

Leaning close to her ear, he whispered in a creepy voice, "We *will* meet again, Detective." He released his grip and forcefully kicked her in the side.

Katie tried to get to her hands and knees, but the pain was excruciating, and she couldn't get enough air in her lungs. She wheezed as she got to her feet. Unsteady at first, she ran to the gaping hole in the wall. It was once again deserted and quiet.

Katie spotted her gun and cell phone. She quickly retrieved them and called McGaven.

"Gav," she barely whispered trying to catch her breath.

"Call in backup and ambulance. He got away. He's wearing dark sweats, medium height, and took off east on Templeton."

Katie and McGaven watched as the EMTs loaded Farrell into the ambulance.

"You really should be checked out," said McGaven.

"I'm fine. I'm angry that he got the upper hand. He must've been waiting for us." Katie was frustrated, tired, and felt at a disadvantage of having Dayton somehow ahead of them. If it was really him.

"You okay?"

"I will be when we catch up to him. I can't figure out how he's moving around like it's his own private world."

"Did Farrell say anything?"

"Just that he was grabbed from behind and hit on the head. No description. And the mail is gone. He's also freaking out about his safety."

"Local Springfield PD is handling that for us. They're doing a canvass and will have a report tomorrow for us."

"Great."

"And," he said looking at the siding of the house, "you went through the wall?"

"Yeah, I have a hard head."

McGaven laughed. "Glad to see that you still have your humor intact."

Katie sighed. "I think we need to go back to the beginning."

"You mean..."

"The Dayton farm."

We will meet again, Detective...

FORTY-EIGHT

Wednesday 0930 hours

Katie drove to the Pine Valley Sheriff's Department in her own Jeep, still reeling from last night. She was relieved that her Jeep was running smoothly and didn't have any maintenance issues from the downhill trek except a replacement of her windshield after the guy in the truck ran her off the road.

McGaven had called her earlier and said that Detective Hamilton wanted to meet with both of them. The morning was turning out to be getting better and better, she thought sourly. Her body ached and she had a couple of bandages covering some minor cuts from the scuffle last night.

Even with everything she had been dealing with, her thoughts weren't ever far away from Chad. She had only talked with him once since he had left. Her heart always ached, but she managed to keep her mind busy, suppressing that emotional pain. When her thoughts turned inward, she reminded herself that there were victims who needed justice.

Katie hurried into the forensic division and could hear voices—it was unusual because the area was generally quiet.

She went directly to their command center. Detective Hamilton and McGaven were already discussing the cases. She was a bit annoyed that they had started without her—but maybe her irritation was based on the lack of sleep.

"Morning," she said.

"Hey, good morning," said McGaven. He seemed to be rested and ready to go.

"Detective," said Hamilton as he nodded his greeting.

Katie looked at the board and the maps of the Dayton farm and Capital Stables. "Do we have an ID yet on the skeleton at the stables?"

"Not yet. And we're having some difficulties finding any information on Thomas Dayton's wife or girlfriend."

"What about Desiree?" she said. "If the body was Dayton's wife or girlfriend, maybe she's Desiree's mom. What about DNA?"

"That's what we're in the process of checking. It takes time, I'm afraid." He paused and looked at both detectives. His expression was serious. "I wanted to talk to you both. You know the shooting victim in front of your house has been identified as Roland Danner."

Katie nodded. "Have you found anything out yet? Matching ballistics?"

"Nothing in the system yet." He pulled some paperwork from a file. "I wanted you two to know everything because it involves your previous cases and Chad." He handed copies to Katie. "I want to keep everything transparent."

"Thanks," she said as she skimmed the list. "So, this is a list from his residence. It says that he had instructions to kill me."

"What?" said McGaven as he read over her shoulder.

"So let me get this straight," she began. "The guy who worked for Lane as a security consultant with Hyde was the jailer for Chad. He was ordered to kill me, but someone killed him first."

McGaven looked at Hamilton. "How does that work?"

Hamilton took a few seconds before he answered. It was unclear if he didn't know the answer or if he was trying to figure out how to relay the information. "It seems Danner was covering all his bases and keeping tabs on what you knew."

"Or wanted to kill her," said McGaven.

"I want you to know," he said looking at Katie. "We're doing everything we can to find out who killed him, but..."

"But you think that it might be possible it's connected to our current case with Thomas Dayton," she said.

He nodded. "I wanted to give you a heads-up before I submit a report to the sheriff."

"Thanks. I appreciate that," said Katie.

"Too many things have been happening to you—the truck and then the shooting in front of your house. Also the shooting at the Dayton property. All of these things have been happening since you've been investigating your current case. You're on the radar front and center. No way it's a coincidence. These previous cases seem to run into your current ones—and especially with Chad in the mix."

"I agree," said McGaven.

"I'm sure you realize this... but you know the sheriff is going to want to put a special detail at your residence," said Hamilton.

"And more," added McGaven.

"Of course," she said. Katie knew that things were coming to a head—and it depended on how they wanted to play it what was going to happen next.

"Thanks for keeping us in the loop," said McGaven.

"And we're working as fast as we can along with forensics," said Hamilton.

"Which means that we need to find Dayton before anything more happens." Katie knew they were running out of time but didn't need to remind her partner.

. . .

Katie and McGaven surveyed the contents of the boxes that had belonged to Dayton, which were found in the garage on the rental property. John had brought in a temporary folding table where the articles of clothing were laid out flat and like items had been grouped together. Two pairs of jeans, four sweaters, five T-shirts, two coats, four bras, six pairs of panties, along with a dog leash and a collar.

"What do we have?" said McGaven.

John joined them. "With the preliminary tests, we know that there are various DNA profiles on most of the items."

Katie was afraid that they had belonged to several different women. "What about the sizes?"

"Interestingly, they are all within two sizes, meaning that the women they belonged to were about the same size."

"Have you been able to lift any trace evidence?" she said.

"We have." John moved to the sweaters. "We found two hair samples and some type of carpet fibers. And three droplets of blood."

"Was there any root attached to the hair?"

"No, but we can tell that one of them was dyed but the other was natural."

Katie sighed. She was disappointed. "So, you won't be able to identify who the hair belonged to unless you have something to compare it to."

"True. But..."

Katie and McGaven stared at the forensic supervisor.

"But... we were able to determine from the blood that they belonged to two different women... and they were related by mitochondrial DNA. Mitochondrial DNA is the circular chromosome located inside the cell structure itself in the mitochondria. It's found in what's called the cytoplasm. Children inherit mitochondria—and as a result mitochondrial DNA—from their mothers."

"Mother," said Katie. "Could it be Desi's mom?"

"Hard to say until we know more, which of course will take time. But that's a fair assessment," said John.

That changed everything. Katie knew they were on the right track, and they needed to keep going—pushing forward and following every lead.

"I'll keep you guys posted when I find out more," said John.

FORTY-NINE

Wednesday 1 1 30 hours

Katie and McGaven arrived at the Dayton farm once again in McGaven's truck, loaded in the back with tools for anything they might need.

McGaven pulled the truck farther into the property in a strategic location where they could view all the locations—houses, barn, stables, drainage area, and back exit. He cut the engine and sat looking out in every direction using his binoculars.

"Maybe we should have requested a deputy to watch our backs," said McGaven.

"We'll be fine. I have your back," she said.

"You know I have yours." He viewed his text messages. "It looks like Farrell is out of the hospital and back home with a Springfield officer watching his place."

Katie thought it was good news and wondered if Chris Farrell had told them everything or if he'd led them into a trap. Nothing on his cell phone indicated otherwise, but there was still a nagging feeling, even though small, that he could be involved.

"Where do you want to start?" said McGaven.

"At the—"

"Beginning?"

She smiled at her partner. "You got it."

McGaven turned over the engine. "Then we need to park close to the main house." He drove over and parked in front of the porch.

They got out and cautiously entered the main farmhouse.

Once inside, Katie said, "So are we allowed to tear up walls and floors?"

"Probably not, but if we need to..."

"We do it," she said. "We need to scrutinize the walls and doorways and even how the floors shore up to the walls."

McGaven was looking around already—section by section.

"Let's split up and cover more areas." Katie was also paying close attention to the structure and how it connected. If there were any tunnel accesses, the house would reveal it if she knew where to look. She had wanted to bring Cisco but with everything that had happened, she decided to keep him safe at home.

"Sounds good," he said.

It was unlikely to Katie, but she checked the bedrooms once again. Everything was still left the way it was the first time she was there with the exception of spray-painted numbers and black fingerprint powder. She bypassed the remnants left behind from forensics and focused on finding some anomaly about the house, indicating a possible entrance to a tunnel. It seemed like the right thing to try to figure out—but now she wondered if they were on a wild goose chase.

Katie went over every inch of the bedrooms—walls, floor, ceiling, closet. Nothing. She was about to return to the main part of the house but thought she should check the bathroom. It was highly unlikely, but she wasn't going to use this time to search the houses and not check every area.

The door was closed. She thought it had always been open when they had been there before, but forensics or patrol might have closed it. She could hear McGaven moving around in the living room and kitchen. It sounded like he was opening cabinets.

She opened the bathroom door, which stuck part way. She pushed hard, the hinges squeaking. It was a good-size bathroom as it was the only one in the house. Upper storage cabinets and the small sink had been removed, but the toilet and clawfoot tub were still intact without any chips or cracks.

The large tub caught her eye. It had dirt inside along the bottom, which seemed strange. Where did the dark soil come from? She touched the silver faucet and turned it—to her surprise the water was active and flowed freely. It must've been from one of the water towers, but it should have been disconnected a long time ago. And the age of the water that had been sitting for years was concerning.

Katie searched the room starting with the floors, walls, and then around the bathroom fixtures. There was nothing indicating anything unusual, or an entrance to the tunnels, if they existed.

She turned to leave and looked back at the tub. Was it her imagination that the placement of the freestanding tub was too far from the wall? She bent down and examined the floor around it. There were clean places and some deep grooves. Running her fingers along these areas, Katie realized that there was something more to it.

"Gav," she said. "Gav!"

McGaven appeared in the doorway. "Find something?"

"I'm not sure. You've done some bathroom renovations before, right?"

"Yeah, just some replacement of stuff in my house. It was so old that I had to replace sinks, fixtures, and redo a shower."

"Take a look at this," she said, moving away from the back part of the tub. "What do you think?"

McGaven bent down, looking at the tub and then how it was installed. "I think you're right. Something is strange."

Katie joined him. "Right here," she said, showing him. "What is this?"

"Let me see." McGaven pulled out his pocketknife and pried away the linoleum flooring near the wall. Underneath was an old service entrance to under the house.

"Is that for the bathroom installation or something else?" she said.

"Not sure, but it seems odd." McGaven kept looking. "See this?" he said.

"What is that? Are those some kind of hinges?"

McGaven maneuvered, scraped, and then pushed the tub over onto its side. "Check this out."

Katie couldn't believe she was standing in the middle of a single bathroom with a freestanding tub that opened a doorway to below the house.

"I think you were right about tunnels," said McGaven.

"Has this been open recently, do you think?" she said.

"I don't think so. It was difficult to open. Probably hadn't been in a while." He stood up. "I'm going to grab a couple of flashlights and some tools. I'll be right back."

Katie waited. She wondered when and who used the tunnel last. Was it Dayton? They needed to see where it went, if anywhere. Just because there was a tunnel or basement access, it didn't mean that it connected to other areas on the farm.

McGaven returned and gave her a flashlight. "You ready?" he asked.

"Yes. Did you tell anyone we were here today?"

"I mentioned it to Hamilton, and I told John."

"Okay."

"You worried about going down there?"

"Not really, but just thinking ahead," she said.

"We'll be fine. If there is anything that seems sketchy and unsafe, we'll immediately backtrack and get out."

Katie moved forward, sat on the floor, and turned the flashlight on, aiming it into the hole. It was larger than she had envisioned. There was no mistaking that it was an entrance into an underground area. It was old, but it was constructed in a way that made it solid and structured. "It looks fine." She eased herself down and dropped to the ground about six or seven feet down. It looked like there had been some type of ladder at one time—there were a few handholds and footholds left so that they could get out.

It was difficult for Katie not to think about those graves on the property. Those tortured, battered, and thrown-away victims. She couldn't seem to get those images out of her mind. The battered, broken, decomposing bodies exhibiting the horrifying things that one man could do would probably be forever burned in her memory.

"You okay?" said McGaven from above.

"It's fine. It'll be a bit tight for you."

"Don't worry about me," he said and dropped in next to her. Due to his height, it was a close fit.

Katie fanned out the light beam, which showed a straight tunnel that seemed endless. The sides were reinforced with rock, which was in line with what Shane had told her at the county courthouse. As she walked, she imagined what it was like for farmers from another era and how these tunnels connected the farms.

Katie kept walking and McGaven strode behind her. She could hear his boots and heavy footsteps echoing in the long chamber.

"Looks like we're heading toward the guesthouse," he said.

"I was just thinking the same thing."

Katie realized that the air wasn't stuffy, which meant there was some type of venting, but it wasn't obvious. Was it something that had been installed originally or was it something more recent?

Katie was about to reach the end of the tunnel when she stepped on something. She stopped and bent down.

"What is that?" McGaven said.

Katie stood up and revealed shackles, holding them by one finger. "These aren't antique in any way."

"Is that blood?"

"I don't know."

Katie put them back where she had found them. "Let's finish the walk and then call John."

"Okay." McGaven's voice now sounded strained, nothing lighthearted about the tone.

Katie continued to move toward the end where she saw a remnant of a chain from a necklace hanging, gently moving. The flashlight shined back at them, reflecting off something. Her mind jumped back to Abigail and her broken body in the fifty-five-gallon drum. She shivered. The images seemed to be getting more intense as their investigation continued. She didn't care about her own safety—she wanted to find Dayton.

When the detectives reached the end, there was an intact metal ladder leading up. Katie thought they must be going to come up in the field somewhere.

McGaven went first. He easily ascended the ladder and when he got to the top, which was a little bit higher than back at the farmhouse bathroom area, he took some time banging against the opening with a pipe he had as Katie watched and waited.

Finally, McGaven was able to open the exit. Light spilled down. They weren't outside—Katie could see some type of a cabinet or door.

"Hey," he said. "We're inside the guesthouse at the built-in cabinet. Actually, right at the location we were sitting when there was a shooter outside." He climbed out.

Once inside, Katie remembered vividly the day of the shooting. They were held against the side of the guesthouse. She looked around with a new understanding, now knowing the tunnels led from one house to the next.

"Looks like we need to get John and Eva out here," said McGaven. "With cover officers."

"I was thinking the same thing. And we need to make sure there aren't any more tunnels."

"We'll let the experts do that under controlled conditions. It might lead to someone else."

"Who else would it be?"

"Well, you never know. We have no idea how many other potential victims there could be here. The tunnel is dirt. Maybe there could be bones along there."

McGaven looked around as if he was looking at the guesthouse for the first time. "Anything is possible."

Katie's cell phone rang. "Detective Scott," she said, listening intently. "But... how?" She remained quiet. Slowly returning the phone to her pocket, her expression was grim.

"What?" said McGaven.

"That was corrections. They said the DA had released Ferris Baldwin shortly after we spoke with him."

"What? Why?"

"We didn't have the authority to continue to hold him there. The best they could do was send patrol by his place. He might already be in the wind."

"That's not good."

"Not when it seems like someone is trying to clean up loose ends. We need to keep everyone safe. Start calling everyone and tracking their locations."

An anxious look crossed McGaven's face. "Lara..."

FIFTY

Katie stood with Cisco at the Dayton property in front of the main house. She had watched John and Eva search every inch of the tunnels, removing various implements—cutting tools, scissors, and more shackles—for testing and searching for fingerprints. The evidence was mounting, but the suspect wasn't anywhere to be found.

We will meet again, Detective...

Katie had quickly gone home, picked up Cisco, and made several phone calls to track their witnesses and potential persons of interest, making sure of their whereabouts. Ferris Baldwin wasn't answering his phone or returning text messages. She knew he was a bit scattered and potentially a flight risk, but there was nothing they could do to make him stay if he didn't want to.

McGaven joined his partner. "Lara is safe and back at home." There was a revolving patrol duty outside that would watch the apartments where she lived.

Katie stared at the farmhouse almost as if she expected

Dayton to casually walk out onto the porch. She could feel his presence and believed the man who ambushed her at the dead-drop location in Springfield was indeed him. But she hated not having proof or evidence to undoubtedly say so.

"What's on your mind?" McGaven asked.

"I'm not really sure what to think," she said.

"You mean Katie Scott is stumped?"

"Not stumped but overloaded with events and evidence."

"Yeah, I get that."

"It's this place." She looked around. "There's so much death and torture. Heartache. Uncertainty. But there's also control and agony. And now forgotten..."

"Wow, when you put it like that... it's really depressing."

"Did you contact Chris Farrell?" she said.

"He was just released from the hospital and is back home."

"Hopefully he won't run," she said.

John approached the detectives. It was hard to read his moods or expressions at times. Katie thought he looked like he had some news, but it was difficult to determine if it was good or bad.

"Did you find anything else?" she asked.

"No, but we were able to extract some fingerprints besides yours," said John.

"Why do I get the feeling you have more news?" she said.

"I do. I just received word from the ME's office that the Jane Doe from Capital Stables has been officially identified as Carla Simone Davenport."

"Oh."

"They were able to find her prints in the military database after they determined who she was from dental records."

"She was in the military?"

"Yes. And that record said she listed her daughter as Desiree Dayton at this address."

Katie felt chills run down her spine. Her instinct had been correct. It was Desiree's mom.

"That's great," said McGaven. "It's another link. Any other evidence from the body?"

"Nothing that could be tested due to the decomposition of the remains, just the clothes she wore. Her neck had been broken, which means it's officially a homicide."

"Why hadn't anyone reported her missing?" she said.

"Maybe no one knew. From the estimation of death, it seems she died between ten to fifteen years ago," said John.

"That would mean she died before Desiree," she said.

"Maybe she was getting close to finding out what Dayton was up to," said McGaven.

"John, can you make sure we get a copy of the reports?"

"Of course. I'll keep you updated." He nodded and turned to finish up with the collection of evidence.

Katie walked toward the house with Cisco staying close to her side. Her thoughts filed through the list of people of interest and victims they'd discovered during the investigation.

- *Lara Fontaine*
- *Abigail Andrews*
- *Thomas Dayton*
- *Desiree Dayton*
- *Ferris Baldwin*
- *Chris Farrell*
- *Carla Davenport*
- *Roland Danner*

Their connections to one another told a story.

"What's going on in that complicated head of yours?" said McGaven.

Katie shook her head. "There's something big we're missing. I mean really big."

"Okay, I'll follow... like what?"

"I don't know. But you know me, I always feel that we should go back to the beginning with the first girl who was found—Abigail Andrews."

"It's always worked in the past."

Katie nodded.

We will meet again, Detective...

FIFTY-ONE

Wednesday 2345 hours

Katie tossed and turned in bed for more than an hour. Everything was flooding her mind and wouldn't shut off no matter how hard she tried. In fact, the more she tried, the more things inundated her conscience. She was psychologically drowning. Her cases and Chad were taking over her life—it was most likely why she wasn't seeing things clearly and objectively. She never wanted to lose that ability to see details, infer clues and timelines, and find the killers.

She flung back her covers and slipped on a hoodie over her pajamas.

Cisco grumbled from his warm comfortable position in the big chair in the corner of the bedroom. He watched Katie but didn't move.

There was an urgency tightening her stomach and almost suppressing her breath. Katie didn't want anything to happen to any of the people involved in the investigation—including her and McGaven. It was almost as if she were fighting something she couldn't see, couldn't touch, and couldn't find. It haunted her, but at the same time it taunted her to keep going.

Katie turned on the lights and went to the front door where she had brought home copies of the cases in a bankers box. She picked up the box and headed to the spare bedroom, which was still set up as a command center of sorts. Her laptop sat on the desk. She reread the notes from the other night with Nick, McGaven, and Denise. It made her smile. There were such great ideas there, and they had actually led her to the post office in Springfield.

It was barely past midnight when Katie began to lay out photos, property drawings, autopsy reports, witness statements, and interviews. She made new notes based on her perceptions of the events in the investigation, beginning with Lara's suicide attempt on the bridge, then moving to McGaven's interview with Detective Jamison about Abigail Andrews, to the skeletal remains at Capital Stables, the ambush in Springfield, and the evidence of torture and murder at the Dayton farm.

Katie looked at photos and property maps of each location. She was looking for something that didn't belong or even a weird anomaly.

The only photo they were able to locate of Thomas Dayton was an old driver's license photo. It appeared that he had never renewed it. Katie stared at his face, his eyes, and the subtle smirk of his mouth. She couldn't take her eyes away from his— even though she had never seen him in person. The feeling that she knew this man and what he was capable of was embedded in her soul. This monster, not really different from the many others she had come face to face with, made her feel different somehow.

She grabbed the other photos and lined them up with people of interest on one side and victims on the other. The only photo she didn't have was Carla Davenport, Desiree's mother. Taking several minutes to look at each person, Katie then ran the timelines of the events and murders.

These cases were a bit different from her previous cases. She almost assuredly knew who the killer was, but not how to catch him.

Was Dayton the killer?

Was she looking at the cases all wrong?

Was she just fixated on Dayton ever since they visited the farm?

Katie stood up, frustrated. She shoved the paperwork off the desk.

"Why...? What am I missing?" she whispered. So many emotions vied for her attention, and it was becoming almost obsessive, which was entirely unproductive.

Katie almost called McGaven to bounce some ideas off him but decided against it. He wouldn't appreciate being woken at this time of night. She bent down to pick up the photos and held Dayton's and Baldwin's together. She studied them closely—the placement of the eyes, nose, mouth, and cheekbones.

"Wait a minute... no..."

Katie rifled through the files and found the timelines and background of both Dayton and Baldwin. She read them through—twice. It mentioned that a Baldwin had worked for Dayton and when she keyed up more information about him, Katie realized that the time Dayton fell off the grid was also when Baldwin had terminated his employment at the farm.

"It can't be..." she said.

Had Dayton been impersonating Baldwin all this time? Was the Baldwin they'd interviewed really Dayton? He had been right in front of them at the rental stables and in the jail. He could have stayed hidden, but he wanted to see what she and McGaven knew. She remembered him acting smug during the interview, saying that Dayton would never leave the area, and that they were like brothers. Even then he was giving hints.

Katie went through the information and double-checked a few things; it all was beginning to make sense. It fit Dayton's profile of being clever and high-minded. It also made sense of how he seemed to know where they were and why he had been watching them. The ambush in Springfield was all planned—he must've waited and hoped that they would follow the clues—like leaving a trail of breadcrumbs. She didn't see the identity of the person in the truck or at the dead drop—it could have been him. She was going to find out once and for all.

Katie didn't have all the information about the shooting victim and Chad's jailer, Roland Danner. She needed his time of death. She frantically searched for Baldwin's discharge from jail. It was the only thing that didn't line up.

Why? How?

Katie found the address that the Pine Valley jail had for Ferris Baldwin: 432 Forrest Lane, Apartment C, Pine Valley.

Katie went to her bedroom and changed her clothes. She was going to that address to see if he was still there, and then would alert the authorities. She wanted to do surveillance as quietly as possible.

Cisco nudged her hand.

"No, Cisco, you have to wait here. I'll be back soon." She grabbed her jacket and made sure that she was ready—for anything.

We will meet again, Detective...

"Yes, we will."

FIFTY-TWO

Thursday 0245 hours

Katie drove by the apartment building on Forrest Lane where Ferris Baldwin resided. She turned around and came back, parking in the next block away from the building. It was almost three in the morning, so everything was dark and quiet. Most people were sound asleep.

Katie quietly shut her car door and scanned the neighborhood. She wasn't going to fall victim to the last time when she was trailing Chris Farrell in Springfield. When she felt everything was clear, she walked to the main entrance of 432 Forrest Lane.

The property was surprisingly well maintained with neat walkways and manicured flower beds. The building was two-story with more than twelve apartments on each level. She looked at the registry and spotted the name Baldwin in apartment C, first floor. At least the address was consistent with what Baldwin claimed at the jail.

Katie looked around and when she was satisfied that the area was indeed vacant, she walked to apartment C. There was a paper taped to the front door. It was a letter for maintenance to clean and shampoo the carpeting.

Katie's heart sank. That sign meant only one thing—the apartment was vacated. Dayton, aka Baldwin, was still a step ahead of the investigation. She was just not fast enough to put the pieces together.

Instinctively, she tried the door, and it was locked.

Katie walked down the hallway and around the corner. She noticed that all the lower apartments had patios and the upper ones had balconies. Looking behind her and where she had walked from, Katie then stepped off the apartments until she reached the patio of apartment C.

There was a sliding door that had a curtain pulled all the way back. She peered inside. It was empty except for some trash and a plastic trash can. Some paint cans and tools were on the kitchen counter. She tried the slider door and found it open. Lucky for her, someone had forgotten to lock it, which was an easy oversight.

Katie eased the slider open just wide enough for her to slip inside. She shut it again. Digging into her pocket, she retrieved a small flashlight. After closing the curtain so as to not attract attention, she turned the flashlight on. Immediately she walked to the trash can and looked inside. There were empty food containers and paper, but what caught her attention were some five-by-eight photos. They had been carefully crumpled and wadded up in balls, but they were still viable as Katie smoothed them out on the kitchen counter.

She directed the flashlight on them. What she saw surprised her. They were photographs of her and McGaven on the farm and another of them walking into work. One photo was of their car at Capital Stables. Dayton had been tailing them and documenting them. And why keep physical evidence of what he was doing? Wasn't that risky? It was as if he was leaving a trail for them to follow.

Katie looked around the small, one-bedroom apartment. She could see indentations on the carpet showing where a couch, chairs, and a table had been located. Sweeping the light across the walls, she found an area where there had been several thumbtack holes. By the placements and level, it appeared to be where Dayton had displayed the photos. There were eight-by-ten-inch and five-by-seven-inch positions. Why wouldn't he use his phone or a laptop?

Katie walked around the apartment thinking about what Dayton had been doing since he took over the identity of his worker. Why hadn't anything popped when he was finger-printed? She realized that he was detained and not arrested, so he wasn't printed as if he had been held in detention. He seemed to have all angles covered. Even though operating this way was risky, he still had proceeded anyway.

She leaned against the counter. Since Dayton had been following them, it made sense that he was at her house and came across Roland Danner. In Dayton's mind, he took the man out because he didn't fit in with his plans and basically got in the way. The previous and current investigations weren't a part of one another; it was just that one of them got in the way of his strategies.

Katie felt pushed into a corner and she didn't know how to get out it. Emotions were high. Her usual world seemed skewed. She needed to push back. Snapping a few photos of the apartment, documenting what and where she found the photos, Katie found a bag and slipped the photos into it.

Katie took one last look around. She was surer than ever that Dayton was masquerading as Ferris Baldwin. It was clever and he'd almost completely pulled off the charade.

Katie slipped out quietly through the sliding door and left all as it was before she had arrived. Hurrying back to her Jeep, she got behind the wheel. Her mind raced even more after what she had found out. She would wait until first thing in the morning when she met with McGaven and filled him in on everything.

Katie drove back home and hoped that she could get a few hours of sleep before morning. Things spun like an endless reel in her mind. How they were getting closer. The best way to trap Dayton. And most important, how to stop him before he took another victim.

FIFTY-THREE

Thursday 0730 hours

Katie had overslept because she'd turned off the alarm. She woke with a start. She jumped out of bed, making Cisco bark. She hurried around the house taking care of morning chores, including feeding Cisco. He showed his unhappiness at not being able to go with Katie by whining and running around near the front door.

She had called McGaven, telling him what she had found out last night and that they needed to take another direction and look at every person on their list again. She was excited and felt confident that the investigation was going to change. Finally. McGaven told her that he had to make a stop first before he would meet up with her at the office.

She was eager to put the photos and her revelation of Dayton and Baldwin into the investigation. Once inside the forensic division, Katie hurried to their office. McGaven would probably be there within the hour.

In the meantime, she added the photos and put together what they knew about Dayton and Baldwin. It was definitely clear where Dayton ended and Baldwin began. The original Baldwin had moved to Idaho; however, there was no footprint of him. It was as if he had disappeared until about five years ago when Dayton used that identity. It was clever and even ingenious, but devious. The real Baldwin was probably dead because alive wouldn't be helpful in Dayton's plan.

Katie spent two hours working and McGaven hadn't arrived yet, which she thought was unlike him. She called his cell phone, and it rang then went to voicemail. She then sent a quick text for him to call her. She sat for a moment staring at the board.

Katie picked up the phone and pressed the records division extension.

"Hey, Katie," said Denise. "What's up?"

"Hi, Denise. Have you heard from Gav?"

"No, I came in at six a.m. Why, is something wrong?"

"Oh, no, he just said he had an errand to run before coming in."

"He didn't say anything to me."

"I'm sure he'll be here soon. I just have some new information."

"Okay. Can you let me know when he gets here?"

"Of course. I'll have him call you."

"Thanks, bye."

Katie hung up. She didn't want to worry Denise. Maybe she was being over-anxious because of everything that had been going on—the things they were aware of and the things they weren't.

"Morning," said John from the doorway.

"Hi."

He walked in. "Everything okay?"

"Yeah, fine. Just waiting for Gav." She looked at the forensic supervisor. His eyes had a way of looking into your soul. There was no way to lie to him. "Have you heard from Gav this morning?"

"No. Should I?"

"I don't know."

"C'mon, tell me what's going on," he said and sat down.

Katie looked at John. She knew that they shared the bond of both being military veterans. "It's this case."

"I understand. Just being on the Dayton farm finding the bodies and those tunnels made me uncomfortable. It's unsettling. I know it must be hard for you trying to find Dayton."

Katie bit her lip as she stared at the board again.

John immediately looked at the investigation where she had added the photos from the apartment. The photographs of Thomas Dayton and Ferris Baldwin were side by side. "Wait a minute. Am I seeing what I think I'm seeing?"

"John, you are too smart for your own good."

"Are you showing that Dayton is really this Baldwin guy?" He was shocked.

Katie slowly nodded. "I can't say with one hundred percent certainty, but you know, I'm pretty sure. This takes the investigation in another direction."

"No kidding." He got up. "I'll have some more tests back this afternoon."

"Thanks, John." She knew that John was very discreet, and he knew more than he let on. He knew how important this new turn of events was in the investigation.

Katie's cell phone rang.

"Gav?" she said, not looking at the number.

"Detective Scott," said a frail voice.

"Yes, this is Detective Scott. Who is this?"

"This is Lara."

"Lara? Are you alright?" said Katie. She was worried about the young woman's safety.

"There's some man who has been following me. I'm scared."

"Is he there now?"

"I... I don't think so..."

"I'll alert patrol to check things out."

"Please, can you come over? I don't want all those police officers here. I left a message with Sean, but he hasn't called me back."

Katie looked at her watch. "I can be there in twenty minutes."

"I don't want to be taken away again."

"Lara, listen to me. No one is taking you away, okay? Keep your doors locked and don't let anyone in until I get there."

"Okay."

The call ended.

Katie was concerned, and she certainly didn't want another body added to the investigation. She was worried about Lara's fragile state. There were more questions she wanted to ask her and if Lara felt safe with her then she might fill in some blanks from that night with Abigail.

She hurried out of the office.

FIFTY-FOUR

When the journey takes you so close to the finale, you can almost taste it, hear it, see it, and feel it in your bones. Your focus becomes more intense and channeled. It's when you know that your hunches, facts, and inferences between the criminal and the victims were coming to fruition. It is all that you could think about—it is almost over.

Thursday 1100 hours

Katie found a parking place in front of Lara's apartment building on Spring Street. Looking around before exiting the police sedan, she stepped out. The area was light with traffic and pedestrians. She thought that there would be more people just before the lunch hour.

Katie hurried up the stairs and stopped in front of apartment A. She knocked. "Lara. It's Detective Scott."

The locked slowly disengaged and the door opened.

"Lara?" said Katie.

"Yes."

"You okay?"

"Please come in." The young woman was wearing pale peach pajamas, bare feet, and seemed to be sluggish and not fully coherent.

"Are you alright?" said Katie.

Lara stopped in the middle of the living room. This time the apartment was neat and tidy. She looked toward the bathroom. "I did what I could, but that's not what he wanted." She smiled. "I always do what he wants, you know."

"What *who* wants?" Katie was suspicious, but she also knew that Lara was most likely on medication and maybe she was begging for help. "Lara, please sit down and tell me what's going on. Have you seen someone following you?"

She nodded. "He watches me."

Katie made sure the front door was locked and then looked out the window. There didn't seem to be anyone suspicious. "I'll have patrol..."

"Please, Katie..." she said. "He's in here..." Lara walked to the bathroom door. It was closed. "You'll believe me now..."

Katie couldn't figure out what Lara was doing. She was obviously delusional. Katie went to the bathroom door to prove to Lara that no one was in there.

Katie opened the door.

Lying on the floor, next to the freestanding tub, on his back, was McGaven.

"Gav," said Katie and ran to her partner's aid, frantic with anxiety. His eyes were closed ,and he wasn't responding but he was breathing. Katie stood up to call for police and an ambulance. She turned toward the door sensing movement—that's when she received fifty thousand volts that thundered through her body, knocking her out.

Hours later

Katie awoke. Her head hurt and her vision was fuzzy. It was dark, as if someone had turned the lights out, but she saw that outside the small window above her it was also dark. She stared at the ceiling and remembered she was in Lara's bathroom when...

"Gav," she managed to whisper. Katie tried to get up, but her wrists and ankles had been secured. She shook her ankles, realizing that they had been tied with rope. A shooting pain telescoped up her legs and back making her head pound. "Gav..."

Katie managed to roll to her left side and could feel McGaven's body next to her.

The bathroom door burst open, and a man immediately put tape over Katie's mouth. She fought him the best she could in her condition, but it didn't help.

"Well, Detective, we do meet again," said Dayton staring down at her. His eyes were dark, almost black. The smile on his face told the entire story—he was satisfied, smug, and enjoying what he was going to do.

Katie felt McGaven stir next to her. He mumbled something that she didn't understand. Dayton walked over to him and taped his mouth, double-checking his restraints.

"Wouldn't want the big guy here to get loose."

Katie watched the man move around the small bathroom as if he were having a wonderful experience.

"I was afraid you weren't going to follow all the clues, but look, here you are. As you probably already know, I don't like messy things or loose ends. So... I'm cleaning it up."

Katie saw Lara at the doorway. She leaned in with a creepy smile on her face. "That's great, baby. Can I do anything?"

"No, darlin', you've done everything perfectly..." He smiled.

Of course, Katie thought. How could she have been so

blind? Lara may have started out as a victim, but somewhere along the way she became Dayton's companion. He knew how to manipulate a person like Lara to his advantage, making her feel needed, strong, and they could do anything together. Dayton had long-term plans and he had been executing them until Katie and McGaven came along. Now they were loose ends as well.

Katie watched Dayton move around. Her biggest fear was that he would kill them in the bathroom, dismember them, and dispose of their body parts. No doubt there were many places to hide bodies that no one would find. He had already done that with previous victims.

Katie surveyed the bathroom trying to see if there was something she could use to her advantage, but it was very small and there was nothing except the usual towel racks and the door hardware.

There was a strange sound approaching. It sounded like wheels running along the floor. It became louder as it neared.

Lara entered with a large rolling laundry bag.

Dayton whistled and hummed as if he were just doing some chores. He pushed the large carrier up to Katie. She knew what they were going to do.

It took about fifteen minutes for Dayton with the help of Lara to load Katie and McGaven into the rolling laundry hamper. It was a tight fit. She faced McGaven who was awake and alert. His eyes kept hers and she knew that he was waiting for the right moment as well. For now, they had to go with the plan. She fidgeted, trying to loosen her restraints, but it was no use. There was no way that she could free herself at the moment.

Dayton leaned in and smiled before he covered the detectives with blankets.

Katie wouldn't forget anytime soon the sneer on Dayton's face like he had already won the battle. It was just beginning.

Her head was beginning to clear, and she concentrated on how long it took before they were loaded into a vehicle—she assumed it was a truck but couldn't be sure. She was running possible scenarios through her mind of how they could escape and what chances they had. It was grim.

They traveled for what seemed like half an hour along very bumpy roads before they stopped and parked. Nothing happened. No one pulled them out. There were no voices.

Katie had managed to get the tape from her mouth by rubbing up against the side of the laundry carrier. She scooted around trying to free her hands.

"Gav," she whispered. "I'm working on freeing my hands. You okay?"

He grunted a "Yes."

"We're going to get out of this," she said. It was more to herself than to McGaven. She was scared and feeling the squeeze of claustrophobia settling in. Fighting back the tears and growing panic, she was ready for battle when it came down to it. She felt her partner move, trying to free his hands.

Suddenly the vehicle shook with them in it. The sound of the tailgate opening cut through the quiet. They were being moved and their time was running out...

FIFTY-FIVE

Thursday 1915 hours

Denise hurried into the forensic division at the Pine Valley Sheriff's Department and made her way to John's office.

"John, I'm so glad you're still here," she said frantically. "I didn't know what else to do. If I should call 911 or go directly to the sheriff. Or..."

"Denise, what's wrong?"

"I don't know. I haven't been able to get a hold of Gav all day. I talked with Katie early this morning and haven't heard from her since. No calls. No texts. Nothing. Something is wrong. Very wrong."

"Take a breath. Sit down. We'll figure this out, okay?" said John. His face clouded and his concern deepened. He tried calling the detectives with the same result as Denise.

"What should we do?" she said.

John went to the detectives' command center and looked around trying to decipher where Katie would have gone and where they were in the investigation.

"What are you looking for?" she said.

"Not sure. I'm trying to see the last thing that Katie was looking at and where she might have gone." He searched papers and looked at the case board. "Wait a minute. She was looking at Thomas Dayton and Ferris Baldwin as the same person."

"Let me see."

"She said she hadn't talked to Gav either, but she left not long after I spoke with her. It was about eleven a.m."

"You don't think she went after this guy?"

"We're talking about Katie."

"But she would have Gav with her, right?" she said.

"Since they are both not picking up, I'd say something is going on." He looked at the board. "And I think I know where to start. Denise, you go home and stay there in case he contacts you. I'm going to look for them."

"But..."

"It's going to be fine, and I'll take backup with me. I'll let you know what I find out."

FIFTY-SIX

Thursday 2030 hours

Katie and McGaven helplessly rode in the laundry carrier, feeling steps and uneven flooring beneath them. The echoing sounds of the stainless wheels rolling over hardwood floors were the only thing they could hear. Katie tried to figure out where they were but there were only a few places she could think they could be. And she didn't want to think about the consequences of where they were going.

The laundry transporter suddenly stopped.

Katie expected that they were going to be shot and then buried. She tried to remain strong and brace for whatever was coming at them. She heard the voices of Dayton and Lara talking. He was saying something about their stash at the rental stables—that was the place where they had first come in contact with Dayton but of course didn't know it at the time. It angered her that they tried to help "Ferris Baldwin" and kept him in protective custody for a while. In the meantime, when he was locked away, Lara had been free to follow his orders.

The blankets were ripped away and the dim lighting was a

welcome vision. There were flashlight lanterns around. A petite brunette woman was lying in the corner—she appeared to be unconscious. It took Katie only a few seconds to recognize the woman from her missing person's report. It was Theresa Simms, and she was still alive. Some partial relief washed over Katie, but it didn't last long.

Katie wasn't shocked that they were in the bathroom in the Dayton farmhouse. It was one of the places she thought they would have been taken to.

"Well, Detectives, this is the end of the line," Dayton said. He leaned forward and ripped away the tape across McGaven's mouth.

"You really think that no one is going to know where we are?" Katie said.

"Nope."

Katie laughed. She was dying inside and scared, but she didn't want Dayton to know that. "So typical."

"Detective, I know all about you and your techniques." He opened the entrance to the tunnels below. "I do my research and I've been studying you for a while. Your last cases..." His eyes lit up. "And your poor boyfriend who got caught in the crossfire and then you couldn't find him. I'm so sorry," he said trying to sound sad, but then he laughed too.

Katie knew he was trying to bait her, but she tried to remain calm even though her body was betraying her with a heightened pulse and a tingling sensation in her extremities. "You're so transparent. You think by killing all these people that you'll eventually be free. You'll never be free. Because your sickness and fantasies will never cease. You will always have to have another victim."

He grabbed McGaven, which was difficult at first, but Dayton managed to shove him into the tunnel. She heard her partner cry out in pain when he landed. Katie wanted to kill

Dayton at that moment, but she knew that if they wanted to survive she had to keep her wits and her head on track.

He then dragged over Theresa's body and pushed her into the hole. Katie wasn't sure if she was alive or dead.

Dayton sneered at her. "Such a pity that you're so attractive, but you're a cop. No loss."

"Coming from a man who would kill his own daughter."

He stopped. For a moment, Katie thought he would strangle her right then. Instead, he said, "Not everyone is fit for life, especially when it doesn't fit into mine. She was a liability, asking too many questions about her mother."

"And you are fit for life?" Katie said.

"Oh, yeah." He picked her up, dropped her on the floor, and then slowly dragged her across the room. "Bye-bye, my sweet." Dayton then dropped Katie into the tunnel.

Katie hit hard, but she managed to protect her head. She could see McGaven lying on his side. "Gav?"

"I think my arm is broken," he mumbled.

Katie sat up, looking toward the opening above them just as the hatch shut and locked, throwing them into darkness. She couldn't see much but remembered the tunnel and knew which direction led to the guesthouse.

Katie scooted toward her partner. "Can you sit up?"

"I think so," he said, groaning in pain until he sat next to her.

"Do you have anything that we can use to cut these ropes?"

"I have a small retractable blade in my pocket."

"Front pocket?"

"Yeah," he barely said. His energy was dwindling, and his voice was becoming almost a whisper.

There was a soft moaning. Katie knew it was Theresa. Some relief washed over her that the woman was still alive.

"Do you have anything else? Like a phone?"

"Nope. You?"

"Nope."

"We'll make do, right?"

"Okay, work with me," she said.

"What else do I have to do right now?"

Katie turned her back to her partner and maneuvered herself so she could reach into his pocket. It took several tries, but she was able to retrieve the pocketknife. "Got it."

"What's going on?" said Theresa. Her voice sounded as if she was having difficulties speaking.

"It's okay. We're police detectives and we're going to get out of here."

"Please..." she kept moaning.

Katie spent almost ten minutes trying to cut the ropes around her wrists. She was thankful that she wasn't shackled, which would have been impossible to escape from.

Strange pounding noises started up from somewhere on the farm. The ground vibrated around them.

"What is that?" she said. The darkness made everything seem surreal and it was difficult to determine where the sounds were coming from. The tunnel made noises echo.

"I'm not sure." McGaven's voice seemed so far away and ever weakening.

Katie managed to break through her restraints. She quickly reached out to find McGaven and worked his restraints.

"Uh," he said in pain.

"I'm sorry, Gav, but I need to free you."

Katie worked quickly and finally freed her partner. She then untied her ankles. "Okay, are you free?"

"Not yet."

"Let me help you."

Katie wrestled with her partner's restraints until he was completely free as well.

"Lara called me and seemed distraught," he said, breathing

hard. "Then when I got there they ambushed me. So stupid. I should've known better."

"Gav, I got blindsided too. I didn't see it until it was too late." She got to her feet using the sides of the tunnel as support and giving some idea to which direction they were going to head. "Last night, I realized that Dayton was masquerading as Ferris Baldwin. That's what I wanted to talk to you about this morning."

"And?"

"He's very clever," she said.

"Not as clever as you, obviously. You figured it out."

"Uh, well look where we are now—but it was only a matter of time. C'mon, let's get to the other side and see if we can get out."

"Then what?"

Katie stopped and checked out McGaven's arm. He flinched and tried not to cry out. "You must've landed on it when you hit. Wait..." she said. Katie took off her belt and made it into a makeshift sling for McGaven. "Here, put this on." She worked with him until it was secured, keeping his arm as immobile as possible. Feeling his body tensing, she knew he was in extreme pain. "We're going to get out of here."

"Please..." said the woman again.

Katie made her way to her. "Are you Theresa Simms?"

"Yeah," she said in a low voice. "How did you know that?"

"Right now I need you to stay calm and move with us. Okay? Can you do that?" said Katie.

"I think so," she said, standing up.

"Are you hurt?"

"Uh, no, I'm okay. Just a really bad headache. I've been drugged and moved, and then I don't know..." She began to cry.

"It's okay. Hold on to my arm. We're going to the end of the tunnel. Okay?"

The detectives with Theresa in tow began moving slowly

toward the other end. It was pitch dark, but Katie used her memory as a guide as they inched forward.

There was a huge boom from above and the sound of pounding.

They stopped and listened.

"What is that?" said McGaven.

"What's happening?" said Theresa.

"I'm not sure."

The sound became louder, like a low rumble of an earthquake. Then Katie realized what it was. It wasn't an earthquake; it was water. To Katie's horror she realized that the water tanks were being emptied into the tunnel.

"Dayton is emptying the water towers!"

FIFTY-SEVEN

Thursday 2230 hours

The hammering of the water filling the tunnel was deafening, making it difficult for Katie to have a conversation with McGaven without yelling at each other. They kept moving forward—now a little bit faster.

Katie could feel McGaven weakening next to her, but she still felt Theresa clutching her arm. They all kept close, but she didn't know how long he would have the strength to walk with two people. The water was muddying the bottom making it difficult to trudge through. Her shoes were soaking wet in ankle-deep water, and she began to shiver from the cold. Not wanting to experience what the tunnel was like under water, she kept them moving as fast as they could, holding tight together.

"What happens if we can't get out through the exit door?" said McGaven.

"Can't worry about that now. We'll figure that out when, and if, that happens." She knew that McGaven was right. Dayton would have made sure they couldn't get out, but there was a solid metal ladder that could keep them out of the water flow—at least for now. There was only so much water in the towers and she hoped that they wouldn't fill the entire tunnel.

McGaven started to fade in his strength. His body weakened, making it difficult for him to stand up straight. He was breathing heavily when he spoke.

"Gav," said Katie when she felt him waver. "Theresa, you're going to have to help me with him."

"I'm okay. I don't want to slow you down. Maybe you should go ahead," he said.

"No, I'm not leaving you behind. We all go together."

They continued to move ahead. It seemed ten times longer than when they had been there previously. The water was beginning to rise almost a foot, which was higher than Katie had estimated. She also noticed that the walls were crumbling in areas, leaving behind pieces of rock and more mud.

"We're almost there," she said, trying to sound optimistic. With every passing minute, it was becoming more futile. It was much more difficult to breathe, and she felt her own strength begin to diminish.

Katie ran into the exit area and felt blindly for the metal ladder. The loud sound of the water and the pitch-black conditions perpetuated the sense of dizziness and being in a watery abyss. It was easy to lose her sense of balance and direction between the loud water and the darkness.

Katie's fingertips touched the ladder. Her relief settled in. "Gav, stay here. I'm going to climb up." She turned to Theresa. "Stay right here, okay?"

"Okay," she said.

Katie hated leaving her partner, but she had to see if they could get out through the other entrance. There was just a hint of light seeping around the shut door. As she climbed to the top, her enthusiasm began to fade.

The water continued to pour into the tunnel. It was getting colder, chilling her to the bone.

Katie reached the top of the ladder, relieved to not be wading through water, but the opening wouldn't move. She ran her fingers around the edge of the opening. She hammered until her hands bled. It wouldn't move. There was something reinforcing it. "No!" She hammered against the trap door in frustration. She wasn't going to give up and they weren't going to submit to a watery grave. She pushed away happy memories of her parents, her uncle, and Chad. It was all becoming too much.

Katie flashed back to the first time they walked the tunnel, and she remembered part of an old shovel lying on its side about halfway into the passageway. If she could get to it maybe she could open the door.

She climbed back down to McGaven and Theresa. "I'm going back to get that old shovel."

"There won't be time at this rate," McGaven said.

"You can't leave us," said Theresa.

The water was almost three feet deep. There was another huge boom, and more water entered the tunnel—obviously the second water tank emptying.

"Katie, you can't do this," he said.

"We don't have a choice. Can you climb up the ladder?"

"Yeah, I can." His voice didn't sound reassuring.

"Theresa, can you follow him?"

"I think so."

Katie helped McGaven and made sure he was in a secure spot before she left him. She could tell that his right arm was painful, and he needed medical attention. Everything now weighed on her ability to get them out before the water filled the tunnel.

She felt Theresa climb up and take hold.

The atmosphere was black as night, and it felt as if she was entering the ocean when there was no moon or sun. The water was high enough for her to swim, making it easier than slogging through the muddied water. She gauged the distance in her mind and stopped at a spot she estimated where the shovel might be. Holding her breath, she dove under the water, feeling around. Nothing. Maybe she was mistaken? Katie made several attempts and wasn't going to give up. She had to find it. There was no other choice.

Taking a few moments to catch her breath before she dove under the water again, Katie pushed her hands along the muddy bottom kicking her feet to propel her forward. The freezing temperature made her entire body numb and her vision was strangely dreamlike in between the chattering of her teeth when she came up for air. It was difficult to keep her wits and trying to focus on if she was up, down, or upside down. Nausea began to set in.

Katie took another dive, and her hand touched a wooden handle. She used both hands on the shovel and heaved it to the surface. The water was now four-foot high and pieces of the tunnel sides were cascading into the water, making it murky and filled with rocks. She felt the jagged pieces hit her torso, arms, and face. She was mostly numb, so at least the impacts didn't really hurt.

Katie hurried as fast as she could to return to where McGaven waited precariously. She felt the ladder rungs and where her partner hung on. The water had almost reached him.

"You find it?" he said.

"Yeah."

Katie climbed past her partner to the top again and began to pound the opening. She spent several minutes until she had to rest from exertion. It wouldn't budge. The wooden handle began to splinter and if she tried any longer it would split into pieces.

Katie was defeated. Tears rolled down her cheeks, but she couldn't tell because she was soaking wet. Her clothes were sopped against her body and her feet were freezing inside her boots. This couldn't be it. She wasn't going to accept it. Never.

They were not going out like this. She had never given up—and now wasn't going to be the first time.

Katie felt McGaven's hand on her ankle.

"It's okay," he said.

"No! It's not!" she said.

Katie made her way down to McGaven and Theresa.

"Katie, you've done everything you could. Only a miracle will save us now."

She hugged him. "I'm going to find a way out until my last breath. Got it?" Katie ran everything through her mind about the tunnel and the property. The houses, barn, and acreage. And the basement.

"The basement," she said.

"What about it?"

"It led to the drainage."

"So?"

"So, it was a way to run the water in case of flooding. And when they originally built this tunnel..."

"They had to have had some way to drain the water..."

"That's right," she said. "It would be near one of the entrances, right? I'm going to see if I can find it."

Katie took a few deep breaths and jumped into the water. It didn't shock her system as it did before because she was already so cold. She moved around near the wall area by the ladder. Her hands rubbed the wall from the bottom to the water's surface. She came up for air and then dove again. This time she found an indentation that was approximately the size of the entrances to the tunnel. She used her fingertips and the wall began to crumble underneath them. Small rocks and dirt began to fall into the water.

Katie came up and the water level was up to McGaven's waist. Theresa hung on as the water rose. "I think I found it."

She took another deep breath and dove in again. This time

she used the shovel to move all the years of dirt and corrosion away from the porthole.

Katie had to come up for air several times until she was able to break through the water exit. First it was a few inches as the water fought against her—then she opened it all the way.

She came up, treading water. "It's open," she said, gasping for air. However, the water wasn't exiting as fast as she thought it should. Watching the water rise, she said, "Gav, we're going to have to go through the exit first." She was breathing hard, and the cold was beginning to get to her. "You okay, Theresa?"

"I don't know... the water..."

"I know, we're going to get out," said Katie.

"How do we know if it's even draining on the property?" said McGaven.

Katie didn't, but they had to try.

"I don't know if I can hold my breath that long with this arm," he said.

Katie thought about that too.

"And we don't know if Dayton is waiting for us."

"No," she said. "He's long gone. I'd bet on it."

"I hope you're right."

"C'mon, Theresa. We all go together." She waited until she felt Theresa's hand on her arm. "Let's go!"

The water was still rising, and they had to act now while they still had the energy.

McGaven took a couple of steps down and then submerged into the water. He began treading as best he could with the help of Katie.

"Okay," she said. "I'll go first. You follow by hanging onto me. Theresa, you do the same."

"Hey," he said, touching her face because he couldn't really see her.

"We're getting out of here, Gav. I promise you." She hugged her partner tight as the memories of their cases rushed in. "You ready? It's going to be like the blind following the blind, but the flow of the drainage will help take us in the right direction."

"Let's do this," he said.

Katie went first and quickly made her way through the escape door. She could feel McGaven holding on to her foot as they moved through, and Theresa's grip was on her arm. They could come up for air with inches of space and then swim back through.

It seemed like they weren't going in the right direction, but she saw some light and thought she could smell the fields outside. Even though it was nighttime, there was still some light. It was like there was some type of phantom helping them through the drainage—gently pushing them to safety.

All three of them came up for air in the pockets and then continued. None of them said anything, wanting to keep their energy up.

Katie felt the water lower around her to a point where she could almost stand up and walk. Then she saw the landscape and knew that they were almost out. She stood up and stumbled toward the field area. Relief overtook her. She didn't know if she was going to laugh or cry or both. Theresa was still at her side. Katie made sure she was able to get through the water.

Turning, she saw McGaven following her example. She rushed to him. His body was weaving a bit as he kept his arm stationary.

"You okay?" she said watching his face. The night lighting made it easier to see him.

"Yeah, I'll live. I wasn't sure for a while though..."

Suddenly they heard a car rev its engine and looked up. It was speeding toward them across the field with high beams flashing.

FIFTY-EIGHT

Friday 0130 hours

Katie and McGaven froze. Theresa was sitting on the ground in a daze; it was unclear if she was hurt or just exhausted and confused by everything that was happening. They were blinded by the light and dreaded that Dayton had come back to finish what he had started. Katie feared what was going to come next. They had just survived the tunnel and now they were cornered without any weapons or cell phones.

The car skidded to a stop and both doors flew open.

"Katie, Gav, are you both alright?" said the first person.

Katie was still stunned. Both men walked into the light. It was John and Detective Hamilton.

Relief didn't completely convey how she felt. "Gav needs an ambulance. His arm is broken. This is Theresa Simms, one of Dayton's latest victims and a missing person. She needs medical assistance as well."

John immediately called it in. Soon the property would be teeming with police cars, fire trucks, and an ambulance.

Katie felt her cold, wet legs weaken in sheer exhaustion as Detective Hamilton approached.

"What about you?" said Hamilton to Katie.

"I'm fine. Just freezing."

"John showed me the wall and the connection between Dayton and Baldwin. That's a new one," he said.

Katie was walking toward the sedan.

"Where are you going?" Hamilton called.

"Dayton is going to kill Lara."

"What makes you say that?"

"She's a loose end."

"Wait a minute," said John.

"I'm not waiting. Give me the keys."

"What makes you think you know where Dayton is going to be? He could be in another state by now," said Hamilton.

"No. I know how this guy operates. There's still time to save Lara and arrest him."

"Katie, wait for backup," said McGaven.

"I can't." She walked toward the sedan.

"No one is going to change your mind, are they?" said Hamilton.

"Nope," said McGaven and John in unison.

"Fine. I'm coming with you," said Hamilton.

"Go!" said John. "We'll wait for the reinforcements."

"Where are we going?" said Hamilton.

"Capital Stables."

"I'm requesting backup to meet us there."

Katie went to the car. "You have extra clothes and a firearm?"

Detective Hamilton opened the trunk. He handed Katie a sweatshirt. She immediately stripped off her shirt and jacket, not caring if they saw her in her bra. The cold air hit her wet skin making her shiver even more. Putting on the oversize sweatshirt gave her some relief, but she was more focused on getting to Lara in time. Even though Lara was an accomplice to Dayton, she was also a very confused young woman living with a mental illness who needed to be in a care facility instead of prison.

The detective opened a duffel bag and retrieved a Glock and a magazine. He handed it to Katie.

"Thanks," she said as she readied the gun, inserting a full magazine.

"I saw the background on Lara Fontaine," he said.

"She's going to be a loose end and I don't want her to end up in one of those graves. She's been helpful to Dayton, but now her time has run out. She's confused and fragile."

She got in. "Let's go!" Hating to leave her partner, she looked back at McGaven, making sure he seemed to be okay. John was with him and that made her feel better.

Detective Hamilton didn't need prodding, he drove the car from the old Dayton property and headed to Capital Stables.

They approached Capital Stables lights out and quietly slipped into a parking spot just outside the main entrance. There was a truck parked halfway past the stables with the engine still ticking, indicating that someone had recently driven up in it. The lights weren't on at the stables, so the truck must've belonged to Dayton.

Hamilton looked at Katie and nodded.

It seemed strange to Katie not having McGaven as her backup. She had changed her mind about Hamilton—sometimes she thought they were good and other times he seemed to dislike her. That night, she watched the detective and knew that he had her back.

Katie whispered, "The area Dayton seems to be attached to is that way."

"We should go opposite ways and round back at where he is." He looked at her. "You sure you don't want to wait?"

"No. We need to go in now to stop him from killing Lara. He'll be in custody by the time patrol gets here."

"Okay then. Stay frosty." He looked back at the roadway and then jogged into the right side of the area while Katie took the left.

Katie was cold and her feet were numb, which made her hypersensitive to her surroundings when she ran through the forest. Her focus was finding Dayton. She had her gun drawn and flashlight ready. Slowing her pace, she heard voices, a man and a woman. He seemed to be arguing and raising his tone.

Katie hurried and tried to keep her approach quiet, so she hoped that Hamilton was doing the same.

She kept close to the tree clusters until she reached the area of the voices. There was a flashlight lantern on the ground, which illuminated the area, but it was easy for Katie to stay within the shadows.

Katie stopped at a tree about twenty feet from Dayton. She watched him try to convince Lara how important she was to him even as they stood in front of a freshly dug hole. It made Katie deeply saddened and disturbed that Lara was such a victim in all of this.

The longer she watched Dayton the angrier she became. She decided to go around and approach him from behind. It would be easier, more effective, and he would definitely not be expecting to see her.

Katie crouched down and moved quickly through the trees. If Dayton did hear anything, he would just think it was some critter moving around in the forest. She kept moving closer, seeing movement from her peripheral and Hamilton's shadow. She knew it was him because he had his gun directed in front of his body.

Dayton's voice became more sinister. "You have done everything I could have ever asked," he began. "You will live on in my heart."

"Really?" said Lara, obviously not fully understanding the situation. "When can I see Desiree?"

Katie clenched her jaw and waited for the perfect moment to restrain Dayton. She wanted to do so much more to the killer and watching him work Lara made her stomach turn. She crept forward.

"I couldn't have done any of this without you," he said.

Lara smiled.

Katie was glad that McGaven didn't witness this display.

She inched a bit more. She was so close to Dayton, she swiftly closed the gap, grabbing the killer from behind and sticking her loaded Glock into the side of his neck.

"Don't move or I'll pull the trigger," said Katie. "Believe me, it would be easy." She surprised herself with how hateful she sounded. Not thinking ahead of what she was going to say it actually came easy.

Lara took a step forward. "What are you doing?"

"Stay back, Lara."

"Why, Katie? Is Sean here?" She innocently looked around.

"You and Dayton left us to die in a tunnel."

"I don't know what you're talking about," the young woman said.

"C'mon, baby, hand me my gun so we can be safe," said Dayton.

Katie eyed the weapon near the lantern. Angry at herself that she didn't see it before she approached.

"C'mon, baby."

"Lara, don't move," she said.

Hamilton moved in as protocol not knowing what kind of weapon Dayton had or what type of traps he might have set up —just in case. "Stay where you are, Ms. Fontaine." He kept his gun trained on her.

Katie pushed Dayton away from her. "Get down on your knees with your hands on your head."

"And what if I don't?"

"Do it now!"

"I don't have to do anything you say. You never identified yourself as a police officer," he said. He began to laugh. "You don't even know the half of it, Detective."

"I'm not going to say it again—get down on your knees."

Hamilton secured Lara in handcuffs and sat her down. He picked up Dayton's weapon and tucked it into his belt.

Dayton dramatically got down on his knees and turned to face Katie. His expression disgusted her.

"So, Detective, don't you want to know what I know?"

"The only thing that you need to know is that you're going away for life," she said.

Hamilton trained his weapon on Dayton as well.

"I feel so sorry for you, Detectives. You think you know so much—but you know nothing. Nothing." He kept a huge smile on his face. "Oh, by the way, where's your partner?"

"Shut up and put your hands on your head."

Katie wasn't going to allow this killer to antagonize her or bait her into something. They were able to stop him before he took another victim and she had to be content with that fact.

"So, how's Chad these days?" said Dayton.

"What? What do you know?" she said, taken off guard.

"Don't let him bait you, Scott," said Hamilton.

"What do you know?" She walked up to Dayton and pushed him down with her foot. "I said. What do you know about Chad?"

"I dunno... you tell me, Detective." He smiled. "You know it's not over, right?"

"Scott, let it go. Backup will be here soon." Hamilton looked nervous.

"What does a killer like you know about Chad?" she

demanded. "What?" She raised her gun higher, aiming it at Dayton's face.

"I mean it, Scott, stand down," said Hamilton.

"No one will ever know if I shot him without provocation. Will they?" she said. "I would be doing a public service. Simple as that."

"No," said Hamilton.

"We have all the forensic evidence for the murders—we know that he's guilty. So, who cares? I mean really, who cares?" she said.

Taking another step closer to the killer, she put her gun in his face, making Dayton's smile disappear. It felt liberating and she wanted to avenge all the victims' deaths with a single bullet. That's all it would take. And the distaste of bringing Chad into the equation was unforgivable. She knew he'd found out some information about her thinking that he could use against her or to provoke her.

Hamilton watched Katie and his expression was grim as he shook his head. "No, I know what you're thinking, but you've been sworn to protect and serve. And this isn't the way."

Katie looked at Hamilton. "You're wrong."

A single shot rang out, echoing throughout the forest.

FIFTY-NINE

Katie and McGaven stood in the parking lot at Capital Stables watching the police escort Ferris Baldwin, aka Thomas Dayton, to a patrol car, putting him in the back. Katie had shot the single bullet into a nearby tree, but she had made her point and enjoyed seeing the look of fear on his face.

When the police cruiser's door shut with Dayton in the back, Katie felt a wave of relief wash over her; she was optimistic once again. She wrapped the blanket tighter around her as McGaven hugged her tight with his one good arm.

"It's over," she said. "It's finally over."

"That it is," said McGaven. "Theresa was physically okay, but she's going to take some time to emotionally recover."

"Now you can go to the hospital and get your cool cast," she said.

"I will. They put a splint on it for now, but I had to make sure that my partner was okay."

"I'm fine."

"Really?"

"I will be." She felt tired enough to sleep for a week. The graves were still vivid in her mind, scattered across the farm in the trees, but she was able to save one of the victims—and that would have to be enough for her.

Detective Hamilton walked up to face McGaven. "You have one helluva partner there. She fooled me for a second," he said.

"Don't I know it. I wouldn't trade partners for anything."

"Thank you, Hamilton," said Katie. "I'm glad you had my back." She hoped that their rift was finally over.

"You didn't need me." The detective smiled, nodded his respect, and then walked over to patrol to get the investigation going.

Lara was escorted to an ambulance transport. She walked like she was visiting a nice place and stared at all the emergency first responders moving around. Her eyes were wide with curiosity.

"What do you think is going to happen to Lara?" said McGaven.

"Not sure what the DA is going to want to do. But I'd imagine that they won't want to prosecute her based on her incompetence to stand trial."

"Then she'll be taken care of in a facility," said McGaven sadly. "The trauma she endured and meeting up with Dayton when she was basically a child has taken over her life. It's such a crime what she has gone through." He watched Lara walk by as she smiled and waved at him as if it was a beautiful sunny day at the park instead of the dead of night in an area where a dead body had been discovered.

Katie looked at her partner. "You okay, partner?"

"I will be," he said.

SIXTY

A WEEK LATER

Katie stood at the top of a grassy hill looking downward with McGaven at her side. He wore his cast on his right arm as a badge of honor and was assigned to light desk duty until it was removed. The detectives watched the funeral for Abigail Andrews where her mother and sister along with some friends could finally put her to rest.

Katie hoped that it brought peace and closure for the family. She watched the service where everyone paid their respects and then the coffin was lowered into the ground.

"Be at peace, Abigail," said Katie before they turned and walked back to the car.

"Hey, I haven't seen Cisco in ages," said McGaven as he glanced at his watch.

Katie laughed. "You just saw him a couple of days ago."

"Yeah, but I need a Cisco fix."

"Well, in that case."

Katie drove into her driveway, the Dayton case still on her mind. Even as some of the memories and details began to slightly fade, they would always be like a ghost in her life, and she would carry them with her forever.

"C'mon, hurry up," said McGaven rushing to her front door.

Katie thought he was acting strange. "Slow down there, partner."

When she got to the front door, she unlocked it and stepped inside.

"Surprise!"

Katie stood at the threshold in shock.

Her uncle, John, Nick, Denise, Lizzie, and Cisco were standing there.

And Chad walked forward, smiling, looking like he had always. "Hi."

"Chad," said Katie almost breathless as she rushed toward him and hugged him tightly. She was excited and surprised, but she was beyond delighted that he was home and was standing in her house. She hoped it wasn't a dream and held him tighter. All the memories and good times rolled back and any of her doubts melted away. "Are you home for good?" she said. She didn't want to let him go.

"Yes, I'm back for good. I start back to work in two weeks. But until then... I'm here with you." His infectious beautiful smile made his entire face light up—he looked well and rested. There was no doubt that Chad was back, and they were going to slowly rebuild what they had lost. He kissed her.

Everyone gave their congratulations and well wishes that Chad was home again. They enjoyed one another's company and shared delicious food. John and Nick were signing McGaven's cast and joking with one another. Sheriff Scott was chatting with Denise.

Katie walked outside, joining Chad as he watched Cisco play with young Lizzie.

"I can't believe you're back. I feel like I finally have my team back," she said.

"You have to know that I would never stay away from you very long. Never."

"I've missed you so much."

"From what I heard, you've been busy," he said. "They wouldn't give me the details, but since I know you, I'm sure it was quite something."

"It was definitely *something*," she said. "I love you." She snuggled up against him, still watching silly Cisco romping around in the backyard with Lizzie.

"I love you more," he said. "I love you so much more."

A LETTER FROM JENNIFER CHASE

I want to say a huge thank you for choosing to read *The First Girl* (Book 11). If you did enjoy it, and want to keep up to date with all my latest releases, just sign up at the following link. Your email address will never be shared and you can unsubscribe at any time.

www.bookouture.com/jennifer-chase

This has continued to be a special project and series for me. Forensics, K9 training, and criminal profiling have been something that I've studied considerably and to be able to incorporate them into a crime fiction novel has been a thrilling experience for me. It has been a truly wonderful experience to continue to bring it to life.

One of my favorite activities, outside of writing, has been dog training. I'm a dog lover, if you couldn't tell by reading this book, and I loved creating a supporting canine character, Cisco, to partner with my cold-case police detective. I hope you enjoyed it as well.

I hope you loved *The First Girl* (Book 11) and if you did I would be very grateful if you could write a review. I'd love to hear what you think, and it makes such a difference helping new readers to discover one of my books for the first time.

I love hearing from my readers—you can get in touch through social media or my website.

KEEP IN TOUCH WITH JENNIFER

www.authorjenniferchase.com

facebook.com/AuthorJenniferChase
x.com/JChaseNovelist
instagram.com/jenchaseauthor

ACKNOWLEDGMENTS

My sincere thank you goes out to all my law enforcement, police detectives, deputies, police K9 teams, forensic units, forensic anthropologists, and first-responder friends—there's too many to list. Your friendships have meant so much to me over the years. It has opened a whole new writing world filled with inspiration for future stories for Detective Katie Scott and K9 Cisco. I wouldn't be able to bring my crime fiction stories to life if it wasn't for all of you. Thank you for your service and dedication to keep the rest of us safe.

Writing this series continues to be a truly amazing experience for me. I would like to thank my publisher Bookouture for the incredible opportunity, and the fantastic staff for continuing to help me to bring this book and the entire Detective Katie Scott series to life.

Thank you, Kim, Sarah, and Noelle for your relentless promotion for us authors. A thank you to my brilliant editor Kelsie and the amazing editorial team—your unwavering support has helped me to worker harder to write more endless adventures for Detective Katie Scott and K9 Cisco.

PUBLISHING TEAM

Turning a manuscript into a book requires the efforts of many people. The publishing team at Bookouture would like to acknowledge everyone who contributed to this publication.

Audio
Alba Proko
Sinead O'Connor
Melissa Tran

Commercial
Lauren Morrissette
Jil Thielen
Imogen Allport

Cover design
Head Design Ltd

Data and analysis
Mark Alder
Mohamed Bussuri

Editorial
Kelsie Marsden
Jen Shannon

Printed in the USA
CPSIA information can be obtained
at www.ICGtesting.com
JSHW021515231223
54207JS00004B/142

9 781835 250204